COOKIES AND CURSES

MIXING UP MAGIC
BOOK ONE

ROSIE PEASE

Editor: Word Whisperer Literary Editing
Proofreader: Jasmine Bryner
Cover Designer: Melony Paradise, Paradise Cover Design

This is a work of fiction. Names, characters, organizations, places, events, and incidents are either products of the author's imagination or are used fictitiously. Any resemblance to actual persons, living or dead, or actual events is purely coincidental.

PAISLEY PRESS BOOKS
WEST WARWICK, RHODE ISLAND

About This Book

Matchmaking, baking and ghosts... a recipe for disaster or a spell for success?

I've never been wrong with cookies or love, and it's made my bakery popular in my small town. Rumors claim my matchmaking skills come from a dash of magic in my treats, but I can ignore the gossip about me being a witch.

But ghosts only I can see suddenly needing my help? That was never a part of my business plan, and solving their problems might be more than I can handle.

If I can't figure out the mystery of why they're coming between the couples I've connected, then not only will my matches not get their happily ever afters but failing could conjure the end of my livelihood too. I can't let the cookie crumble on my career.

Ghosts, it's time to meet your baker.

AUTHOR'S NOTE

Dear Reader,

Thank you so much for picking *Cookies and Curses* as your next read. I hope you fall in love with the characters and Heartwood Hollow as much as I have.

Originally published in 2019 in the Matchmaker's Grimoire series, *Cookies and Curses*, the subsequent books in the series, and all of Heartwood Hollow were magically transported out of Upstate New York when I signed on with a small publisher. Although these books are self-published once again, changing the series name to Mixing Up Magic and moving the setting to small town New England brought a new dimension to the stories, and I'm happy with where it ended up.

It's no secret that the town is full of secrets, and I can't wait for you to uncover them all.

I love hearing from readers. If you'd like to reach out to me, you can do so across social media @WriteRosiePease.

Happy reading!

Cheers,

Rosie

CHAPTER 1

Elizabeth burst into Suncraft Bakery. "I got the job! Joanie, I got the job!" she shouted, her brown curls bouncing against her shoulders as she came to a stop in front of the counter.

I glanced at the overhead lights. I would have sworn the room brightened as if in response to her mood. Actually, it was entirely possible. Things like that had a way of happening around here.

Her wide smile was infectious, and I easily returned it. "That's wonderful news! I knew your interview would go well."

She side-stepped down the row of pastry cases and poked the glass in front of her repeatedly. "And it's all thanks to you and your spiced snickerdoodle cookie, Joanie." Elizabeth had come in a half hour before her interview two weeks prior and bought the cookie upon my suggestion. I'd chosen that one to spice things up a bit. "They said they liked my spunk."

"And that's what will make you a great—what was it?— assistant activities coordinator at the nursing home?"

She nodded enthusiastically. "I'll be working in the senior center too."

"How wonderful! You'll have them up and dancing in no time."

Elizabeth chuckled. "I don't know about dancing, but I have some great ideas that I think they're going to enjoy." She pulled her hair up into a ponytail, securing it with a hair elastic she had been wearing around her wrist. "Hey, do you still have those cookies? I need to buy one to celebrate. It did help me get the job, after all."

"Sure do." I nodded at where her finger was on the glass. "You didn't even realize you were pointing right to them. They're one of the specials this month."

I bent over and reached into the case, then pulled out one of the larger cookies for Elizabeth. I was genuinely happy for her landing her first real job after graduating college early in December. She'd been nervous about the interview. She had plenty of skill, passion, and experience. All she needed was a small confidence boost.

I had a reputation in town for being a witch. The good kind. I'd never agreed with the claim, laughed at it, really. I wasn't a witch, but I knew how to read people and played up the rumors about me for the benefit of others. When I handed Elizabeth the snickerdoodle cookie the day of her interview, I'd winked. That's all she'd needed.

I dropped the cookie into a bag and handed it to her. "Anything else I can do for you today?"

She pressed the bag to her chest and smiled. "You want to find me a guy? I have a job. Soon I'll have an apartment. Then all I'll need is a man. People talk. I know you got Beth and Carl together last month, and Chelsea and David are getting married soon. Everyone knows you had a hand in that."

Smiling, I shook my head. Elizabeth wasn't wrong. Matchmaking came easily to me. In my four years of living in Heartwood Hollow, I'd matched over a dozen couples. The skill was hereditary. I'd grown up in a small town, not unlike this one, and my mom was the town librarian. She spent her entire career in that one library and was responsible for at least a hundred matches during those nearly thirty years. When I asked Mom about it after I matched my first couple in high school, she'd told me how she did it: "You just know something about somebody when you see what books they bring up to check out." I could only take her at her word—though I loved to read, I didn't know books like I did baked goods—but I imagined there was a little more to it than that. I was a watcher. The way someone entered the bakery, viewed the treats in the case and picked something out, and said goodbye told me a lot about a person. Over time, I'd established friendly relationships with many of my customers. Like with Elizabeth.

"You don't need a man to complete your life. There's time. You're young still."

She sighed loudly and rolled her eyes. "And you're too young to say that. You're what, not even thirty? That's what my mom said too. Doesn't stop me from wanting one. Can't you poof someone for me?"

I laughed, ignoring the age comment, although she wasn't wrong with that either. I was only twenty-seven. "*Poof?*"

"Yeah, or whatever it is that you do. Please?" She handed me her money for the cookie.

I rang her out and gave her back her change. "It doesn't work that way. I can't pull someone from thin air. The perfect guy doesn't magically appear in town just because I want him to."

"I know, but—"

"There's someone out there for you. It takes time. But if I find him, I'll tell you. I promise."

The smile that had gotten lost when she was talking about wanting a guy reappeared. She'd find someone eventually, with or without my help.

"Thanks. I gotta run—I haven't even told my mom or brother yet—but I'll see you soon."

"Good to see you, and congratulations."

Elizabeth spun on her heels, then walked toward the exit. She called over her shoulder, "And thanks for the cookie!" as she pulled the door open and stepped down onto the sidewalk.

At that moment, my assistant, Sarah, walked into the shop from the kitchen, the door swinging shut behind her. "What was all that about?"

"Elizabeth got the job she interviewed for."

"Oh, how wonderful!" Sarah clapped.

"She bought a cookie to celebrate."

Sarah wiped her hands on her purple apron. "I wondered what was keeping you."

"Keeping me?" I glanced in her direction with an eyebrow raised.

Sarah tapped at her wrist. "Yeah, don't you realize what time it is?"

I looked at the clock on the register. "Ack! I need to get going! Can't be late for teatime."

I grabbed my small purse from under the counter and then slung it around my neck so it crossed over my body.

"Everything's already boxed up," Sarah said. "I'll help you load it."

She walked back into the kitchen, and I followed quickly behind her, untying my apron in the process and hanging it on the wall hook by the mixing station.

"Thanks." I grabbed three packed and tied-shut yellow boxes and pushed the back door open with my hip.

"I got it." Holding two boxes herself, Sarah held the door open, and I continued down the concrete steps to the parking lot. It was my second delivery of the day—I'd already dropped four dozen muffins off to the two town diners before the bakery even opened—so my bike was ready and waiting under the second-floor landing for the apartment above the bakery. I carefully placed my boxes into the bike trailer that reminded me of an old shopping cart, then Sarah handed me her boxes over the stair railing before dashing inside to get me one more. I held on to that one after she gave it to me. Its delivery didn't require the bike.

"I'm going to take lunch after the deliveries, so you're on your own for the next hour and a half. Call if you need me."

"Sure thing. I'll take mine when you get back. Enjoy your ride. It's a great day for it."

I looked up at the sky. Not a cloud in sight. "It sure is."

Pastry box in hand, I walked across the parking lot to another back door that sat kitty-corner to the bakery's. I knocked gently with my foot. The heavy white door swung open, revealing a skinny blonde in black yoga pants and a hot-pink sports bra.

"Wonderful! You're here. Ladies, Joanie's here." Kimmy, the owner of the yoga studio, ushered me inside to applause from a small class full of women in clothing similar to hers.

"Good to see everyone." I placed the box on an empty side table and popped the tabs at the sides so it opened up completely. I slid the tray out of the box and began to unpack the five dozen cookies.

When I was done, Kimmy handed me a check. "Thanks for these. The girls really love cheat day."

As I slid the check into my purse, we said our goodbyes. I

didn't have the heart to tell her how many of her clients stopped in after every class they took.

I exited the studio, then jogged over to my bike and hopped on, immediately taking off. Libby would have a fit if I was late for tea. First tea, anyway. The inn had two every other day and a high tea on Sundays.

At the end of the parking lot, I turned left on Founder Street toward Mill River. The road split into three at the intersection, and I headed straight toward the paved driveway of the Riverview Inn. The manicured lawn sprawled out on either side of me with large maples lining the driveway. In late winter, Libby and her husband, Billy, tapped the trees to make syrup and sugar. I regularly tried to incorporate the maple products into my baked goods. Most of my special flavors had been maple based last month to celebrate their latest harvest. They were always some of my favorite treats of the year, especially the maple cream whoopie pies.

Libby was waiting for me on the porch of the stately brick home. A mini-mansion, really. It had once been the home of Heartwood Hollow's founder, Alfred Dunmore. He'd made his money in the logging industry, building a sawmill with waterwheel and dam downriver over a hundred and fifty years ago.

"You're just in time," she called as I pulled my bike to the side of the driveway closest to the path for the stairs.

I waved. "Sorry, I had a customer come in when I should have been leaving, and it's cheat day at the yoga studio." I still had a few minutes before I would consider myself late. She liked to have everything ready with plenty of time for her guests to arrive and see the elaborate spread. Teatime was open to members of the public, not just the guests of the ten-room inn.

"Isn't every day cheat day?" Libby giggled as she hopped

down the steps to wrap me in a motherly hug as she did every time I saw her, despite her being not much older than me.

I returned her hug and then reached into my trailer for two of the boxes. "It is for me." I let out a slight chuckle.

"And look at you! Still so skinny! Too skinny if you ask me." She took the top box from my hands and walked around the side of the inn toward the kitchen door.

I looked down at my frame as I followed her. I was petite, sure, but *skinny* wouldn't be the word I'd use to describe myself. Perhaps she'd said that since I didn't look like I snacked on sweets all day, even though I did. I was told once I started working with it day in and day out, I'd lose the taste for the yummy things I made. Four years into this business— plus culinary school and baking for any and every occasion when I was a kid—and I still liked eating it all.

"So what do we have today?"

"Well, you have your typical variety of scones—ginger, blueberry, and cinnamon. We also have some spiced snicker- doodles, mini whoopie pies, and lemon drops." I placed my box next to hers on the kitchen counter.

Libby busied herself with opening the first box. "I do so love your lemon drops. Are you staying for tea this time?"

When I first moved to town I'd been a frequent guest, but now I could rarely sneak away from the bakery. "Wish I could, but I still have to get to Town Hall and the real estate office."

"Oh, new townspeople! I wonder which house they bought. There's only a few for sale. Find out for me, will you? I love to know what's going on, but the inn keeps me too busy most days. We've got a full house today." She moved on to the second box and began to arrange the cookies on tiered tea trays she had already laid out.

"That's great to hear. All the work you and Billy consistently put into this place really shows." I turned for the door. "Any requests for Friday?"

"Surprise me. I trust you. Have a good day, Joanie."

"You too, Libby."

After closing the door behind me, I pulled my bike back onto the driveway then climbed on. I still had two more deliveries to make, and my stomach was already rumbling.

My next stop was Town Hall, where I had to drop off twenty-four pieces of mocha almond biscotti for today's meeting of the town's selectmen. Several residents in town had told me that meetings were much more entertaining to watch before I came to Heartwood Hollow and started providing snacks. They claimed my food mellowed the selectmen out too much. I chalked it up to the best discussions and decisions happening on a full belly. Everyone got cranky when they were hungry.

I grabbed the box of biscotti and pulled a bag out of the remaining box in my trailer. Careful not to trip, I walked up the tall marble steps to the columned porch and waved at Courtney, my best friend, through the window looking into her office. She jumped up from her desk chair. Moments later, one of the large white doors opened, and Courtney held it for me as I stepped inside. She waved me toward the meeting room, and once there, I plopped the box down on the center of the table, where the selectmen would find it in a couple hours.

"Can't stay today," I said as I entered Courtney's office a moment later. "I still have another delivery to make, but I brought you something."

"You are a godsend," she replied. "Jill called out today, so I can't take much of a lunch break. This is just what I needed." She took the white bag from my hand, opened it, and peered inside to see the hand-sized chocolate chip cookie. "My favorite! Oh, before you go. Drew and Megan had their baby, a little girl."

"That's wonderful! Congratulations to them."

"Thought you'd like to know since you got them together. That makes it—"

"Six now," I answered for her. "Gotta run. Let's catch up soon and do a girls' night. It's been too long." I jogged out her door and then the building's, waving toward her window before I carefully navigated the steps. I'd slipped on them once and never wanted to repeat that. It had hurt to sit for the next week.

I rode my bike down Main Street toward the real estate office at the end of the street. It was a quick delivery of two dozen cookies as a welcome to the neighborhood present to celebrate a closing. It was one of the first partnerships I had made when I moved to town. Give the new people free cookies and hope to gain a customer from it. So far, it had worked well. I'd have to remember to tell Libby during my Friday delivery that someone had purchased the red house by the hospital.

Circling back on Main Street, I turned left on Founder Street and pedaled over to Leafs and Grounds, the local coffee shop. I could see the corner of my bakery from its entrance. The proximity had proven dangerous over the years. I was addicted to the marshmallow rice treats there. Sure, I could easily make them myself, but something about these was so perfect, and who was I to try competing with perfection? I grabbed two of the plastic-wrapped treats off the counter as I placed my order. A creature of habit, I almost always chose the same thing. A pesto, tomato, and mozzarella panini with a bag of chips to go. Sometimes I got soup, but that was only when I could split a sandwich with Courtney.

I took my food back across Main Street to Founder's Park,

directly next to the bakery. It wasn't much of a park at all, despite the name, because of its small size. There was little more than a few benches amongst the bushes and flower boxes. It had a tourist info booth sitting in it, a free little library box, and it was where the town placed Santa's cottage soon after Thanksgiving each year for the holiday season. A man in a beige trench coat entered the little park with his dachshund and tipped his fedora in my direction, nodding slightly as he did. Quiet but always polite, he was another park regular. Came here every day at the same time, no matter the weather. I waved and smiled at him in return. He sat on one of the other benches and let the leash out a bit for his dog. Other than him, I rarely saw people using the park outside of the holiday season, but this was one of my favorite places in town. I loved sitting outside and watching the people come and go along Main Street while I ate.

After finishing my lunch, I rushed back to the bakery. For more than just Sarah needing her lunch, I had a feeling it was exactly where I needed to be.

CHAPTER 2

The problem with that sort of feeling was it didn't come with a timer. Alone up front a couple hours later, the sound of the door sliding open alerted me to someone entering the bakery. Four years of running the bakery and I still hadn't invested in any sort of bell. I had yet to need one. I always managed to find myself exactly where I needed to be when a customer came in.

"Good afternoon, Joanie," Ashley, one of my regulars, said slightly out of breath.

"How are you doing today? How was school?"

She gave me a half-hearted smile. It wasn't like her at all. "You make me feel like I'm back in school when you ask that, and I don't mean as staff. No one got sent to the principal's office today, but I wrote out a ton of late passes this morning. I swear the nicer days lately have everyone stopping to smell the spring flowers." She thumped her purse onto the counter.

"You okay? You seem a bit out of sorts." Taking a better look at her, I noticed her blonde hair was hastily thrown into a ponytail, and she'd already wiped off her usually impeccable makeup, not that having no makeup made her any less pretty. Her bright-pink manicure had a few chips too.

"I feel out of sorts. And to top it off, I had to park down the street. I can't parallel park, and the lot behind you is full of yogis. Actual yogis, not their cars. I jogged here. I need my afternoon pick-me-up wicked bad. What do you have?" she asked, not even looking at the case in front of her.

"I think I have what you need." Ducking down, I reached into the cookie case. I stood back up holding a hand-sized black and white cookie. "Here you go."

"That is massive. You've really outdone yourself with the size this time, Joanie. I love black and white cookies." She took the cookie from me and immediately had a bite.

"My gram calls them half-moon cookies." Doubting that she'd eat the whole thing while we chatted, I turned and grabbed a white wax paper bag for her. "The white part's the moon, and the black part's the sky."

"I can totally see that." She looked down at the cookie, a look of concern on her face. I handed her the bag, and she brightened. "Thanks. You always know just what I need." She carefully placed the cookie inside and then licked the remaining frosting off her fingers. "What do I owe you?"

"Two seventy-five. Tax included."

Ashley opened her purse, and her face dropped.

"Ashley?"

"Okay, I swear I didn't put this in here. It magically showed up in there all by itself." She pulled out an old hair-brush and placed it on the counter. "It just appeared on my nightstand last night and my dresser the night before. You want to know why I'm out of sorts?" She pointed to the brush. "That thing. It's creeping me out."

Hovering my hand over it, I asked, "May I?" Ashley

nodded, and I picked up the silver-plated brush for an inspection. It was slightly tarnished but in otherwise good condition. The bristles, probably some type of synthetic material, were all intact. I flipped the brush over and studied the back's intricate pink-painted rose design. It likely had a matching mirror at one point. My gram had a similar set when I was a kid. Probably still did.

"Is it yours?"

She shrugged. "Not really, but I guess so? It was mailed to me in a box with some other stuff. I didn't recognize any of it. A lot of it was old. Older than I am, definitely." She handed me exact change for the cookie and grabbed her purse off the counter.

I hadn't been expecting that explanation. "How strange. Well, hang in there."

"Thanks. I always feel better after coming to see you." She held up the bag with the cookie in it. "I think you really put magic in these things." Ashley turned to leave.

"Hey, you forgot your brush." I held it out to her.

She spun around on her heels. "Keep it. That way it can't follow me home. And if it somehow does, I'm burning it."

"Um, okay. Thanks, I guess. Have a good rest of your day." Sure I could find it a home somewhere, even if over at the antique store, I placed it next to my bag on the shelf beneath the counter where customers couldn't see it.

Seeming lighter somehow, Ashley smiled and then walked out the door. She waved at me as she passed the storefront window. I considered her a friend. After four years of her coming into my bakery after work nearly every school day, I knew her pretty well. Plus, she was one half of my latest matchmaking endeavor.

On paper, Ashley and Rich were perfect for each other,

but for whatever reason, they hadn't made that ultimate connection. Something was standing in their way, and it was my mission to figure out what so they could be together. If I could put my finger on it, I knew I'd be able to fix whatever was coming between them.

CHAPTER 3

Ashley's departure heralded the after-school rush, as several more people came in, teachers and students alike. Ashley wasn't the only person who liked an afternoon treat. But after the post-school rush, the bakery slowed down. It always did on Wednesdays. Like clockwork. We alternated who got to leave early as a result. It was nice to get an extra hour sometimes.

"Are you sure you don't need me to stay?" Sarah asked as she put on her sweater and slung her bag over her shoulder. "You already let me take a longer lunch. I don't mind if you'd rather go home early."

"It's okay. I have a feeling I might be needed here."

"Why does that make me feel like I should stay too? Your witchy senses are rarely wrong."

I raised an eyebrow at her.

She gave me a sheepish grin. "What? They're wicked accurate, even your matchmaking. What else would you call it?"

I sometimes forgot how much stock she put into the

rumors. "Experience and a bit of luck. There's nothing witchy about that."

"If you say so. But thank you. That should give me time to make soup for Jill. She's sick today."

"Oh right, I didn't see her at Town Hall. You're going to make soup?" Sarah didn't bake, and she certainly didn't cook. If she could make soup, it was news to me.

She cracked a smile. "Okay, so I only need to heat it up. That totally counts."

"Tell her I hope she feels better soon."

"I will."

"Oh, green tea with honey. That will help."

"Thanks again. I'm covering for Lauren tomorrow, so I'll see you in the morning." With that, Sarah headed home, leaving me alone in the bakery.

The truth was, I looked forward to the last hour of the day on Wednesdays. With so few people coming in, I used the time to have a relaxed closing. Tomorrow would be busier as people geared up for the weekend.

I'd already consolidated and covered the remaining baked goods with covers that would keep them fresh until morning. Most of the till had been counted and placed into a bank envelope for deposit. The kitchen was swept, its counters clean. I still had a few minutes left before I could flip the sign from *open* to *closed*. I wouldn't do it until the exact top of the hour to give anyone the last-minute chance to come in and buy something to satisfy a craving or buy the forgotten dessert for dinner.

Dusting a display shelf, I had my back turned to the checkout counter when a slight rattling against a nearby surface followed by a scuffling noise caught my attention. I glanced up, curious, but saw nothing so resumed dusting. The moment I did, it happened again. After finishing the shelf, I walked back around the counter and saw the brush Ashley had left with me three feet from where I had placed it.

I picked up the brush. It had moved, but how? Why? I placed it back on the counter where I had first put it and tried to slide it myself. It wasn't difficult, but there was some resistance. It wouldn't just slide on its own. I lifted the brush and gave it a slight shake. Nothing rattled.

The front door opened, and Rich walked in. I quickly plopped the brush back next to my bag on the shelf beneath the checkout counter.

"Hi, Rich, how are you today?"

He smiled politely. "I'm good, yourself?"

"Oh, the usual." Just a brush that moves on its own. "What can I do for you?"

"I hope it's not too late. Can I place an order for tomorrow?" Rich took off his glasses and then wiped them with a small cloth he'd pulled out of his pants pocket. He glanced up at me with his ebony eyes that were as dark as his skin. Such a handsome man, clean-cut. A good man too. I regularly heard positive things from students coming into the bakery after school. I had no doubt he was the perfect match for Ashley, and I was never wrong. He placed his glasses back on his face, then tucked the cloth into his pocket.

"Sure thing. What do you want?" I grabbed my order pad and a pen off the counter behind me.

"My AP history students have a big test in the morning, and everyone knows your muffins will give them a boost of luck."

"Aww, that's sweet of you. How many are in your class?"

"Eight. Last fall, Robbie got a near-perfect SAT score, and he had one of your muffins for breakfast that morning."

I smiled. Like Elizabeth sharing her news about her job this morning, Robbie had come running in here to tell me his score, waving the envelope with the results in his hand. "I heard about that."

"Word got around school, as it usually does. So it's become ritual for me to give them something special, but it slipped my mind, which is why I'm here now. Did you know that there's only one teacher in the school who will still give tests on Tuesdays? Everyone else makes sure you're open, just in case."

"Just in case?" I repeated.

He leaned in slightly as if to tell me a secret. "Yeah, you know, just in case the good luck is real."

"Oh, I see. So eight muffins, or do you want one for yourself?"

"Just the eight." He chuckled. "I don't have a test to take." He looked down and straightened his bowtie. Could this man get any more adorable? I could see he was toeing around something else. I had a good idea what. He didn't have a test, but maybe he needed a bit of luck.

"I saw Ashley today. You missed her by an hour."

Something shuffled and hit the floor near my foot with a slight clank, loud enough for only me to hear. Perhaps Ashley hadn't been wrong about the brush showing up in her purse. I suspected that it had moved on its own. Again. I had placed it down in a spot where it couldn't move accidentally. And if it wasn't an accident, then something or *someone* had moved it.

"Oh yeah?" His eyes lit up a bit. "I had cross-country practice. They have a meet on Saturday in Snowhaven."

Beyond the small flicker in his eyes, Rich didn't take the bait. Rather than press him on it, I asked, "Do you need good luck muffins for that too?"

"How about some pastries for after? They might run faster knowing what's waiting for them at the end on the bus ride home."

"I can do that." I wrote it down on the order form with the muffins.

"Thanks." He sighed, long and hard, then scrubbed his face with his hand. "Fine. I came in here for more than the muffins. Ashley. How did she seem? Is she okay? Did she say anything about me?"

At the mention of Ashley's name, the scuffling noise resumed. The brush was on the move, sliding across the floor. Such a curious thing. I'd need to study it further when I got home.

"Well, if you're asking if she's come in for a special treat to soothe an aching heart or spice up her love life, the answer is no. What's up? I thought things were going well."

"They were, and they are . . . sometimes." I cocked my head to the side, urging him to continue. "I like her, and I think she likes me. She lights up when I visit the junior high and stop in to see her in the office. We've been out a few times, and the dates haven't been bad, but—" He paused and shook his head rapidly as if chasing away a thought. "I don't know, maybe I'm reading too much into it."

Perhaps their problem was that they were each too into their own heads. If they'd let go a little, they'd be perfect and wouldn't be having a problem. "You should try talking to her about it. Clear the air."

"I guess you're right."

"Of course I am. Haven't you heard I have a knack for these things?" I winked at him and grinned broadly to play up the shtick.

He shrugged. Boy, he was a tough cookie today. His Ashley troubles were really getting to him.

"Hold on. I know just the thing." I reached under one of the tray covers and pulled out a spiced snickerdoodle, the kind Elizabeth liked so much and claimed had given her the confidence and spark she'd needed for her interview.

"Here." As I handed Rich the cookie, I spotted an old man standing silently in the back corner of the bakery. A thick silver-white mustache stood out against his dark skin, and his tightly curled hair was more white than gray. He was wearing an outdated small-checkered suit coat over a green button-up shirt and pleated brown trousers. His hands rested casually in his pants pockets, but he stared at Rich with an intensity I couldn't decipher.

Rich dug out his wallet and tried to hand me a five-dollar bill, but I couldn't stop looking at the older man. I had no doubt about it. This man, whoever he was and however he was connected to Rich, was a ghost. I'd been able to see them since I was a kid. Some I saw regularly, like the man walking his dachshund earlier. But this ghost was new to me. Added to the possibly possessed hairbrush, I had to wonder, what was going on?

"It's on the house, Rich. You need it."

He pursed his lips and raised an eyebrow at me. "You know I don't believe in this, right? A cookie isn't going to make me magically feel better."

Trying to stay focused on my living customer, I crossed my arms and lifted an eyebrow of my own. "Says the man who bought good luck muffins for his students."

He threw his arms up in surrender and laughed. "I don't, truly. There's no such thing as magic. But they believe it, which is what matters."

"Fine. And for the record, I agree with you. It isn't magic, but who's never felt better after a cookie?"

Rich bit into the snickerdoodle, one hand under his chin to catch crumbs. "Mmm . . . this is good." He took another bite, closing his eyes as he chewed. He licked his lips slightly, then thanked me.

"See? Feeling better already."

"Gotta hand it to you. You're right. I am. Maybe there is a bit of magic in your cookies." He stole another bite as he looked at his watch. "Oh goodness, it's getting late. I'm sorry to have kept you."

"Oh, it's okay. I still have a bit to do before I can officially call it a day." I glanced at the corner of the bakery. The ghost was still there, still staring. Who was he to Rich?

"Well, I'll let you get to it." Rich tapped on the counter. "Have a good night."

"You too." I walked around the counter to follow Rich and his ghost toward the door. The ghost paid no attention to me even though I was hot on his heels. He hadn't realized I could see him, which was fine by me. It wasn't something I had wanted to draw attention to. One didn't wave to a third person in the corner when there were only supposed to be two people in the room. I was already dealing with the rumors about my being a witch. Although those seemed to bring me more business, I didn't need new rumors spread through town about my seeing ghosts, especially when those would be true.

Rich and his ghost exited the shop, and when the door shut, I locked it behind them and flipped the store sign to *closed*. Still eating his cookie, Rich walked down the sidewalk, the ghost following him. But when Rich reached the corner, the ghost blinked out of sight.

I knew he wasn't gone for good, though. I'd be seeing him again, for sure.

Once Rich was out of view, I drew the shades and turned around, hands on my hips.

Now, where was that brush?

CHAPTER 4

At the end of the day, even a slow one like Wednesdays, the exteriors of the baking cases were covered with fingerprints, handprints, and smudges. I'm sure some didn't like this daily task, but I always enjoyed it. The mess and grime were signs of people's eagerness to have one of my goodies. My favorites were those down low from children who regularly placed both hands flat against the cases, and sometimes their faces too. I always laughed at nose prints. They reminded me of my cat, Saffy, smooshing her face against the living room window at home so she could get closer to the outside.

The cases sparkled once I was through with them. Now it was time to sweep. The last thing I needed was some sort of insect infestation from crumbs left on the floor. As I swept, I searched for the brush, which I had heard move several times while Rich was here. I spotted it on the floor along the base of the counter a good seven feet away from where I'd put it. Wanting to see if it would move some more, I left it alone and continued sweeping but kept an eye on it.

It didn't budge. Once I'd finished sweeping, I placed the

broom back in the kitchen closet and then returned to where the brush lay to pick it up. I grabbed my bag and then dropped the brush inside. It was coming home with me. I wanted to run an experiment on it using something my grandmother had shown me when I was a teenager. But first I had to deposit the day's till at the bank, so with purse and bank envelope in hand, I left the bakery.

Outside, I made sure my bike and trailer were locked around one of the security stanchions that would keep a car from accidentally hitting the building. I had driven my car today, a rarity, and didn't feel like loading the bike into the trunk. All it meant was I'd have to walk to work tomorrow, which wasn't out of the ordinary.

I hopped in the car and tossed my purse onto the passenger seat, then placed the bank deposit envelope on top of that. With all the change inside—I only deposited coins once a week since they had to be rolled first—it was heavy today.

I backed out of my spot and then left the parking lot, turning right onto Founder. The bank was close, right at the top of the street, but its proximity to Leafs and Grounds made it one of the more dangerous treks I had to make. I had to remind myself that I still had a marshmallow rice treat to prevent myself from checking to see if the coffee shop had more as I drove by.

Mine was the only car in the bank's customer parking lot when I arrived to make the deposit. For most, that would have signaled the bank was closed, but someone manned the business window for an extra half hour each day. I grabbed the deposit envelope and my purse, then darted into the bank. The faster I could get in, the sooner I could get home and figure out that brush.

"Joanie!" the teller called, waving as I approached her

window.

"Rachael. It's so good to see you. How are you doing? How's Mark?" Rachael and Mark had been my sixth match after I moved to Heartwood Hollow. They'd gotten married two years ago after a short engagement. It was the first wedding I attended as a guest since arriving here, but I had made their cake too.

"Oh, we're fine, just fine. I was hoping to see you today."

I set the deposit envelope on the counter with a *thunk*. "You were? How come? I haven't seen you in a few days."

"I've been sick," she answered with a smirk. Her cheeks blushed slightly.

"Aw, I'm sorry to hear that."

"Oh, no, it's for a really good reason." Her grin widened into a broad, excited smile. "Mark and I are having a baby! I'm pregnant!"

"That's wonderful news. Congratulations!"

"We just started telling people. I thought for sure I'd be found out sooner with as much as I've needed to call out lately. This morning sickness has been awful." She unzipped the bank envelope and began stacking the coin rolls.

"Come by the bakery tomorrow. I'll whip up some gingersnaps and lemon-ginger scones. They'll help settle your stomach."

"Oh, you're the best. Thank you. I told Mark you'd have something to help."

I was sure she'd heard the question a bunch from those they'd told, but I had to ask. "Do you know what you're having yet?"

She shook her head. "Not yet. It's still too early. We're really hoping for a little girl." She'd moved on to counting the bills, then ran them through a sorter to confirm.

I smiled. I had a feeling they were going to get exactly

what they wanted.

Rachael looked at her computer and keyed in a few things. Her rosy cheeks revealed the slightest glow. If she hadn't begun to tell people already, they would have figured it out for themselves soon enough.

The tiny printer next to her kicked to life, and out popped a receipt. She handed it to me. "Here, you go. Anything else I can do for you?"

"Nope, that's it for me today, but do pass along my congratulations to Mark."

"Oh, I will. And I'll be in tomorrow for those ginger treats, so I'll see you then."

"Have a good night." I grabbed my purse and headed back to the car.

When I sat down in my seat, the brush was sitting on the passenger side floorboard. I hadn't even realized it wasn't still in my purse. What a curious object.

By the time I pulled into my driveway two blocks later, I could no longer see the brush. Once out of the car, I walked around to the passenger side and opened the door. I had to bend all the way over to feel underneath the seat. The brush was in the most inconvenient spot from this angle. I snatched my purse off the passenger seat and then opened the rear door. Hoping I could grab the brush from here, I bent down and reached under the seat again. I swear the brush had moved once more. It was as if the brush didn't want to go inside my house with me. Or maybe there was somewhere else it wanted to be—Ashley's. I needed to get this brush inside or else it probably would end up back at her house. She only lived a street away. I leaned down and turned so my shoulder almost touched the back footwell. Then I reached in as far as I could and finally felt the handle of the brush.

"Ah ha! Got you." Anyone watching would have laughed

when I pulled a brush out and not some small critter that had jumped into and hidden in my car. Actually, that had happened once with a squirrel who was desperate for the bag of peanuts I had on the seat. I ended up having to bait him out with a peanut butter cookie.

"Look," I started as I placed the brush into my bag, "I don't know what your problem is, but you don't have a choice right now. You're going into the house whether you like it or not." This would have been a lot easier if it could tell me what was wrong.

Holding the brush in place so it couldn't jump out of my open purse, I dug out my house key. Saffron, who I called Saffy of Saf for short, was waiting for me in the front window, sitting on the back of the couch. As I approached the lock with my key out, she ran to the couch arm closest to the door to greet me like she always did.

"Did you see all that?" I asked the calico cat once I was inside, giving her a quick pet all over her head. "Of course you did. I hope it gave you a good laugh."

Saffy sat up straight on the arm of the couch and stared me down, judging me, no doubt. I swung my bag off my shoulder and tossed it onto the couch. She dove for it and stuck her head into the main pocket.

I closed the door behind me and kicked off my shoes. "Do you think there's something going on with it too?"

Saffy didn't answer, not that I expected her to. Although if any cat could talk, it would be her. She continued to root inside my bag. I hoped I didn't have anything important inside. She knew to leave my marshmallow rice treat alone.

"Gram told me about a recipe once that I hope will help. I'll be in the kitchen. Keep an eye on the brush. I'll be right back."

After sliding on a pair of slippers, I walked into the

kitchen. I kept my feet covered whenever I cooked or baked, even at home. I'd heard one too many stories of kitchen accidents to ever feel comfortable with bare feet around hot foods, heavy dishes, or sharp instruments.

First things first. I grabbed a pork loin from the fridge. That wasn't for the recipe, but it was for dinner.

As that roasted in the oven, I dug through my drawers. I knew I needed a white candle, some sage, a silver candlestick, and . . . and . . . to call my grandmother.

"Hey, Gram. It's Joanie."

"Joanie, dear. It's not Saturday. Is everything okay?"

Was I really that stuck on my routine that I only called her on Saturdays? "I'm fine, but I'm having a bit of an issue with a *thing*, and I think you'll be able to help me."

"Are ghosts coming to you again?"

Gram didn't hold back punches. It had been years since I'd last mentioned seeing them to her. Probably not since she and Mom helped me move out of my college dorm and into my first apartment. I'd always been able to see them, but it hadn't been a problem until I hit puberty. Then they began to seek me out, and I couldn't handle it. Gram helped me rein them in. Now I only saw them if they were out and about on their regular business. Like the man and his dog and the ghost following Rich today. No help needed on my part. At least until today. What was it about that brush?

"Well, no, but maybe?" I wasn't sure. "A friend gave me a hairbrush, and it moves on its own. I think it might be possessed. But there's something about it that makes me need to know by who. I remember you showing me a spell back when everything was first happening. I've got my white candle—"

"For purity and divination, yes."

"And my sage. Is it okay to use cooking sage and not a

stick thingie?"

"A smudge stick," she corrected me. "It's not ideal, but it will work. You could use rosemary too if you have it. Set it in a little dish and light it with a match you've just blown out. Flame would set it afire and burn through it too quickly. You only want it to smoke, so a match ember should do the trick."

I slid my sage next to the white candle. "And I have the silver candlestick that you gave me when I got my first apartment."

"There should be two. One for the white candle and one for the black, the black being for protection along with the silver."

"A black candle! That's what I was forgetting. Thanks. Is there anything else?"

"Are you finally starting to believe in your powers?" I could picture the look she was giving me. A raised eyebrow, head tilted toward me slightly, lips tight, and her free hand on her hip.

"Powers? Gram, you know I don't believe in witches."

"Says the girl who's asking me for help with spell work."

She had a point. But I wasn't a witch. I saw ghosts and was a decent matchmaker. Wasn't that enough? Why did I need to add a black pointy hat and flying on a broomstick to the mix?

"I'm willing to try anything, Gram. This brush has moved in both my shop and in my car."

At that moment, a commotion arose in the living room—the sounds of change clanking against the floor, the thump of my bag following the change, and finally a loud *thunk*, which could only be Saffy jumping to the floor from the couch.

"I gotta go. It's on the move again, and Saffy's after it. Thanks for your help!" I clicked the phone off, then dropped it onto the table before darting out to the living room.

Saffy skittered after the brush, hot on its heels as it slid across the floor to the front door.

"Stop it, both of you!"

The brush froze, and Saffy, her claws failing to find purchase on the wood floor, slid to a halt right in front of it. Now inches away, my pudgy little furball sniffed at the brush and repeatedly tapped it with her paw. Sniff. Swat. Sniff. Swat-swat-swat.

I shook my head at the messy but cute scene. "Saffy, leave it."

She looked up at me, blinked, then tapped the brush again.

"I'm serious. We don't know what we're dealing with. Leave it alone."

This time, she backed up and jumped onto the arm of the couch and stared at the brush. Her guard was up. I chuckled. Good guard cat.

Then I realized how much of my bag was strewn about the floor. Change, lip balm, *my* hairbrush—even my bag had been dragged a few feet. I rushed into the kitchen and grabbed my dustpan and broom from the closet. Who knows how many crumbs had been dumped onto the floor. My bag was a pit.

Several minutes later, the coins had been collected and deposited back into the change pocket in my bag, the lip balm and hairbrush were back in their rightful places, and the crumbs had been eradicated. At least the marshmallow rice treat had been spared. When I returned from putting the broom and dustpan back into the closet, the brush had moved again. Now it was directly in front of the door. Saffy still perched on the couch looking down at it, but at least she wasn't touching it anymore.

The oven timer sounded, and I headed into the kitchen

for dinner, telling the brush and my cat, "Let's not have a repeat of what just happened out here while I'm eating, okay?" I plated my dinner and placed it on the table. After cleaning up the living room once already, I didn't feel like eating in there like I usually did. The last thing I wanted was for the brush to start moving again and for Saffy to use me or my dinner as a springboard in an attempt to go after it. It felt weird to be eating alone at the table. I only ate here when I had company over.

After a few minutes, I tried to get Saffy to come join me by putting food in her bowl but she didn't come running like she always did. That brush had done something no one else had been able to do—distract her enough that she forgot about food.

Once I'd finished eating, I put away the leftovers and then packed my bag for tomorrow with all the supplies I'd need for Gram's recipe. I had everything she said I needed except for a black candle. The bakery had them, though. We kept all sorts of seasonal decorations in the closet. I had gotten black ones for Halloween.

Saffy and the brush were in the same spots when I walked back into the living room.

"Saffy, I'm going to bed." After this strange day, all I wanted to do was climb into bed and read a good book.

Usually she'd race—and beat—me to the bedroom. She was such a pillow hog before eventually settling in between my knees. Tonight, though, she'd barely glanced at me before returning her gaze to the brush.

"Fine, you two can stay there tonight. Just don't break anything."

I headed upstairs, hoping I'd get answers in the morning.

CHAPTER 5

At some point in the middle of the night, Saffy must have grown bored with guard duty. I found her curled up in between my knees early the next morning. The brush must have kept her up late as she had no interest in getting up and following me downstairs like she usually did. She merely stood up, turned in a circle three times, and lay back down when I slid my legs out from under her.

"Your breakfast will be waiting for you when you're ready. I'm taking the brush with me, so no worries there."

Her only response came in the form of faint snoring. I swore she slept more soundly than I ever did.

After getting dressed, I cautiously crept down the stairs, unsure of what I would find. I hadn't heard any ruckus overnight, but I wasn't taking that as a sign nothing had happened. I peered my head around the wall at the landing of the stairs that separated it from the living room.

Nothing. Everything was clean. Just as I had left it. Good.

Now it was time for tea. The spring weather had me craving something floral. I added some lilac loose leaf into a tea ball and then threw that into my travel mug.

As I waited for the water to boil, I dipped into my half bathroom off the side of the kitchen to finish getting ready.

"Well, hello. What are you doing in here?"

On the corner of my vanity sat the silver-plated hairbrush from Ashley. If I hadn't seen it move on its own yesterday and last night, I would have been thoroughly concerned about my sanity since I had left it by the front door. I certainly hadn't expected it to show up in my bathroom, but it was probably comfortable in what was likely a familiar setting. Ashley's dresser must have had a mirror since she had found it there one morning.

I took the brush with me as I exited the bathroom. The water was boiling now, so I poured some into my mug, then stirred in a spoonful of local honey. It was the only way I sweetened my tea. I got enough sugar in the bakery. After letting the tea steep for another minute, I pulled the tea ball from my thermos.

With that ready, it was time to go. I grabbed the bag with the supplies for Gram's recipe—I was not going to call it a spell no matter what she said—off the kitchen table for later. Bag, tea, and brush in hand, I headed through the living room. Slinging my purse over my shoulder and dropping the brush inside it, I opened the front door.

The predawn air was chillier than it had been yesterday, but It was nothing I couldn't handle, especially knowing that I'd be in a toasty kitchen soon. I breathed in the fresh air, took a sip of my tea, then began my ten-minute trek to the bakery.

Within minutes of flipping the lights on, my four bakers arrived to help with the day's load. We started on muffins as we did each morning. I had to deliver two dozen to each of the two diners in town first thing. Once we had those in the oven, Gina started on the pastries, Bryan took over muffins, and Lily used a portion of the muffin batter to pour it into loaf tins to bake into dessert breads. Sam was already filling cupcake tins with strawberry cake batter. We'd had a special order come in for a class birthday party and needed those for an early pickup. I began the cookies, one of my favorite things to make . . . okay, I liked making it all.

Once the diners' muffins were out of the oven, I boxed them and loaded up the bike trailer. By the time I got back, my team would have half of the day's muffins and cookies baking or already done and pastry shells cooling and waiting for cream.

My first delivery was always a quick stop. Carter, the owner of Double Aitch Diner, ran a tight ship. Although he had supported my bakery since the beginning, I always felt a bit in the way as I weaved my way around a sea of eggs cracking, meats and veggies being chopped, and soups for lunch already coming together. I nodded at the four cooks as I passed and dropped the two dozen muffins at their designated spot where they'd wait to be grilled with butter or served as is. Taped to the top was a list of what kinds the boxes contained and in what quantity.

Donna was unlocking the door when I pulled up at the second diner. Olde Templeton Diner was much smaller than Double Aitch, with only three tables and six spots at the counter. Despite its size, there was regularly a line out the door on weekends.

"Mornin', Joanie, what do ya have today?" Donna walked over to the specials board. I knew with that one question Donna was in a chatty mood. Other mornings she was content to read the list on the boxes.

She wrote as I spoke. "Six corn, six mixed berry, six chocolate chip, six lemon poppy."

"Good mix, good mix." She shuffled toward three coffee pots sitting empty in the kitchen window. She brought them to the small counter sink, filled them, then dumped one in each machine and set them to brew. A moment later, she plopped a heavy, white ceramic cup in front of me.

"Oh, I really shouldn't stay today, Donna. I—"

"You can take five more minutes to talk to one of your oldest customers and have a cuppa. The kids are perfectly capable of filling éclairs."

"That they are." I hopped onto a counter stool. They weren't kids, and it would be more like fifteen or twenty minutes, but people didn't say no to Donna Templeton twice.

"So did ya see the new man in town?" she asked as she poured me a cup of coffee, then began filling plastic baskets with jam and butter packets for each table.

"No, I haven't yet." I hadn't known the newest town resident was a man. "I take it you have?"

"He came in here for breakfast with his daughter yesterday. How'd you not see him? Don't cha make deliveries to the real estate office to celebrate these things?"

"Must have missed him. He wasn't there when I dropped off the cookies."

As she distributed the filled jelly baskets, she gathered the glass sugar pourers, then placed them onto the counter. "Guess it's just him and the girl." She unscrewed all the caps before reaching under her counter for a partially used bag of sugar to fill them with. "Don't know if the mom's dead or if they're divorced. Must be a doctor or something. He's working at the hospital."

"Oh, I have a delivery there today. Perhaps I'll see him." It wasn't likely. For a small town, we had a big hospital.

Donna continued as if I hadn't spoken. "Fine fellow, he is. I will watch him eat scrambled eggs any day. He's too young for me, but I have no problem looking." She sighed.

The sugar pourer she had been filling overflowed. "Ah,

look at me going on and on. You get. You have things to go do. Go on and have a nice day. Hope you see that hot doc."

She shooed me off the stool.

"Good to see you, Donna. Call the shop if you run out of muffins and need more. I'll send Sarah over. I bet she'd be happy to hear all about the hot doc."

She beamed with the prospect of new gossip. "You do that, Joanie. She always has the latest news."

My baking team was exactly where I thought they'd be in the process when I got back and then some. They could handle the place without me, but this also meant they were used to Donna keeping me awhile at the diner. She liked to talk, but she had a heart of gold too. She refused to charge me for my coffee. I'd heard, "Nope, I'm making you drink it. The least you can do is let me take care of it for you," numerous times.

I jumped into the baking frenzy and whipped up some more pastry cream, then worked on another several batches of cookies alongside Sam, who had already finished the day's cupcakes and was waiting on them to cool. My standard cookie varieties were already in the oven, along with the day's muffins for the shop, but these were the monthly specials— the spiced snickerdoodles and lemon blossoms—as well as the ones I thought might do the trick today. Yesterday it was black and whites. Today it was gingersnaps, both crunchy and soft. I was primarily making them for Rachael, but someone else might have needed to settle their stomach or perk up a bit. It was either/or with those. Funny how one food could have such a range of effects.

Sarah arrived as my team finished prepping the scones for baking. I followed her into the shop, and we went about our morning routine as I filled her in on the orders that had come in yesterday after she left. With the morning light streaming in, we grabbed trays of baked goods from the kitchen and loaded them into the display cases: one for cookies and cupcakes, a second for muffins and scones, and finally a refrigerated case for the sweet pastries.

Officially ready for the day to begin, I checked in on my bakers once more as they cleaned the kitchen while waiting on the last of the treats. I headed into our closet-sized bathroom to clean up. Having a little flour on me was normal, but I tried to look presentable at all times. One never knew who'd stop by the shop on any given day. I redid my ponytail, washed my hands, then walked back out front to switch the sign to *open*.

The day continued on like any other Thursday. The cupcakes were picked up bright and early by the excited birthday boy himself and his mother. Rachael's husband, Mark, picked up the gingersnaps and lemon-ginger scones I had made for her. She was missing work once again with severe morning sickness. Hopefully these would help her get back on her feet.

I eagerly anticipated Rich's arrival. I had placed the brush back under the checkout counter, and I wanted to see if it would have the same reaction today as yesterday. He arrived mid-morning during his free period for the muffins. The ghost wasn't with him, and the brush didn't react to his presence whatsoever. I found myself slightly disappointed by that. Although I didn't get to talk with him for long, Rich seemed to be feeling better about the Ashley situation, which was good at least.

My baking team headed home shortly after Rich left with his muffins, leaving Sarah and me alone in the shop.

"Feel like making the deliveries today, Sarah?"

"Me?" She pressed her palm to her chest. "Are you sure?"

I loved making the deliveries. It got me around town and

allowed me to talk to people more than staying in the shop did.

"Absolutely. There are only two. I have to run one to the hospital a little later—a care package for a patient—so I thought it would be good for you to get some more experience. It's been a while since you last helped me." Usually I had someone on the baking team do them if I couldn't. I liked them to see their efforts pay off.

"Great! So where do I need to go?"

Sarah followed me into the kitchen. As I boxed the three dozen cupcakes needed for the orders, I filled her in on the birthday at the local historical society and the retirement party at the fire and police station for one of the town's two dispatchers.

Sarah opted to drive her car for the deliveries. Although she joked that the bike trailer was embarrassing, I didn't fully buy it. The trailer wasn't that noticeable.

By the time she returned, I had almost finished creating the care package to take with me to the hospital. The order said to pack a mixture of "soft treats" with no other guidelines. I ended up including a few muffins and several of my softer cookies on a small circular tray. Nothing too chewy or with a crunch.

"I'm going to grab lunch at the hospital cafeteria while I'm there, so you're in charge for a bit," I told Sarah as I finished tying a ribbon around the gathering of clear plastic wrapping at the top of the bundle.

"Scoping the scene for the town's newest hot doc?" She raised her eyebrows repeatedly.

I chuckled. "Word sure travels fast around here."

"It's Heartwood Hollow." Sarah rolled her eyes, then gave me a look that said I should know better. "People talk. Especially about new people. Especially when they're hot. Now maybe people will stop talking so much about *you*."

After over four years of living here, I was still one of the newest residents in town. "What could anyone have to say about me? I bake. Run my shop. Make deliveries. Go home. Repeat. I'm not interesting."

"Your baked goods bring good luck, and you've single-handedly raised the population by six, soon to be seven, people because of your matchmaking."

"Ah, you heard about Rachael?"

"Of course I did. We went to high school together. But don't change the subject. I don't know how you do it, but there's some sort of magic in what you do."

"There's no magic." I'd never discussed the rumors about me before. There was nothing to say. At least, there hadn't been. After last night's discussion with Gram and knowing I had supplies for a divination recipe in the closet and a possessed brush on the shelf beneath the register, I was feeling a bit uncomfortable about it all. Perhaps there was some truth to those rumors after all.

"Sure . . ." This wasn't the first time Sarah had referenced their existence in the four years she'd worked for me, though, and she didn't believe my answer at all.

I half rolled my eyes and shook my head.

"Okay, okay. I'll drop it . . . for now."

Needing to put an end to the conversation, I said, "Gotta go. See you after lunch." I grabbed the care package and walked out the front door, stopping quickly to grab the brush. If it went crazy while Sarah was alone in the shop, I'd have a hard time convincing her there was nothing witchy about me.

CHAPTER 6

The hospital at the southwest edge of town required a bit of a hike uphill, but the day had warmed up to a comfortable sixty-some-odd degrees—warm for Heartwood Hollow and the entire Fiddlefern Fjord region this time of the year but perfect walking weather. Besides, walking around with a nice display of treats was great advertising for the bakery.

When I got to the third-floor nurses' station, Rich's mom greeted me. After not seeing the ghost with Rich this morning when he picked up the muffins, I had wondered if the older spirit followed other members of Rich's family. Beverly, however, was alone. Although this didn't confirm or deny my suspicions, I had a feeling the ghost only visited Rich. But why?

Since I wasn't a friend or family member of the patient getting the care package, I wasn't allowed to go to the room to deliver it. Bev, as she liked to be called, promised she wouldn't let anyone else get a hold of my treats and that she'd take care of it personally. I thanked her and then headed to the first-floor cafeteria. I'd worked up an appetite walking here and couldn't wait for lunch. The food here was surprisingly good, and since most of it was buffet style, it was hot and ready. Perfect for my rumbling stomach.

Tray full of food in hand, I approached the cafeteria tables and noticed Ashley and Rich sitting together eating lunch. It wasn't uncommon to see school staff and faculty at the hospital. The elementary, middle, and high schools shared a campus next door. Many teachers came for a quick lunch during their free periods. I couldn't tell what they were saying, but it looked like things were tense. Rich wasn't smiling. He almost always smiled. The ghost stood behind him, one hand tightly holding on to Rich's shoulder. Had the old man been alive, I'm sure it would have hurt Rich a little. The ghost's other hand was clenched into a fist, index finger extended and pointed at Ashley. It was as if the ghost was goading Rich, egging him on, adding fire to the situation.

I had to step in and shift the conversation before it could grow any more heated. This had the potential to jeopardize this match, and I didn't want that. Although anyone else seeing their discussion right now would likely wonder if these two should be together, they were perfect for one another. I had yet to be wrong. This wasn't like them at all.

I approached the three with my food-filled tray, hoping that saying hello would be enough of a distraction. Their reaction to my interruption would allow me to judge how awry things had gone. As I got closer, the ghost behind Rich lifted up his head, and we made eye contact. It wasn't a coincidence. He saw me, and this time, he knew I could see him. But even so, he still held on to Rich's shoulder, encouraging him to press the issue of whatever they were talking about.

The ghost wouldn't deter me. I wouldn't let him get in my way. As I took my next step, a ready to say hi with a smile on my face, I heard a slight *thunk*. Not registering what the sound could be, I took another step. My foot slid out from under me . . . and my tray flew into the air. I landed with a thud on the floor, my food all over me.

"Oh my God! Joanie, are you okay?" Ashley leaned over and handed me the few napkins she had. "Here, wipe your face. It's drenched."

Rich jumped to his feet. "I'll go grab some more napkins."

The ghost . . . was gone. If nothing else, I had made the ghost leave with my accident. Already the tense atmosphere had lessened.

"How clumsy of me." I plucked a lettuce leaf from my shoulder and tried to laugh off my accident, but thank goodness Rich was getting napkins. I was covered in food, and my shirt was no doubt ruined. The oil stains from the salad dressing would never come out of it. So much for having lunch.

Ashley held out her hand. "What did you trip on?"

I handed her my tray and my purse. As I got to my knees, I spotted the culprit. The brush had—probably literally—jumped out of my bag and landed in my footpath. I grabbed the brush and showed it to her.

"This."

"Why am I not surprised?" Ashley refused to take the brush from me, so I plopped it onto the table. She leaned away from it. "I should have burned it."

Focused on another piece of food clinging to my arm, I startled when a hand appeared in my line of sight. At first, I expected it to be Ashley since she was right there and had been helping me with my things, but then I noticed the hand lacked a colorful manicure and was way too big to be hers.

"Here, let me help you." Whoever it was pulled me onto

my knees and then, using my forearm, lifted me up to my feet.

When I saw who had rescued me from the floor, I let out a small gasp. This must have been who Donna and Sarah had meant by the new hot doctor, but I didn't think he was actually a doctor. He wasn't wearing scrubs or a medical coat. And I couldn't even be certain if he was the new man in town. The hospital drew people from around the region for work. He was somebody one noticed, though, and I hadn't seen him before.

Out of the corner of my eye, I caught sight of Ashley with a big grin plastered on her face. She gave me a thumbs-up. What, was she trying to play matchmaker? That was my job, although what a right job I was doing of it. A rush of warmth spread up my neck and across my face.

At that moment, Rich returned with napkins. "I've—"

Ashley shushed him with a flap of her hand and tilted her head toward us. Rich nodded once slowly in recognition and sat down. We had an audience.

"Are you all right? I can call for a doctor," the man asked once I was safely on my feet.

"Oh, no. I can assure you I'm fine. Just a bruised ego, that's all."

"Well, I'm glad you are okay. That was quite a fall."

"Thank you. For the help, I mean."

"I'm Ken Dawson, the new community liaison here at the hospital, and you are?"

"Joanie Sunevall, town baker and today's cafeteria klutz."

It was then we realized he was still holding on to my forearm. He dropped it as he stuck out his hand. "Baker, you say? Did you make those cookies in the gift basket the real estate office gave me?"

I took his hand in mine and gave it a quick shake. "Sure did."

"My daughter is going to be so excited I met you. She loved your cookies. She let me have two of them, but that's only because I told her there were raisins in them."

I laughed out loud, throwing my head back. A piece of lettuce slopped to the floor. After a short moment of mortification as we both looked at it by my foot, I glanced back at Ken and snorted a laugh.

He chuckled politely, likely not wanting to laugh in my face, but next to us, Ashley and Rich had devolved into a fit of giggles.

Taking a deep breath to calm myself, I brushed a strand of slimy hair that had fallen out of my ponytail behind my ear and finally took the opportunity to study Ken's face. His warm greenish eyes drew me in and shined with amusement. If I hadn't just run my fingers through more salad dressing, I would have said that had been a pretty good attempt at flirting on my part. It wasn't something I did often. I helped people meet others and get dates. I didn't go on them myself.

"Well, I should really get going. I need to go home and change my shirt before walking back to the bakery. I can't work smelling like a Caesar salad."

"And I need to head back to my office. It was"—he picked another lettuce leaf out of my hair and one off my shoulder—"*ice* to meet you, Joanie."

"I gotta give you credit. That was punny. It was nice to meet you too." Heat rose to my cheeks once more.

"Had to, sorry." He shrugged but had a big smile on his face.

"All right, well, you have a nice day." I patted him awkwardly on the chest. "Rich, Ashley, it was good to see you. Sorry for interrupting your lunch." I wasn't really but felt I had to say something. However, the truth that *I had to get rid of a ghost* wasn't the right thing.

"I'll have to stop by the bakery soon," Ken said. "Get some more cookies for my daughter. She'll be thrilled."

I smiled at him. "I'd like that, and I promise I won't be covered in my lunch next time."

CHAPTER 7

"Hey, Joanie, it's a little late for you to be coming in. Having the usual?" Gary asked when he saw me in line at Leafs and Grounds. I held up a wrapped marshmallow rice treat, the last one they had. At least something was working in my favor.

"Nope, just this today. Had a bit of an accident and had to go home and change. Missed lunch. Have to get back to give Sarah her turn."

"You, uh, spill batter or something on yourself? We're not going to have a cupcake shortage this afternoon, are we?" He rang up my treat. "That will be two thirteen."

"You could say that, but no," I replied, handing him two dollars and a quarter. "It wasn't at the bakery, so no shortages there."

"Oh, glad to hear it. Hey, do me a favor and tell Sarah I said hi, will you?"

"Sure thing." It was no secret that Gary liked Sarah, but she didn't see him that way. They weren't a match, at least, not yet—timing was an important factor in such things—but that didn't mean life wouldn't put them together eventually.

"Thanks. Hey, I owe ya one. Next one of those is on me." He pointed to the square treat in my hand, which I had already begun to unwrap. "I know how much you like them."

"They're absolutely delicious." I moved out of the way so the next person could order. "You have yourself a good day."

I exited the coffee shop and slowly walked back to the bakery while eating my marshmallow rice treat. There would be no saving half of it for later. I had plenty of perfectly good reasons to drown my feelings in crunchy, sticky perfection. Mostly, I was hungry and humiliated. Even a ghost had laughed at me on my way home to go change.

Concern lightly etched Sarah's forehead. "You weren't wearing that when you left. And your hair is wet. I thought you went to the hospital. You okay?"

"I ended up wearing my lunch instead of eating it. Figured it was best for me to go home and clean up a bit before coming back here." A major understatement. I couldn't have come back to work without a shower. Saffy had been so confused when I got home, but then she took one whiff of me and let me do my thing. They must not have used anchovies in the hospital's Caesar dressing or else she would have been all over me.

She refused let me leave my explanation at that. "What happened?"

"I saw Rich and Ashley in the hospital cafeteria. When I went over to say hi, I tripped holding my tray full of food." I wasn't going to tell her what I tripped on, though.

"Oh no!" She covered her open mouth with her hand but then tried to stifle her giggle.

I slung my purple apron over my head, then wrapped the ties behind my back. "And to make matters worse, I met the new man in town . . . *after* it all happened. He picked lettuce out of my hair. And made a pun out of it, saying it was 'ice' to meet me. It was iceberg lettuce. It was mortifying." I sighed. "He's not a doctor, by the way. He's the new community liaison at the hospital."

"You know I'll never remember that. Plus, *hot doc* has a much better ring to it."

"His name's Ken. Oh, and Gary told me to tell you hello from him."

"Nope, hot doc all the way," she replied, ignoring my comment about Gary. "Except to his face, of course."

I put my purse under the counter as Sarah stepped around me.

"I'll see you after lunch. Can I bring you back anything?"

I waved her off. "Nah, I'm good. I'll grab a cookie if the rice treat ends up not being enough."

She popped into the kitchen, and a minute later, the back door latched shut. She returned a half hour later, catching me red-handed as I shoved the last bite of a gingersnap cookie into my mouth.

I unzipped my purse, then removed the brush from the center pouch. "Man the front end, will you? I have an experiment to do in the back."

"Okay," she said automatically. "Wait, experiment? What are you doing? Why do you need that brush? There's no hair in it, is there? That's not sanitary, and you know it." She fired her questions in quick succession, then paused a moment. "Do I want to know?"

"No, probably not," I answered with my hand already on the door to the kitchen.

Letting the door swing shut behind me, I walked to the closet where I had already stowed the candle, sage, and candlesticks from home. There were several boxes on the closet floor, labeled *holiday*, and after digging through two, I finally pulled out a black candle from last year's Halloween decorations.

Sarah peeked through the round window in the kitchen door, but she wasn't tall enough to get a good view. She quickly backed up as I stood and approached the door.

I popped my head back into the bakery. "And, no, there's no hair in the brush. I already checked."

Hands on my hips, I turned around and faced the kitchen. I wanted answers. Now.

Although I had planned to do this after the bakery closed for the day, once the brush jumped out of my purse and tripped me—and I truly believed it purposely jumped—I refused to wait any longer. No time like the present. I needed to find out if it was possible for me to call the spirit forth. From there, I'd figure out what else to do.

Once I struck the match, I lit the candles. Then I blew out the match and held it to the dry sage. Like Gram said, it was just enough to make smoke. I walked to the corners of the room wafting the smoke outward with my hands. Memories of Gram doing this came to the forefront of my mind. At my house when I moved in a little over three years ago, in my second apartment, my first one, all my dorm rooms, and as far back as I could remember when Mom and I would spend New Year's Eve with her. "Cleansing the house and starting the year off right," she'd say as she, my mom, and my aunt smudged the house while us grandkids ran and opened the front and back doors to let the old energy out and the new energy in at the stroke of midnight. I hadn't done that in years. Funny how I never questioned it when I was a kid.

I set the brush between the two candles and spoke the recipe my grandmother had taught me. Why that had stuck in my head and not all the ingredients, I didn't know, but that was how my mind worked sometimes, even with food recipes.

It had caused many interesting flavor combinations over the years. Some not so good, but others made the rotation in my shop.

As I recited the recipe, the brush rattled. For a moment, I thought it was working, that I would finally get some answers for Ashley and myself. But as quickly as it had begun, the brush stopped moving.

"Drats. Well, I guess I'll have to call Gram back tonight. Mom might have an idea too." I'd call her if Gram didn't know what else to try.

Then the hairbrush began to spin, and in the air above it, a blurry apparition took shape. It looked vaguely female. It lasted only a minute before it vanished, almost looking like it had been sucked back into the brush.

"So there is someone in the brush! I was right! Okay, come on out and tell me who you are." I repeated the recipe, and although the brush now seemed to pulse with energy, nothing happened. Not even a rattle. I spent the next ten minutes trying to think of what I could do that would draw the spirit out of the brush. I tried anything and everything, but nothing worked. The ghost wouldn't appear before me.

A gust of air swept through the kitchen, one large enough to force me to turn and check the back door. We never left it open, but maybe it hadn't latched all the way when Sarah came back from lunch. It felt as if someone had just walked inside on a blustery day. As I expected, the door was still closed, but the breeze continued.

"Is that your way of trying to scare me?"

Now the room was literally humming, but I recognized the noise. I looked up and saw the ceiling fan oscillating. Was the ghost trying to get me to cool down and knock it off?

"It's not going to work. I will find out who you are."

Our pedestal fan by the counter turned on next, and

something I couldn't identify thumped. I guessed the spirit wanted to play games, but as long as I won, I was okay with it having a little fun. I hoped this would somehow force the ghost to show itself.

Then one of the stand mixers turned on. I couldn't let that run with nothing in it. That would burn out the motor, and those were expensive. I jogged over to it and turned it off. Undeterred, I immediately tried to entice the spirit out once more. I refused let that little distraction stop me.

Big distractions, on the other hand . . .

White specks danced in the air. First a few and then a little more.

"What the—" This couldn't be good.

I turned around to see flour trickling from a container on a shelf above the pedestal fan getting caught up with its breeze. The container was on its side, the lid flipped open. That must have been the thump, it tipping over. I leaned toward the fan to turn it off, but it wouldn't respond. Its on button hadn't been pressed. I'd have to unplug it, but I'd be risking another mess by crawling on the floor to reach the outlet behind one of drying racks. The fan hadn't been on in the first place, so I doubted that would even stop it.

I carefully reached up for the flour. Before I even had my fingertips around it, the lid shifted. The container dumped flour on top of the fan, sending it everywhere. I closed my eyes and tried to cover my face, but it was to no avail. I was covered in stuff for a second time today.

All of a sudden, the fans, the noise, the energy—it all stopped. The flour still in the air began to float to the floor.

At that exact moment, Sarah ducked her head in, a broad smile on her face until she saw the mess. "Um, Ken is here to see you."

"Oh, can you tell him I'll be there in a minute?" I couldn't go into the bakery looking like this, especially after the way I had met him a few hours before.

"Take two. You'll need it. Do I want to know what just happened here?" she asked, her gaze darting about the room.

"No"—I looked at the hairbrush on the counter. It was spotless despite being surrounded by flour—"but I think I lost."

CHAPTER 8

I dashed into the bathroom off to the side of the kitchen to wash up before greeting Ken. I surveyed myself in the mirror. Covered head to toe. Or at least head to belly button with a little—okay, a lot—more on my shoes. I wiped as much as I could off my head, whacking myself a little too hard a few times, but couldn't get much out of my hair. If anything, I'd made it look like it was graying so I could play some part in a school musical. I vowed to stock the small medicine cabinet above the sink with face soap after this.

I took off my apron and then tossed it in the hamper we had in the corner. We had several spares, so I grabbed a black one and tied it around my waist. It didn't have a bib but my shirt had the flour outline of one. Oh well. This was as good as I was going to get. So much for hiding the evidence of my mishap.

The fan blades had completely stopped revolving by the time I reached the door leading to the bakery. The flour had settled too, but I had tracked footprints throughout the kitchen. This would be such a pain to clean up.

Pushing the door open, I took a deep breath and tucked a

stray lock of hair back behind my ear. "Hi, Ken. What a pleasant surprise. I wasn't expecting to see you so soon."

Ken looked up from the cookie display case, a smile already on his face. "Hi, Joanie." He quickly looked away, sucking in his lips that were threatening to break into an even broader grin. It was adorable.

There was no use ignoring the obvious. "I promise you it's not an everyday look. I had a little mishap in the kitchen, that's all."

"And I thought you promised you wouldn't be covered in food the next time we saw one another." He chuckled. Guess I hadn't done as good a job washing up as I had hoped. "Sorry. Did you trip again?"

"You should have seen her a few minutes ago," Sarah interjected. "She definitely tried to clean up for you."

"Sarah, you're not helping," I mumbled as I passed behind her to get to the display cases. "And, no, I didn't trip again."

"She was doing a spell back there," Sarah said.

The last thing I needed was for Ken to take her seriously. "Sarah, would you mind getting some prep work done on the cupcake order we had come in?" I asked.

Sarah looked at me and cocked her head. "What order?"

I widened my eyes and shot a look over at Ken.

"Oh, that order. Yeah, no problem." She scooted out from behind the counter and into the kitchen, but not before shooting a wink over her shoulder at me.

I turned toward Ken. "Sorry about that."

"So a spell, huh?"

"She exaggerates. I was trying to solve a bit of a mystery by doing an experiment, that's all."

He leaned against the case. "I take it, it didn't go too well?"

I feigned offense. "What gives you that idea?"

Ken wiped the side of his nose with his index finger. "You still have a bit there."

I pawed at my nose. "Better?"

"And there. And there." He pointed to spots on my ear and shoulder.

I laughed. "And what if I meant to get covered in flour?"

"I'd say that was a very interesting experiment. Did you figure out what you needed to?" I appreciated his playing along, but the telltale warmth of a blush crept up my cheeks.

"I think it yielded some unexpected answers"—like that he was somehow involved. Why else would the brush ghost disappear upon his arrival?—"but I don't know what to make of them yet. So what can I do for you?"

"Well, I wanted to come check out the place after meeting you at the hospital. Part of my job is to get out into the community and establish relationships with the various businesses in town. Figured I'd start here . . . and pick up some cookies for my daughter since she liked the others so much."

"I'm so glad you liked them. How is your daughter handling the move? Does she like it here?"

"I guess okay. She's seven. So in a way, it's easier. She's already made a few friends."

"That's wonderful. And how about you?"

At that moment, Sarah popped her head back into the bakery, effectively ending that part of the conversation. "I'm done with what you asked me to do. I even swept up the floor." Considering there hadn't been any cupcakes, sweeping was all she had done. "Oh, you're *still* here," she said to Ken but raising her eyebrows at me.

"Sarah!"

"Sorry. Big mouth." She came and stood at the end of the counter.

Prompted by Sarah's comment, Ken glanced at his watch.

"Oh, I need to go pick Ivy up from practice—she's doing spring soccer—but I'd love to talk to you some more. Dinner tomorrow? I can get a sitter. One of the high school volunteers at the hospital is a well-known babysitter in town, apparently."

Sarah laughed so hard she could barely breathe. She drew in a breath and doubled over. "Joanie doesn't date. Ever."

"Sarah!" Did she have to make this more awkward than it already was?

"Sorry." She shrugged. "Me and my big mouth again. But it's true. You've lived here over four years, and you've never gone out with any guys. Not even for coffee."

I chuckled good-naturedly. Her big mouth was going to get her in trouble one of these days. But right now, she had talked herself into a corner she couldn't escape from. "And you'd know so much about coffee, right, Sarah? When was the last time you grabbed a mocha? You wouldn't be avoiding a certain cute coffee guy, now, would you?"

Her smile dropped slightly, but she quickly recovered. "Oh, I like spicy Joanie. I blame it on the gingersnap I caught you snacking on earlier. But, I admit, you got me there. I'm wounded." She clasped her hands to her heart and broke out in laughter once more.

Ken had been watching our good-natured sparring match like a ping-pong game, his head bobbing side to side. By the end of it, once he realized neither of us was mad at the other, he was laughing too.

I needed Sarah out of the shop. She couldn't be our audience for this. Her big mouth would mean everyone would find out the "hot doc" and I were going on a date before I had enough time to process it. I turned serious. "Would you mind pulling out another bag of flour from storage?"

"Yeah, sure, since most of what we had ended up on you and the floor."

"Wipe the counters, too, please," I called to her back as she had one foot already in the kitchen. I turned back toward Ken. "So about that date—"

He held up his hands. "I'm sorry if I assumed. If you don't date men, that's okay."

"What?" He'd gotten that idea from Sarah's response to him asking me out? "No, I do. I do. I just haven't in a while. I would love to get dinner with you." I smiled.

His grin widened. "Great, it's a date, then. Tomorrow night. Can we meet here, or I can pick you up at your house if you'd like."

"How about my house? It will give me time to clean up in case I happen to have any more accidents"—I swept my arm down in front of my flour-covered self—"in the kitchen." I wrote my address down on a blank order slip and handed it to him.

"Great. Six thirty?"

I nodded. "Perfect."

"I'm looking forward to it." He glanced at his watch again. "Okay, I really do have to be going."

"Wait, let me wrap a few cookies up for your daughter. That was one of the reasons you came here, right?"

"Oh, uh, yeah." He gave me a sheepish grin.

I barked out a laugh. "Busted."

"No, really, she'd kill me if she found out I came in here and didn't get her something," he said as I started gathering cookies.

"Does she have a favorite?"

"Can all of them count as a favorite? But no raisins."

"Got it." I continued grabbing cookies, then placed them

in a box. "I think I went a bit overboard," I said, giving him the box.

"She's going to be thrilled. Thank you. What do I owe you?"

"It's on the house. Think of it as a welcome to town present."

"No." Ken shook his head. "There are way too many cookies to be free. Plus, you already gave me a welcome present when I closed on the house." He pulled out his wallet. "Please, I insist."

"Okay, fine, but only because you insisted," I replied, ringing him out but giving him an undisclosed, generous discount.

"Thanks, Joanie. I will see you tomorrow." He nodded at me and headed for the door.

"I'm looking forward to it." I gave him a small wave as he looked over his shoulder.

"Me too."

Once he'd passed the bakery window, I called out to Sarah. "It's okay to come back in now."

Something scraped across the kitchen floor. Sarah pushed open the door a moment later. "Joanie has a date, Joanie has a date," she teased in a sing-song voice.

"How long were you spying?"

"Spying? Me? I can't see through that window. I'm not tall enough."

I put one hand on my hip. "I heard the chair."

"Shoot. I saw enough to know he's a good guy. You'll have fun together. I'm happy for you. Now, I am *not* going to clean the rest of that up by myself without some answers."

I played innocent. "Answers?"

She was smarter than that. "Yeah, starting with, can you please explain this?" She pulled the hairbrush from behind her back. "This doesn't help your whole 'I'm not a witch' thing. You know that, right?" She led me into the kitchen.

"But it's true. I'm not a witch."

Sarah turned and raised an eyebrow at me.

"I'm not. But sometimes weird things happen around me. That's all." It was an understatement, but I wasn't about to blow weird out of the water by telling her I saw ghosts.

She sighed. "Okay. Good enough for now. So witch stuff aside, what's with this brush?"

"Well, you know how I'm kind of good at matchmaking, right?"

"Of course I do. The whole town does. Several babies can thank you for being alive right now."

"I think this brush has something to do with why Ashley and Rich aren't together yet."

"They really would make such a cute couple, but why would this brush have anything to do with it? What happened in here?"

"That I'm not sure about yet, but the brush was Ashley's. And this"—I waved my arm, displaying the surrounding mess —"is one of those weird things that I mentioned. I'm going to have to investigate further on Saturday when they both don't have to work. They're supposed to be together. I just know it."

"Because you're a witch?"

Now it was my turn to raise an eyebrow at her. I held out my hand for the brush, which she plopped into my palm.

"I know, I know." She sighed. "You're not a witch. Now how about we clean the rest of this up? I'd like to get home tonight."

I held up my index finger, then darted back into the bakery where I switched the sign from *open* to *closed* after a quick glance at the clock to make sure it was time. I tossed the brush in my purse and zipped it shut, knowing the brush wasn't the only problem. The ghost that followed Rich also played a key part in keeping Rich and Ashley separated. But were they part of the same issue, or were they connected to two completely different things? And I couldn't forget how everything stopped the moment Ken stepped foot in the bakery. That couldn't be a coincidence, could it? I needed to learn more about this ghost following Rich, the brush, and the new man in town.

I stepped back into the kitchen and placed my hands on my hips. "All right, let's get to work."

CHAPTER 9

Fridays in the bakery usually sped by. They were busy with people placing orders or picking up treats for the weekend. But that didn't mean they didn't drag sometimes. That was the case with today, and I blamed it entirely on being excited for my date. Or was it nervousness? Maybe it was both.

Sarah had been completely accurate when she blurted out that I didn't date. She only knew my dating history from the four plus years I'd lived here, but I hadn't been on a date since my second year in college. I'd had a decent handle on my ability to see ghosts back then, but I still couldn't always tell the difference between someone alive and someone, well, not. Ghosts weren't see-through. They didn't have a blueish glow around them, and they didn't float or walk through things. To me, they looked normal. Alive. Over the years, it had caused quite a few heads to turn when I struck up conversations with those around me who no one else could see. I'd done that on my last date, tried to talk to someone who I thought was a waiter. Well, he didn't bring me my dinner, but he did bring about the end of the date.

Fortunately, it had been with someone I had met online and not someone I had to face every day in class. I didn't know what I would have done if I had to do that. I wouldn't have been able to avoid him. You can't get a baking degree online.

After that incident, I swore off dating, even after I had a firmer grip between the living and the dead. I hadn't been surprised by one in years. Ghosts usually had this calm demeanor about them. The ones I saw now, anyway. My gram and mom had banished the bad ones from interacting with me, but before they did, *calm* was not how I would have described them. The ghosts also didn't talk back without the use of a lot of energy. They lived out their days in familiar routines, like the man with his dog, or followed loved ones, like the man who followed Rich.

There was something charming about Ken, though, that broke through my no dating rule. Maybe it was how he had helped me in the cafeteria when I was drenched with salad dressing or the way he tried not to laugh at my flour-covered self. But whatever this was, I wanted to see where it went. At least for one date, anyway.

Sarah had the early part of the morning off, my treat for her staying later to help me clean the kitchen, but she arrived right on time—a mocha in hand—for me to make my deliveries for the second half of the day.

"Are you excited?" she asked giddily.

"Um . . . does excited feel a bit like wanting to puke and jump up and down at the same time?"

She nodded. "It certainly can."

"Then, yes, I'm excited."

Sarah clapped her hands, then took off her sweater and stashed it in the kitchen closet. She came over to help me finish packing the last delivery box. "I know I teased you in front of Ken, but I really am happy for you. It's nice to see you like this."

I sealed the box and picked it and another up. Sarah grabbed the third off the counter and followed me outside to my bike.

"Thanks." I nodded toward her drink. "And I see you took some initiative in the guy department as well. How's Gary?"

She sighed. "He wasn't there. I swear I didn't know that when I went in, though. I'd have been going when he wasn't working all along if that were the case. I've missed my good coffee."

We loaded the trailer, and I headed out on the bike.

Billy, Libby's husband, met me in the kitchen. He was a pleasant guy, not overly chatty, and said Libby was out getting flowers for the tables' centerpieces when I arrived. The spring flowers were in full bloom, and their garden was bursting with pale purples, pinks, and yellows.

As I left, I could just make out Libby, in overalls and a wide-brimmed hat, across the wide expanse of a lawn amongst the flowers. I waved in a broad sweeping motion in case she happened to stand up from her gardening and see me.

My next and last stop was Town Hall, where I had to deliver a birthday cake and cupcakes to celebrate the town manager's birthday.

"Hey, Jill," I said as my best friend's assistant greeted me at the entrance. "Feeling better?"

"Loads. That green tea and honey suggestion helped. Thank you."

"I'm glad." I lifted the box in my hands a bit higher. "This going anywhere special?"

"They can come in here, Joanie," Courtney called from her office. "I'm going to hide it in the closet."

"You got it." I walked into my best friend's office as she stood and headed for the closet.

"The party isn't until this afternoon," she explained. "We may have scheduled a few extra meetings for the town manager so he wouldn't be on to us. Then again, he could be on to us because we scheduled so many meetings. Either way, he's not here, and I don't want to ruin the surprise—if it is still a surprise—when he walks back in."

She opened the closet door. "Actually, might as well have you put it in so we don't have to move it more than necessary."

I slipped the box onto an empty shelf, and Courtney closed the door.

"Hey, do you have time for lunch today? The party is pretty much all set, so I can go split a sandwich with you or something if you're able."

It had been ages since we caught up properly. "Absolutely. You ready now?"

"Sure, let me grab my bag."

"All right. I'll meet you outside. I'm going to go move my bike."

I pulled my bike around the corner of the building to behind a storage shed attached to Town Hall. It wasn't locked up, but at least it was out of the way and random passersby couldn't see it. I'd been told numerous times that it would be just as safe sitting out front, but that made me feel like I was asking for trouble. Bikes disappeared all the time near the college campus I had lived on. I hadn't outgrown the belief that my bike wouldn't be there when I got back if I left it out in the open.

I waited for Courtney at the bottom of the steps. She came out a minute later. "Are we walking? Who am I kidding?" She laughed. "Of course we are. It's a great day."

"Actually, I can't believe I'm asking this, but do you mind driving? I didn't tell Sarah that I was taking lunch."

"Sure, not a problem." We walked around back, then hopped into Courtney's silver hatchback. She drove the few blocks to the coffee shop, where we ordered a sandwich to split and each got a cup of soup.

We stood at the end of the counter and waited for our order. Once it was called, we made our way to a table in the back corner of the shop, closest to the open patio doors. The patio had yet to be set up for the season, but if today's weather was any indication, soon we'd be sitting out there.

"I have a bone to pick with you," Courtney said as she sat down.

That instantly set me on high alert. "Why, what did I do? Oh, geez"—I covered my face with one of my hands—"you heard about the incident at the hospital, didn't you? It was so humiliating!"

Courtney's eyes widened. "I had not, but now you need to tell me. But first, why didn't you tell me you had a date? I'm your best friend. You're supposed to call and tell me these things."

"How did you already find out? He only asked me out last night."

"Do you really need me to tell you? Did you forget our assistants are roommates?"

I winced. "Man, Sarah has a really big mouth."

"And so does Jill, but I encourage it by asking her for the latest scoop every morning." She laughed.

"You're terrible," I joked. "And I am sorry I didn't tell you. I'm still kind of surprised it happened." I took a bite of my half of the sandwich. The pesto to mozzarella to tomato ratio was divine. I chewed slowly, savoring the bite.

"All's forgiven as long as you call me as soon as the date is over."

"Deal."

"Now, tell me about this 'incident.' Did it involve hot doc?"

I'd have to break her out of the habit of calling him hot doc if this went beyond a single date. I nodded and told her the whole story, stopping short of admitting what the something was that fell out of my bag and tripped me. Telling her that a haunted brush purposely landed in front of me would have been too much for her. I didn't need my best friend thinking I was crazy, or worse, to lose her like I had my last one because of this ability.

We spent the next half hour catching up before we both had to get back to work. She drove us back to Town Hall, and we said goodbye in the parking lot. I grabbed my bike—it was right where I had left it—and rode to the bakery.

"Oh, good, you're back," Sarah said when I strolled into the bakery from the kitchen. "How was lunch?"

"How do you know I had lunch?"

"Jill told me."

I sighed. "What have I told you about being on your phone while at work? What if a customer walked in?"

"I know, but when you didn't come back, I wanted to make sure you had gotten there. And I didn't use my phone. I used the shop's."

Sarah's responsibility pleasantly surprised me, and I chided myself over my lack of it. "I should have called you, I'm sorry. Thank you for your concern."

"I figured you would go since you were seeing Courtney, but I had to check. Can I go to lunch now?"

"Sure. Oh, one more thing."

She turned back to face me, her hand already pushing the door into the kitchen. "Yeah?"

"Can you not discuss my dating life with Jill? Courtney already knew about tonight. Kinda takes the fun out of being able to tell people myself."

Sarah looked down. "I'm sorry. It's my big mouth. I was happy for you, that's all. He's so delicious! But don't worry, I didn't tell her anything about your witchy business."

"Good, since there's nothing witchy about it."

"Keep telling yourself that, Joanie, and maybe you'll start to believe it." She walked through the door, leaving me alone in the bakery.

The afternoon both crept and flew by. A steady pace of customers kept us busy for the most part, but whenever someone wasn't there, the minutes crawled. Today was one of those days when, if I really had magic, I'd have used it to speed up time.

Finally, I was locking up the bakery and ready to drive home. I had taken the car this morning so I could have as much time to get ready for my date with Ken as I could get. It had been so long since I'd been on a date, I expected several outfit changes and requiring extra time to make sure my makeup looked natural and not like I was trying too hard—a fine line to walk for someone who rarely bothered with more than lip gloss and clear mascara.

Saffy greeted me on the arm of the couch after running along the back from her spot in front of the window. Tail shaking, she pranced into the kitchen, leading me to the cupboard where her food was kept.

"Here you go, Saffy." I scooped half a can of soft food into Saffy's special bowl. I placed the remaining half in the refrigerator for tomorrow.

Saffy turned around to see if she had her audience. She hated to eat alone when I was home.

"I can't watch you eat tonight. I'm going on a date and have to get ready."

Saffy cocked her head and stared at me.

"I know, I know. Words you've never heard me speak in your life."

I headed upstairs to hop in the shower. When I came out, Saffy was sitting on the foot of the bed. "What, are you going to help me pick something out?"

She stood and circled her spot three times before lying down. But she kept her head upright, eyes trained on my closet.

By six o'clock, I had tried on five outfits before settling on the little black dress I had put on first. I should have trusted Saffy's fashion sense. It was the only one she had meowed for. She probably liked the idea of how much cat fur would show up on it if she got close enough to it.

Once I was dressed, I darted back into the bathroom. I pulled the top half of my brown hair back into a small pony-tail and let the rest fall in loose, natural waves to my shoul-ders. For makeup, I applied black mascara and pink lipstick, with a bit of blush. Despite having to wash it all off once because I'd been a bit heavy handed, my second attempt didn't turn out half bad. I had a steady hand from years of decorating cakes, but I knew not to mess with eyeliner when I was so nervous.

Now I had to wait for Ken to arrive.

Longest ten minutes ever.

CHAPTER 10

At exactly six thirty, footsteps on my porch preceded a loud knock. I rushed over to the door, then took a deep breath to calm my nerves before opening it.

I greeted Ken with a big smile. "You are right on time. Come on in. I just need to grab my purse and we can go."

"Wow, you look beautiful." Ken handed me flowers. "These are for you."

"Oh, thank you so much!" I sniffed the bouquet of peach-colored roses. "Let me go put these in water."

I shuffled into the kitchen, afraid to trip over myself even though I was wearing flats. Still holding onto the bouquet, I grabbed a vase from the cupboard over my refrigerator. Once it was filled with water, I set the flowers inside and placed the vase on top of the fridge so Saffy wouldn't be able to eat the bouquet while I was gone. With as much as I liked flowers, I had learned from that mistake one too many times when I first got her.

I stepped into the living room to find Saffy sitting in the center of the floor, appraising Ken. Ken, bless him, was crouched with his hand extended toward her.

"She won't come to you. It's only your first time here. She doesn't think it's worth making friends unless she knows they're going to come back. You actually need to come back to prove it to her." I grabbed my purse as Ken stood up. "Ready to go?"

Ken nodded. "Sure am." He turned to my Saffy, who was still staring at him. "It was nice meeting you. I hope to see you again." My heart melted at how he was trying to win her over.

Saffy stood up, walked away, and jumped onto the couch, where she took up her spot by the window.

We drove the few blocks to the town parking lot off Main Street and walked to Nick and Etta's, one of two Italian restaurants in Heartwood Hollow. Although the other had food just as delicious, the atmosphere made Nick and Etta's the one most people chose for a nicer date. The restaurant was a few storefronts down from my bakery, and like my bakery, it was long and narrow—three tables wide, six tables deep, with two more tables in the back for larger groups. We were sat to the side, diagonally across from a husband and wife and their young daughter in a high chair. The toddler turned to watch us as we sat down and were read the specials by our teenage waiter, Todd. She was still staring when Todd left. I waved to her and said hello.

"I remember when Ivy was that age. She'd smile at everyone."

"She's so cute. Those cheeks!" I flipped a page of my menu. "Is this your first time leaving your daughter with a babysitter?"

"Here, yes. But it was a rare occurrence where we used to live. We didn't get out much. Me even less so."

"Oh, I see," I replied, noting the slight tension toward the end of his statement.

He laughed. "But enough about Ivy. I told myself I wouldn't only talk about her tonight and scare you off by all of my single dad talk."

"I don't scare that easily," I commented, noticing that the family of three was no longer alone. They were now joined by an older woman—a ghost. The little girl was entranced.

Our waiter came for our order. Chicken parm for me with the house white wine, and chicken marsala for Ken with a draft beer from one of the local breweries. We made idle chitchat until dinner arrived, finding out more about one another. Talking to him was easy.

Dinner arrived on large plates with heaping portions. As we ate, I found myself distracted by the little girl and the ghost, who were now playing with one another. The girl seemingly giggled at nothing, much to the delight of her parents, who I'm sure were happy to be able to enjoy their meal together, but I knew better. The innocence of children allowed most to see ghosts without realizing there was anything different about them. For some, like me, this continued well past childhood.

The ghost made faces at the toddler. I chuckled, gaining the attention of both the girl and the ghost, who I assumed was the little girl's grandmother. The ghost seemed surprised I could see her, and a grin just for me grew on her face. I waved.

"Joanie, did you hear me?" Ken asked.

"Hmm?" I hadn't. Whoops. Strike one for me. "No. I got caught up by the baby. Sorry." I resolved to pay better attention to my date. I turned to find him staring at me smiling with a faraway look on his face, making me feel like he didn't mind my being distracted at all.

He looked at the little girl. "She does seem so happy, doesn't she? I loved when Ivy would giggle at nothing."

As easy as Ken was to talk to, telling him his daughter had likely been laughing at ghosts probably wasn't first-date material.

"Do you want kids someday?" he asked.

"I love kids." Truthfully, I had no idea how to handle kids, but I loved each one who came into the bakery.

"They're great. I wouldn't mind having another one or two."

"I bet you're a great dad."

"Hope so. Ivy—" He laughed. "Nope, not gonna do it. I'm not going to show you how sad my life is because all my stories are about my kid."

"Oh, I highly doubt that. You just aren't used to telling them anymore. I'll get them out of you yet." I felt compelled to place my hand on top of his where it rested on the table. It was warm and slightly rough. He smiled at my touch, and I gave him one in return.

"Thanks. So what I was asking before was, do you want dessert? We don't have to. I'm sure you get enough of it when you work."

"Oh, I can never have enough dessert. I eat it whenever offered. Morning is my favorite time of day because I can taste test everything we're baking for the day."

"And yet you look as if you tired of it years ago and haven't touched a crumb since."

Todd returned then for our order, which gave me time to think of a response. I knew Ken had meant it as a compliment, but I felt slightly awkward. It was a stereotype that all bakers were pudgy and then some.

"Aww, thank you," I finally said. "You're not the only one to comment on that. You'd be rolling me out of here if I didn't usually walk and ride my bike everywhere."

He pointed to my head and mimicked removing a lettuce leaf. "Does that mean that yesterday . . ."

"I had to walk home with salad-covered hair? Yes. Thank goodness few people saw me."

"And again with the flour?"

"It was a . . . special day for me." I laughed. "Saffy didn't know what to make of me taking three showers yesterday."

When our desserts arrived, I dug in. The tiramisu here was to die for.

Ken had gotten the same. "You were right on with this recommendation."

"What can I say? I know my desserts. The key to not getting sick of them is to never order what you work with. But it helps that I experiment regularly with new flavors at the bakery too."

"Ivy loved the cookies, by the way."

"She hasn't eaten them all already, has she?"

"Gosh, no. Although, she would have had I let her. Have to ration them. And there I go again."

I placed my hand back on his, having removed it at some point between ordering and receiving dessert. I gave it a slight squeeze. "It's okay to talk about her."

"Thanks. I'll work on my conversational skills for next time."

The idea of *next time* sent a happy shiver through my body. Dinner had been lovely. I could see going on another date with him, and this one wasn't over yet.

Todd came over with our check, and Ken insisted on paying for all of it. He handed the billfold back to the teen, saying it was all set. He turned to me. "Can I interest you in a walk down by the river before the movie?"

"Absolutely."

The evening had grown cool. But it was a clear night, and

the weather wasn't stopping anyone from enjoying one of the first nice Fridays of the season.

Music grew louder as we approached the park. Soon two guitarists came into view. They strummed along to the beat of a single drum held between the knees of a third man sitting on a stool. Several people danced around them in an area lit up by twinkling lights strung between two light poles and a tree. I swayed to the beat as we walked.

"This town is charming."

"Just wait until your first festival. You've not lived until you've experienced one of those."

"I'm looking forward to it."

"The next one is coming up in a few weeks."

At that moment, a man danced up next to me, a broad grin on his face, and spun me halfway around as he continued past me.

"Whoa, are you okay?" Ken asked.

I laughed it off. "Yeah, I tripped. Must have been a rock or something." There wasn't a good way to explain a friendly ghost who was enjoying the music as much as I was.

"You seem to do that a lot." Ken wrapped an arm around my side. "Now I'll be ready to catch you in case it happens again."

I smiled up at him. "Thanks."

After stopping to listen to the music for a few minutes, we continued to follow the path through the park, the guitar notes fading the farther we got up river and the drumbeat dying out soon after. The silence was comfortable, as easy as it had been to talk to him. I was grateful every moment didn't have to be filled with conversation. After a full day of being at the bakery and chatting with customers, I liked being able to turn off and have a bit of silence so I could recharge.

The path meandered away from the river and toward the

street as it came closer to the park's border with the inn. Both the inn and Riverview Park had once been owned by Alfred Dunmore, the town's founder. He founded the park upon his death through a provision in his will. As such, the line of sight from the inn remained almost the same as it had been one hundred fifty years ago. It made the property seem expansive even though it was much shorter on this side.

We turned up the sidewalk once we exited the park and headed toward Main Street to the one-screen theater. It showed close to first-run movies and rotated three throughout the day, preventing many of us in Heartwood Hollow from having to drive the thirty minutes to a multi-screen theater unless we really wanted to see something right away.

Halfway up the street, a block away from the theater, Ken's phone rang.

"Sorry, I have to see who this is," he said as he dug his cell out of his pocket.

"Sure, go ahead." As if I was going to tell a father he couldn't check his cell phone when he wasn't with his daughter.

"Hey, is everything okay?" I knew it was the babysitter with that one question. He went silent a moment as he listened to why she had called then scrubbed his hand up the side of his face. "Yeah. Okay. It's fine. I understand. I'm on Main Street and can be there in a few minutes."

No doubt about it, date night was getting cut short.

"Yeah. Bye." Ken turned to me. "Bad news."

"Is Ivy okay?"

"She's fine, but the babysitter has to go help her grand-mother because the dog escaped again. I'm sorry." He rubbed the back of his neck. "That sounds like some horrible excuse I've made up to get out of our date."

"Is your babysitter Lichelle Walker?"

"How'd you guess?"

"Otis gets out all the time. Even I've been roped into a search or two. Great dog, but he can jump any fence they put up. Claudia even had an electric fence installed, and it doesn't bug him a bit."

Ken breathed a sigh of relief. "You knowing I'm not trying to pull a fast one makes me feel slightly better. I really am sorry to have to end the date early. I was having a good time."

"Me too." I couldn't hide the disappointment in my voice. "But I'm glad nothing's wrong with Ivy."

"Can I drive you home?" he asked as we backtracked toward the town parking lot.

"Oh, no, that's all right. It's a nice night. I don't mind the walk. And it will get you home to Ivy all the sooner."

He asked me if I was sure a few more times on the walk to his car. Finally, we reached his navy sedan. "Well, here we are."

"Yes, and before you ask again, yes, I'm okay with walking home."

"Let's do all of this again sometime soon, okay? But without the interruption next time."

"I'd like that." Hoping for a goodnight kiss, I shifted forward and put more weight on my toes so I'd be ready to lift onto them.

"Enjoy the rest of your night, Joanie." Ken stuck out his hand.

So much for that kiss. Taking his hand in mine, we shook. I hadn't ever ended a date like this before. "You too." I stepped back from the car so Ken could open his door and began walking away.

"Joanie?" Ken asked from much closer than expected.

I turned. "Yes?"

He rubbed the back of his neck. "May I kiss you goodnight?"

A slow smile crept onto my face. I tucked a strand of hair behind my ear. "Yes, you absolutely can."

He leaned in and gave me a small peck on the cheek. Not what I was expecting, but not unpleasant either.

"Goodnight, Ken."

"Goodnight." He climbed into his car and closed the door.

I waved as he drove out of the parking lot and walked home, disappointed but understanding. Tonight made me wish I could use my matchmaking skills on myself, but they didn't work that way.

Several minutes later, I arrived back at my house. Saffy sat waiting for me at the window. I wondered if she had even left that spot. She wasn't used to me going out at night.

I unzipped my purse to dig for my keys. I was probably one of the few who actually locked their door in town—another holdover from having lived in a city when going to school.

Sitting at the top of my bag was the hairbrush Ashley had given me. I had forgotten all about it being in there. Fortunately, it hadn't acted up. Was the ghost gone, or was it because I had been with Ken?

I finally found my keys—how was it they always slipped to the bottom of my bag?—then unlocked the door. Saffy came running, her tail shaking as it always did when she was happy. I thought she'd dive headfirst into my bag, but nope, she ignored it. Instead, she headbutted me right in my stomach and turned to rub against me. It was her way of checking up on me and making sure I was okay.

"Well, that didn't quite go as planned. But it wasn't a bad date. I think you might even see him again sometime. What are your thoughts on kids?" She pulled away from me. "He has a daughter," I clarified, giving her a quick scratch under her chin.

Once she'd had enough, she scampered into the kitchen, hoping for more food.

With Saffy's non-reaction to the brush, I knew it would be safe in my bag overnight. I zipped it back up, the hairbrush still inside, confident it wouldn't be able to get away somehow.

Tonight I had to feed my sassy cat and get out of this dress that was now covered in fur. My bed was calling me.

Tomorrow I'd get my answers.

CHAPTER 11

By the next morning, word about my date had spread even further. I swore by lunch, half of Heartwood Hollow would have heard I'd gone out with the new man in town last night. Someone must have seen me. After speaking with Sarah yesterday, I didn't think she'd go blabbing right away. I'd give her another day or two. That was the one thing about her. She usually spoke first and thought later when it came to gossip. But she was a great worker, one of my best, and had been with me since before the bakery had opened.

But somehow Donna knew, and even Carter at Double Aitch mentioned it when I dropped off the diner's muffins and picked up my check for the week.

"So I heard you went on a date last night," Sam said when I walked in after making the first round of deliveries. We only had one midday delivery, a birthday cake for Gina's mom, so I'd told everyone to go home once the baking was done. Gina had already planned on leaving early to get ready for her mom's party, but Lily and Bryan jumped at the chance to leave as well. Sam offered to stay just in case, and I put him to work decorating the two-tier cake I had crumb-coated, stacked, and covered in fondant that morning.

"I did," I admitted, "but how did you find out?" I hadn't expected him to be a gossip. Sam was a no-nonsense, tell-it-like-it-is, college-bound high school senior. He had come to me a year ago to formerly ask about interning with me because he'd wanted to go to culinary school. That hadn't been the first time he'd mentioned it though. The first time I'd met him, back when he was a freshman, he'd told me about the high school graduation requirement. I'd already written him a glowing recommendation letter for three schools he'd applied to, including my alma mater. I hoped he'd get in there. He'd flourish in the city with all it had to offer.

"Um," he hesitated. "My boyfriend was your waiter."

I hadn't known. I'd wondered, but it wasn't something I'd considered asking with our boss/employee relationship. And besides, it didn't matter to me. He was Sam.

"Thank you for trusting me enough to tell me." I opened my arms toward him. "Can I give you a hug?"

He dove into my embrace. "Of course."

"I'm proud of you." I patted him on the back.

"Then you're going to be really proud of me when I tell you I got in to my top choice." My school.

"You did? I knew you could! Congratulations!"

"Thank you! I owe so much of it to you."

I dropped my arms and placed a hand on his shoulder. "Are you kidding me? You were talented before you ever set foot in this bakery. This is all you, Sam. Now let's go look at your decorations."

"This is great work, Sam," I told him after he showed me the flowers he'd shaped and sculpted. "Are you busy this morning?"

"I'm meeting Todd for lunch. Why, do you need me to stick around for a bit?"

"How would you like to deliver this cake with me?"

His eyes widened with excitement. "Really?"

"Absolutely. You've earned it."

"That'd be awesome."

"Great! Let's go fill Sarah in on the morning." She'd arrived while I was inspecting the cake and had gone straight into the shop once she got here.

Before I could give her the daily update, she demanded to hear how that date went first. I told her about my getting ready to appease her for the moment, then gave her bits and pieces as we raced through the morning's first customers. Sarah expressed concern over Ken's getting a call to leave early, but when I told her it was because of Otis, she understood completely.

Sam watched the morning's transactions with rapt attention. I'd have to ask him about picking up a few shifts in the shop for the summer so he could see the business side of things.

After the morning rush, the stream of customers fell to a steady lull.

"Hey, Sarah. After Sam and I make this delivery, I'm going to head home."

"Okay." She nodded, but I didn't think she understood that I probably wouldn't be back today.

"I'll call Lauren in. You'll be in charge for the rest of the afternoon."

The reality of it hit her then. "I've never been in charge for that long."

"But you've done nearly half of that length already all by yourself on days I make deliveries and take a lunch. You know how to close too. You've got this."

"I've got this," Sarah replied quietly to herself. "So what are you up to today?"

"I have something I got to do." Widening my eyes, I hoped she'd let me leave it at that.

"Something witchy?" Hint not taken.

Sam's mouth parted slightly. This was what I'd wanted to avoid.

"Sarah!" Now she was spreading the idea of my being a witch to others with her lack of a filter. But I was sure I could trust Sam to not go spouting off rumors.

Undeterred, Sarah asked, "Well, is it?"

"If that's what you need to think, then, yes."

We spent the time waiting for Lauren to arrive by finishing up a few details on the cake. She arrived a half hour after I called her, looking tired. Another part-timer, she worked whenever Sarah didn't, although Sarah had picked up several of her shifts lately. I'd have to ask her if she was okay the next time it was just her and me in the shop together.

I packed up a half-dozen muffins and placed them on the floor of my back seat. Sam carried the cake out to the car, where he carefully slid it into the trunk of the station wagon and secured it in place with tie down straps I had installed especially for deliveries. After all the work Sam had done on the cake, I wanted him to have ownership over the delivery.

I hopped into the driver seat, and Sam climbed into the passenger seat. We had to drive several blocks to Gina's house for her mom's sixtieth birthday party.

"If you're worried, I'm not going to tell anyone about what Sarah said," Sam assured me as I pulled out onto Founder Street.

I glanced at him out of the corner of my eye. "I'm not a witch."

"You're not the only one who's had rumors circulate

about them around town. I know how it feels, and the ones about me are true. I haven't come out wide but I'm slowly starting to tell people who aren't my family." He shrugged. "Who am I to feed the rumors about someone else?"

"You're a great guy, Sam. Thanks again for telling me."

"You're welcome. And even if you were a witch, I wouldn't care. You're just Joanie."

"Thanks, Sam." We pulled up to Gina's house. "Ready for your first delivery?"

Sam took a deep breath. "I think so."

"Come on, let's get your cake out."

Sam made a flawless delivery. I hadn't doubted he would. He was going to be successful someday. We parted ways at Gina's house. It was a shorter walk home for him from here than from the bakery. Sam, like me, regularly walked to work, but I'd picked him up a few times at his house in the mornings when the weather was bad.

I drove to back to Main Street and parked in front of Nick and Etta's. Rich lived above the restaurant. Perhaps he had been the one to see me on my date. But he didn't seem the type to go spreading that sort of news around. I grabbed out the box of muffins from my car, then climbed the stairs to the second-floor apartment.

Rich's roommate, Tim, answered the door and told me Rich was over at his mom's. Fortunately, I knew where Dev lived.

CHAPTER 12

On the outskirts of town, across from the grocery store, Bev's house stood two stories tall with a flat roof. It looked like a giant, olive-green cube. I pulled behind Rich's car in the driveway and turned mine off. I got out and walked up the front steps.

"Joanie?" Rich asked when he saw me standing on the stoop after opening the door.

"Hi Rich, how are you? How was the cross-country meet?" From my vantage point, I had a clear view of the living room into the kitchen. The ghost stood in the doorway between the two rooms. He looked up and saw me—and my purse where the hairbrush was—and blipped out.

"I'm good. Our team came in fifth, but one of the girls placed second in her individual event. What are you doing here?"

"I've brought some muffins for your mom. When I ran into her at the hospital the other day, she mentioned it had been a while since she last had any." I shrugged. "Thought she might like some."

"You should have given them to me when I picked up the

pastries this morning. You didn't have to come all this way," he said as if I'd driven hours and not the two minutes it had taken.

"That's actually what made me think of it. I did try your apartment first."

"That's awful kind of you. Please, come on in." Rich moved so I could step into the living room.

"Rich, who was—" Bev cut herself off as she came around the corner and saw me. "Oh, hi, Joanie. What do I owe the pleasure?"

I held up the box. "Brought you some muffins."

"Oh, child, you have no idea how you've just made my morning. Come in, come in. Please, sit. Rich, take the box from her and set them in the kitchen." She waved me into the living room. "Can I get you anything to drink?"

"A water would be fine, thanks." I removed my light jacket and sat on the couch, placing my jacket on the armrest and my purse on the coffee table in front of me. It was a nice room, light and airy. The yellow wallpaper with tiny blue flowers helped to brighten up the whole space. The couch and a loveseat across from me matched the flowers on the wallpaper. Photos dotted the walls. Many were of Rich as a child and teen. Then I spotted one with someone else I recognized.

"Here you go," Bev said as she placed the water next to my purse.

"Bev, I couldn't help but notice all the photos in here. Is that you in that one over there?" I pointed to the one that had the ghost in it with who I assumed was a young Beverly.

Bev glanced at the photo, but I doubt she had needed to. "It is. I was about twelve in that one."

"Is that your dad?"

With the mention of the ghost's photo, the brush inside my bag started to shake.

"It is. His name was Daniel." The purse shook from the brush's movement. "Do you need to get that?" Bev asked as if my bag was vibrating thanks to a cell phone inside it.

I rolled with her train of thought but kept my eye on the bag. The truth was more than what could be believed. "Oh, no, it's fine. Please continue."

"My dad was a good man. Born, raised, and died here. He worked at the car dealership, which at the time was owned by a friend's dad, before it became a company-owned place. He did well for himself, especially as attitudes toward Black people started to change in town. It wasn't always easy, as I'm sure you can imagine."

"No, I imagine it wasn't."

"He worked hard, and he loved us kids—my brother, me, and his nephew, my cousin Marcus. I think he was happiest when his grandkids were born. He adored Rich. But I grew up with the feeling that he never really loved my mama. They were two of the few Black twenty-somethings in Heartwood Hollow when they got together. My mom's brother married my dad's sister a few years after my parents got married. That's just the way it was if you didn't leave here. There wasn't a whole lot of choice if you wanted to stay here, if you catch my meaning. They were kind to one another, and I don't doubt that she loved him, but I don't know. Now that I'm older, I'm wondering if he settled for her."

My purse shook so violently, it tipped, knocking over the glass of water.

Rich jumped up. "I'll grab some napkins." His words and actions gave me a small sense of déjà vu.

Wherever the spirit had gone, it was back now with plenty

of energy. My bag wasn't light. "Oh my goodness, I am so sorry. Let me check that this time."

"Oh, it's all right, child." Bev dismissed the spill with a small wave. "No harm done."

I grabbed my purse and unzipped it to glare at the brush while pretending to fiddle with my phone.

Rich returned and handed me a few napkins, a smile on his face. "Didn't I do this for you the other day?"

I patted the area dry. "At least it's not salad dressing," I joked.

"Can I get you another water?" Bev asked.

"No, I should really get going and check in with Sarah at the shop. But thank you." I stood and put on my jacket, then grabbed my purse.

"Thank you so much for the muffins. You really know how to brighten up someone's day. I work so much and never get down to Main Street anymore. Let me tell you, those muffins across the street"—she pointed in the direction of the grocery store—"don't hold a candle to what you can do with yours."

"Aww, well, thanks for your kind words. Make sure you share with Rich." I let out a small chuckle.

Bev laughed as she walked me the few feet to the door. "If he finishes everything I told him to do, maybe he'll get one."

As she pulled open the door, I asked, "I'm sorry if this is a sad subject, but I don't see any recent photos of your father. Has he passed?" I, of course, knew the answer but wanted to find out when it had happened.

Bev nodded. "That he did. Back when Rich was twelve. Heart attack. And he had seemed so healthy too."

"I'm sorry to hear that."

"Rich reminds me so much of him sometimes. Funny

how that happens. Just wait until you have kids. You'll see what I mean."

"I'm sure I will," I said, not knowing if kids would ever be in my future. "You have a good day." Turning away from her, I opened the screen door and then stepped out of the house.

"You too."

I walked to my car and sat down in the driver's seat. Plopping my bag next to me, I unzipped it once more.

The brush pulsed with energy.

"You would have chosen then to act up again, wouldn't you?" The brush said nothing, not that I'd been expecting it to. "Let's see what you do when we get to Ashley's."

CHAPTER 13

I had been living here and making deliveries long enough to have learned where many people in town lived. Heartwood Hollow was missing a good event hall for things like baby and bridal showers, so the majority took place in people's homes. I had last been to Ashley's house two years ago. Ashley and her three roommates had thrown a bridal shower for Rachael, the bank teller, who had once lived here too. Now she lived across the street with her husband.

I pulled in front of the house, then grabbed my purse and walked up the porch steps of the old Queen Anne.

Ashley must have seen me coming. She opened the door as if she had been waiting for me. "Hey, Joanie, how are you?"

"Hey, I'm good. I've come to ask you about that hairbrush of yours."

"What about it? If you're trying to give it back, I don't want it." She held her hand up, palm facing me. "I told you I'm going to burn it."

"Oh, no, not that. I'm just wondering where you got it."

"That's the weird part. I got a box in the mail. Probably

about yay big." She moved her hands about a foot apart from one another. "A note inside said the stuff was found in the person's house and whoever sent it thought it was mine. Don't know why. There wasn't a name, but there was a return address label on the box."

"Interesting." I took a deep breath, and my tone turned serious. "Ashley, I don't want to scare you, but I think the brush might be haunted." I purposely avoided using the word *possessed*. It was a darker word, and I didn't get those vibes from the brush. Plus, I wanted to avoid alarming her too much.

Ashley didn't seem surprised in the slightest. "Why else do you think I was so glad to get rid of it?"

I laughed. She had a point.

"It's taken you this long to figure it out?" she continued. "Your tripping at the hospital pretty much confirmed it for me. I saw it. It threw itself out of your bag."

Well, at least I hadn't been wrong about that. "Oh, I've known. You wouldn't believe some of the things it's done beyond that."

Ashley crossed her arms.

"Okay, you would."

"I did have it for a week before you got it."

"Only a week?" That got me thinking. "Do you still have the box?" Recycling was biweekly.

"Yeah, I didn't know what to do with the other stuff, so it's all still in there. Before you took the brush, I'd considered mailing it all back saying they had the wrong person. But none of the other stuff is like that brush. I mean, none of it moves, anyway."

"We should go for a drive to check out where the brush came from."

Her eyes lit up. "I'm game. I want some answers too. It's

not mine. I don't recognize any of it. How did some random person pick me and my address?"

"Did you recognize the address?"

"No, but the address is on one of those county roads across the river."

"Do you have time now? Sarah's watching the bakery. It won't take long."

She shook her head. "I can't today. I volunteer to socialize the cats on Saturdays since I can't have pets in the house." She pointed to the logo on her red polo shirt. The yellow interlocking cat and dog design matched her recent manicure. I wondered if she'd done that purposely.

"No worries." Looked like I was heading back to the bakery after all.

"How about tomorrow?" she asked, her tone hopeful.

"Sure." As long as today had gone well, I bet I'd be able to get Sarah to watch the shop again.

"Sounds like a plan. Say, like, eleven?"

I nodded. "Works for me." At least that would give me some time in the bakery to help Sarah with the early after-church crowd.

"Great. I'll see you tomorrow."

"See you tomorrow." I turned and walked the few steps down to the walkway, then stopped and called over my shoulder, "Do you need a ride to the shelter?"

Ashley laughed. "I'm good, but thanks. You aren't the only one who likes to ride her bike all around town."

"Good point. I think I'm going to go ditch my car at my house." I waved as I slid into the car, then peeked into my bag. The hairbrush had barely reacted to Ashley's presence, if at all.

Back at my house around the corner, I swapped my car for my bike and then pedaled down to the bakery to find a rush of customers as I rode past toward the parking lot. But instead of running in through the kitchen to help, I walked around the front and entered as if I didn't own the place. Sarah and Lauren worked in tandem to serve the line of customers, and I wondered how long it would take for one of them to notice I was here.

That answer came fifteen minutes later when I was next in line, several people still behind me. Lauren didn't look at me as I pretended to have difficulty with choosing what I wanted from the case. It was only when she handed the peanut butter cookie to me that she realized who I was.

"Oh my gosh! What are you doing here?"

Sarah's head shot up as she was ringing out her customer, and we made eye contact.

"I came in to check how things were going," I answered. "Quite a rush you have going on."

"And you didn't think to, I don't know, help?" Sarah said, somewhat frazzled. She turned to her customer, a smile plastered on her face. "Here's your change. Have a wonderful day." Her tone had completely changed to one that was calm and professional yet friendly.

"I wanted to see how you'd do, and you're doing great!"

Sarah smiled as both she and Lauren took their next customers.

I walked into the back, hung up my coat, and ate my peanut butter cookie. For a moment, I contemplated joining Sarah and Lauren out front, but Sarah needed to realize she was more than capable of running things herself. I had never taken a sick day before, but what if I needed to? What if I ever wanted a vacation?

Several minutes later, Sarah came into the kitchen and slumped against the wall. "That was exhausting! I don't know how you do it."

"Some days I don't know either, but you survived and thrived! The pace will slow down now that the brunch rush is over. You want to go grab something to eat while Lauren and I are both here?"

Sarah rubbed her eyes with the palms of her hands. "That would be amazing. I need a latte." She stood up straight and darted to the closet for her bag. She had only one arm through a sleeve of her sweater before heading out the back door.

I entered the shop to find Lauren leaning against the back counter, sagging slightly. She stood upon noticing me. "You look beat. Why don't you take fifteen? Grab a snack from one of the cases. How about one of the lemon blueberry scones? They're refreshing. Might do just the thing for you."

"Thanks, Joanie." Lauren gave me a small smile. "You've not steered me wrong yet with your recommendations. I'm going to grab a bit of fresh air too." Lauren took a scone from the case and then made her way to the kitchen, her feet dragging slightly against the floor as if she were too tired to lift them all the way. I could tell something was on her mind. It wasn't like Lauren to drop shifts, and today she seemed . . . off, more so than just being tired from the rush.

I surveyed the bakery. Smudges covered the three cases, and the countertop had scraps of purple-and-white string scattered about from their tying the boxes closed. Large crumbs lay in a heap on the floor by the checkout counter, likely the result of someone dropping a treat they didn't want in a bag or box. All in all, the shop was messier than how I would have liked it to look, even in a rush, but the girls had done well.

I darted to the kitchen closet to grab the broom and dustpan.

By the time Lauren came back, I had finished sweeping

up the floor and wiping the top of the counter. Her feet were no longer dragging, and her demeanor seemed brighter. She had retied her hair into a fresh ponytail, and if the damp hairline was any indication, she had splashed water on her face.

"Thanks. I needed that more than I realized."

"I'm glad it helped. Sometimes you just need to step away for a bit." I hesitated before asking, "Is everything okay? You've seemed stressed lately, and I can't remember the last time you called someone to cover a shift for you until recently."

"Honestly?" Lauren sighed, deep and long. "Not really. My college classes are kicking my butt. I had a group project that had to be turned in this week. That's why I asked Sarah to cover my shift. The rest of my group could only meet that morning, and even though they said they'd"—she made air quotes—"fill me in, I didn't trust them to. It was too much of my grade."

"What can I do to help? Do you need fewer shifts? No shifts? You name it."

"School ends in a month. Do you think I could work Saturdays only or something until then? I don't want to not work. I need the money so I can afford the gas to get to class, but finals are coming up, and—"

"Say no more. I'll talk to Sarah to see if she wants more shifts."

"Thanks. I really appreciate you being so cool about all this. I just don't think I can handle more right now. Sorry."

"It's okay. We've all been there. And once summer gets here, you can get back into the swing of things. Do you want to head home, or do you think you have the rest of the shift in you?"

"I can handle it. You called me in because you needed me. I won't let you down." Lauren smiled a real smile for the first time that day. The room brightened slightly in response. The yellow walls felt cheerier. It wasn't a play of the light outside. There wasn't a cloud in the sky.

"Great! I knew you could do it."

I could sense Lauren wanted to hug me, but a customer walked into the shop at that moment. Lauren bounced around the counter to help the middle-aged woman.

Sarah came back from lunch several minutes later with three cups in a cardboard cup holder. "Courtesy of Gary," she chimed as she set the tray onto the back counter.

"I've so needed this," Lauren said on a sigh.

Lemon blueberry scones only helped so much. Sometimes one needed a caffeine pick-me-up too. I'd learned that back in culinary school when I first started drinking coffee. Before that, I only drank tea.

Sarah picked up one of the drinks and handed it to Lauren. "Peanut butter mocha."

Lauren took a sip. "Oh, this is delicious!"

Sarah lifted a second drink from the tray and then handed it to me. "French vanilla blueberry coffee with milk and agave, and a caramel mocha for me." Sarah drew a long sip from the last cup. "Ah . . ."

I lifted the lid and blew on my coffee to help cool it down. "This smells divine. Thank you."

"So what did we do to get free coffees?" Lauren asked.

"Honestly? I think Gary was happy to finally see me. He told Duke to get me whatever I wanted. I was planning on getting you both drinks anyway, so . . ."

"Sarah!" I chided.

"What?" Sarah shrugged though a slight blush crept onto her cheeks. "He said *anything*. He didn't bat an eye when I ordered a sandwich to eat there too."

"Oh, so this has been sitting a bit?" My eyes widened with anticipation.

"Yep, should be all set for you to drink. I know you worry about burning your taste buds."

"Fabulous." I peeled back the top and took a sip. It was as good as I hoped it would be. Not what I usually would go for —I still preferred tea unless something struck my fancy—but it was tasty.

"So do you two think you can handle the afternoon without me?" I asked, trying to gauge Sarah's reaction to being left alone again for a few more hours.

Sarah opened her mouth to speak, but Lauren answered for them both. "We've got this."

CHAPTER 14

Rather than bike back home, I hooked my bicycle up to the trailer and secured it to a wood column supporting the stairs leading to the apartments above the bakery. Something was telling me to take my time going home. It was a gorgeous day, and I didn't mind the walk.

I strolled away from the bakery, then turned left on Main Street once I'd crossed the street, proud that I had capable staff who I could trust to run the shop. Maybe I could take a vacation. Eventually. Someday.

I was passing the Heartwood Hollow General Store, a one-story glass-front building toward the end of the street when Rich walked out. The ghost, who I now knew to be his grand father Daniel, was right behind him.

"Hey, Rich, how are you?"

"Joanie, that's twice now today. You aren't following me, are you?" He smiled widely, a hint of laughter in his voice.

"Not this time," I said, the tone of my voice matching his. "I promise it's completely coincidental. What brings you to the general store? Still helping your mom?"

He held up a clear grocery bag with a yellow smiley face

on it. I could easily see a caulking gun and two tubes of caulk inside. "Yeah, helping her reseal a few things in her kitchen and bathroom."

"You're a good son, Rich. Your mom is lucky to have you."

"And me her, but today, you've totally overshadowed anything I could do. I'm going to have to start bringing her your muffins when I go visit."

I threw my head back and laughed. "Sorry, I didn't mean to upstage you."

"Oh, it's all right. She was so happy to have the muffins. Thank you for doing that for her. I think she enjoyed talking about Grandpa Dan too. She doesn't get much of a chance to."

I quickly cast my gaze over Rich's shoulder. Daniel was listening with interest. His awareness intrigued me. Usually ghosts didn't get too involved. They hung back and watched —unless they could play with a child who was able to see them, like what had happened at Nick and Etta's the other night—but this was the second time the ghost seemed to want to hear more, never mind his interaction with Rich at the hospital. Was it because he knew I was watching? When ghosts didn't know I could see them, they mostly ignored me.

"Glad I could give her the opportunity. I didn't know my dad and wish I had stories to tell about him." Talking about my absent father was not something I wanted to do. "Actually, I'm glad I ran into you."

"Oh, yeah?" His eyebrows raised.

I placed my hand on his upper arm as I stepped aside so the ghost man walking his dachshund could pass by. Daniel watched me curiously as if only then remembering I could see him. Guess that took the having an audience theory out of the running.

"Yeah, I wanted to talk to you about Thursday. How are things between you and Ashley? Things seemed a bit tense before my accident. I dropped by her house after I left your mom's this morning, but she didn't have the time to talk."

"Oh, right, yeah. She volunteers on Saturdays at the animal shelter."

At the mention of Ashley's name, the hairbrush in my bag started to dance about. I hoped Rich and Daniel wouldn't notice.

"You know? It's strange," he continued. "We were getting snippy with one another about the stupidest things all through lunch, and I couldn't take it anymore. I was getting ready to leave when you fell. Are you okay? I meant to ask you that earlier. It wasn't pretty."

I waved him off and smiled. "I'm fine. No harm done."

"Oh, good. Good. But, anyway, after you left, it was like nothing had happened. We were totally fine, and Ashley and I had a great rest of our lunch. I even walked her back to the junior high since my kids were taking that test I told you about. I wasn't proctoring it, so I had time to kill."

By now, the brush was peeking out of my bag. I pressed my purse tightly against my side to keep it from jumping out. "That's really good to hear. You two will figure things out."

"Hope so. I really like her, ya know? Just sometimes it feels we're so different. I mean, we are—look at us—but I never thought that mattered with us." He shrugged. "Maybe it does."

It saddened me that people in this day and age would judge a relationship on how the couple looked. "Have people been saying you shouldn't be together?"

"Well, no, but there must be people who think it."

If we'd been in the bakery, I'd have given him a cookie. It was a cookie that had started it all. I'd first felt their match the month prior. They'd come into the bakery separately, one right after the other, after school. Both had their eye on the last maple-glazed oatmeal cookie in the case. Ashley had beaten him in by a step, so the cookie was hers. When he groaned at losing out on it, she took it from me and broke it to give him half. At that moment, I knew. My toes tingled, and the sensation worked its way up to my stomach, unleashing a swarm of butterflies.

I couldn't speak to what he was talking about, but I knew one thing. "Love doesn't see all that unless you let it. Don't let it. You two are great for one another."

Rich drew his lips to the side in contemplation.

"Talk to Ashley. Hang out with her. It's the only way you'll find out."

As we continued talking, the brush continued to go crazy. I was moving around so much, trying to keep it in my bag, it must have looked like I was doing a bathroom dance. Rich was either oblivious or too polite to mention it, but Daniel noticed, and his gaze fell to my bag and the brush. His eyes widened with recognition.

Seeing this, I placed my hand on the brush head and began to draw it out. Why was the brush reacting so strongly to Rich when he talked about Ashley, and how did Daniel know it? It was from his era. I guessed his wife, or even Bev, could have had a similar one back then.

Wanting to figure out my next steps, I was ready to be on my way and bid Rich and his ghostly grandfather goodbye when I heard my name.

"Joanie!"

Rich and I turned to see who had called me.

I waved as I spotted Ken and his daughter.

The two looked both ways before crossing the street, hand in hand.

"Hi, Ken. How are you doing today?" I smiled at him,

then stooped slightly. "And this must be Ivy. I've heard a lot about you. It's nice to finally meet you."

Ivy looked up at her dad, her wide blue eyes asking the question she didn't voice.

"This is Joanie. She's the baker lady who made the cookies."

"I loved the cookies," Ivy said, jumping up and down, her voice growing excited at the word *cookies*. Cookies made me feel the same way.

"What else do you say?"

She stopped bouncing and gave me a shy grin. "Thank you."

"You're very welcome," I answered, straightening. I turned my arm out toward Rich in a displaying fashion. "Ken, have you met Rich yet?"

"No, but you look familiar . . ." Ken scratched at his temple with one finger.

"I was there on Thursday when you came to Joanie's rescue," Rich supplied. "I got the napkins."

"Ah, that must be it." Ken stuck out his hand.

Rich took it in his and shook it with three steady beats. It was then I noticed Daniel was nowhere to be seen. How strange. When had that happened? It wasn't like Ken could see him, so why disappear? I glanced down at my hand on my bag. The brush had settled back inside it. A normal brush once more just like during our date.

"It's nice to officially meet Joanie's knight in shining armor," Rich said.

"Well, I don't know about that. A real knight would have been able to catch her." We all chuckled at Ken's response.

"My daddy's not a knight," Ivy interjected, looking at me and Rich and then directly up at her dad behind her. "He doesn't have a horse!"

"Good point, kiddo." He clapped her shoulder. "Say, Joanie, Ivy and I were on our way to the park. Would you like to join us?"

I did. It was a beautiful day, and I wanted to spend more time with Ken. I turned to Rich. "Looks like I'm being called away. It was nice chatting with you."

"Have a good day, Joanie. Again, it was nice to meet you, Ken."

Ken, Ivy, and I continued past the general store, heading toward my shop on the way to the park. Rich walked in the opposite direction. Before we got too far away in going our separate ways, I cast a glance over my shoulder. Daniel had reappeared, following Rich, but he, too, was looking over his shoulder. I couldn't be certain, but I believed his gaze was set on my purse.

The mysteries of Daniel and the hairbrush were growing increasingly complex. When would I finally have some answers?

CHAPTER 15

"Daddy, can I get a cookie?"

"You have lots of cookies at home still."

"But Joanie's here, and she made me want a cookie. And she can get me a cookie. Can't you?" Ivy looked at me with big blue eyes, her hands clasped in front of her and her shoulders swaying front to back. "Please?"

Ken sighed.

"I really don't mind," I told him. "Lauren and Sarah are working today. We can run in and grab something."

"Yay!" Ivy bounced up and down.

"Are you sure?" Ken asked. "I don't want to mooch off your generosity any more than I already have with her cookies."

"Absolutely. It's fine." I gave him a reassuring smile. If it made Ivy happy, I was okay with a little bribery to get her to like me.

Ivy skipped ahead of us, naming off every type of cookie that she liked, from chocolate chip to sugar to peanut butter blossoms and more.

"Have you even had one of those?" Ken asked after a more interesting flavor combination.

I had to give her credit, she was coming up with ideas that could actually work. The next time I was with her, I'd have to carry around a notebook in case she spouted the next great combination.

The bakery was less chaotic when I walked through the front door this time. Sarah and Lauren looked up with smiles, Sarah's widening as she saw who I was with. I bet she'd give Lauren an earful about it once we left. More gossip I'd be at the center of tomorrow.

"Hello, ladies, back again. This is Ivy, Ken's daughter."

"Hi, Ivy," both girls chimed.

Ivy grew shy and clung to her dad, partially shielding herself behind him.

"Come on, Ivy," Ken said, shuffling to the cookie case, pulling her along. "Which one do you want?"

Lauren met us down at the case as Ivy pointed to a spiced snickerdoodle. Lauren reached in, grabbing the largest cookie. Ivy held out her hand expectantly, but Lauren glanced at Ken for the go-ahead.

"How about we put this in a bag and you can eat it when we get to the park?" Ken suggested.

"Okay, Daddy."

Lauren slipped the cookie into a white bakery bag and passed it to Ken.

He tucked the cookie inside his coat. "What do you say, Ivy?

"Thank you." Over her momentary shyness, she came out from behind her dad.

"Thanks, ladies. We're off to the park." I figured it would give Sarah something to feed off in her quest for relationship news.

We headed out of the bakery, and once we reached the sidewalk, Ivy resumed skipping ahead of us.

"Can I treat you to some coffee?" Ken asked.

"Oh, you don't have to do that."

"Please? Eliminate some of that mooching guilt for me."

I didn't have the heart to tell him I'd already had coffee today. I'd get something else warm, that's all. Perhaps a nice chai tea. "Okay. I'd like that."

"Ivy, wait for us at the corner, please."

Ivy bounced on her toes, waiting for us to catch up to her.

"We're going to cross the street and go to the coffee shop," Ken told her as he stuck out his hand for her to take.

She crossed her arms. "Can I get a hot chocolate?"

"What? You just got a cookie."

She stomped her foot. "But now I want a hot chocolate." This kid drove a hard bargain, but Gary made a mean hot chocolate. It was one of my favorite drinks in the winter.

Ken looked to the sky. "Okay."

Ivy dropped her arms, letting one fall to her side and taking Ken's offered hand with the other. Once we were across Main Street, Ivy let go of her dad's hand. She bounded ahead of us we continued up Founder, stopping in front of Leafs and Grounds.

"She has me wrapped around her finger," he muttered.

"I can see why. She's a cute kid. And you can tell she adores you."

"Thanks. I certainly hope so," he replied. It seemed like a loaded statement. One I didn't feel was my place to pry into at the moment.

"Joanie! How are you today? Come for your marshmallow rice treat? We might have one or two left," Gary called as I entered the coffee shop.

Tempting, so tempting.

"Yes, yes, she is," Ken answered for me as he approached the counter.

Ken placed an order for himself and Ivy, then looked at me expectantly.

"I'll take a hot chai tea, please."

Ken paid and continued to talk with Gary as we waited for our order. I overheard his work position being mentioned, and I assumed he was making connections for the hospital. Ivy sat at one of the nearby tables, legs swinging underneath the tall barstool. Even my legs would have swung when I was sitting if I let them.

Holly, one of Gary's several baristas, placed our order on the counter. "All set."

Gary and Ken shook hands, and Ivy jumped down from the chair, landing with a hard thump. "Can I have my hot chocolate now, Daddy?"

"It's hot. How about I hold it until we get to the park," Ken suggested.

"Okay." She darted around three tables, weaving her way to the exit instead of taking the clear aisle in front of us. She waited for us by the door, then led the way out of the coffee shop.

We turned right on Main Street once we reached the corner, passing the bookstore, ice cream parlor—which wasn't open yet for the season—a couple more storefronts, the library, and several houses before reaching the park entrance.

Ivy ran straight for the swing set once we made it through the wrought-iron arch that marked the official entrance for the park, even though the whole thing was open to the sidewalk.

"Ivy, don't you want your cookie and hot chocolate?" Ken called as he and I headed for a bench, then sat down.

"In a minute," she shouted as she pumped her legs to start her swing in motion. "I want to swing right now!" Next to her, a teenaged ghost sat gently moving the swing she was on. To Ken—and given her age, likely to Ivy as well—it looked like it was swinging softly in the breeze off the river, but I knew better. The girl wore a calico-patterned dress from the mid-1800s and black shoes. With as many ghosts as I'd seen over the years, I'd gotten good at placing them in their correct era. The ghost girl smiled at Ivy but didn't seem to notice me watching.

"Okay, have fun," Ken called. "Don't forget that they're here."

"I won't!" She'd managed to get a good swing going and was getting higher and higher.

The ghost looked impressed, but part of me wondered if she was jealous since she couldn't do it without drawing too much attention to what others saw as an empty swing. Did ghosts get jealous? Likely the bad ones could, but it had been years since Gram blocked those from me. I guess it was possible for all ghosts, though. After all, Daniel had shown me they could be surprised. How did he know that brush?

Ken bumped my free hand with his, and when I looked down, he was holding a wrapped marshmallow rice treat.

"You didn't think I'd forget, did you?" he asked.

"Thank you. You have no idea how much I like these."

He chuckled. "You're a baker. Can't you make them yourself?"

"Sure I could. I've done it before." I placed my chai tea next to me on the bench and unwrapped half the treat. "But Gary must have a secret ingredient, because I can't replicate them. Mine are good, but these are perfect."

"Feel like sharing?" I could tell by the tone in his voice that he was teasing me.

I laughed. "Not with these."

"Glad I got one for myself, then. I didn't think you'd share with the way Gary pointed out to you how many were left." Ken dug a second from his coat pocket.

I took a bite of mine, watching as he unwrapped his. I wanted to see his reaction. He bit into a corner and ripped off a section.

"Mm, okay, I can see why you like these so much."

"Careful, they're addicting."

"I believe that," he said through a mouth full of rice cereal and marshmallow.

We sat in comfortable silence for a few minutes eating and drinking while watching Ivy swing.

When the swing reached its highest point, Ivy jumped off, her knees buckling as she hit the rubberized ground. She bounced back up and shook her hands off, then ran toward her father.

"Daddy!"

"Ivy!" Ken mimicked her tone.

"Can I have my cookie and hot chocolate now?"

"Sure thing. Why don't you sit?"

Ivy squeezed in between Ken and me, then took her hot chocolate and cookie from Ken's hands. She sipped her drink and had several bites of cookie, alternating between the two. After a few minutes, she jumped up—nearly dropping the rest of her snickerdoodle—took one more sip of her hot chocolate, and handed both back to her dad before running off again to play. This time she sped toward the slide.

With her well out of earshot, I turned toward Ken. "So can I ask what happened between you and Ivy's mom? It's okay if you don't want to talk about it, but I am curious."

"For a long story short, Ivy's mom, Kelly, wasn't ready to

be a parent—or a wife, really. We tried to do the right thing and got married, but it didn't work out."

"Oh, I'm sorry to hear that."

"It's okay. It was starting to get tense with my doing everything for the three of us, even after the divorce. I'm twenty-seven. I have plenty of time to find the one. Being a single dad gives me an extra set of responsibilities that might make it harder, but I wouldn't trade having Ivy for anything."

"She's lucky to have you." Even with all of his talking during our date on Friday and now, it hadn't dawned on me all that dating a single father entailed. Could I do it? I wanted my own kids, but I didn't have experience with them beyond those in my shop. Ivy already had a mom. I didn't want to tread on that relationship or have either of them thinking I was. Was I ready for that sort of relationship? I'd just met Ken, and he was great, but he came with extra baggage. I wasn't sure if I could handle it. Perhaps I needed to step back and be his friend for a while.

"She's a good kid, a bit spoiled as you've probably noticed, but I'm trying to work on that. On my end, anyway. I've been lax on it since the move, trying to smooth things over. Can't do anything about Kelly."

I cocked my head to the side as I studied him. "I thought you said things were going well here."

"They are, but I'd like to keep it that way." He gave me a crooked grin and gave a small shrug, one side of his mouth rising slightly higher than the other.

Rapid footfalls approached, then came to a halt in front of us. "Daddy, I'm hungry. Can we go get something to eat?"

Ken looked at his watch. "Well, would you look at that."

"What?" Ivy asked.

"It's almost dinnertime." He leaned toward her, his hands

on his thighs and his elbows bent outward. "How about we find a place to eat on Main Street."

"Can we go to the Dawg Pound and get a hot dog and french fries?"

"Sure thing." Ken turned toward me. "Would you like to join us?"

"Oh, no, that's all right. You enjoy the time with your daughter."

"You sure?" He didn't sound ready to end our time together.

"I've already set something in the slow cooker for tonight. But thank you." I hated to disappoint him, but I was looking forward to the pierogies and kielbasa that I had prepped this morning.

"All right, kiddo," Ken said, standing. "Let's go to Dawg Pound. It was good to see you, Joanie. This was nice. Hope we can do it again sometime."

Unsure of what to say, I nodded. I didn't know if I was ready to date him, and I wasn't ready to become some sort of female role model for Ivy, but could we still do this if we were only friends?

"Bye, Joanie!" Ivy chirped.

"Bye, Ivy. It was nice to meet you." I gave them a small wave and watched them walk toward the park exit. Once they disappeared up Main Street, I turned back to face the playground. The ghost had disappeared from the swings. I sat in quiet contemplation for several minutes as the sun glistened off the river bordering the opposite side of the park.

Ivy was a cute kid, and Ken a great guy. Maybe I just needed to spend more time with them to realize I could give this a shot.

CHAPTER 16

I stopped at the bakery one more time after leaving the park. Sarah and Lauren were cleaning up for the evening. I felt bad for what probably seemed like me checking up on them, especially after pretending to be a customer the first time, but I had to tell Sarah I needed to be gone for part of the day tomorrow and that she'd be in charge again. After a smooth afternoon, Sarah was fine with running the shop again. This would put her at over thirty hours for the week. If I kept having weeks like this, I'd have to start thinking about whether I'd make the leap to bringing her on full time if she wanted it.

Before I left, I put in a call to Gina, who had done spot shifts for me in the past, to see if she could stay after her baking shift. Although she agreed, I felt guilty that I'd be overworking her. The situation upped my resolve to ask Sam about picking up shifts this summer.

Saffy greeted me as she always did, running from her spot in the window to sit on the arm of the couch as I opened the door, but today after I pet her, she dove for my purse and shoved her head inside.

Curious about how strong her reaction to the brush was, I pulled my purse away, but she followed it, then immediately stuck her head back in once I stopped. Next I tried lifting it, and she practically stood on two feet to keep her head inside the bag, making the bag heavy with her chubby resistance. I lowered it, and not paying attention as she took a step forward to stay with it, she fell off the couch.

"Whoops! Careful, Saf." Undeterred, she jumped right back up and stuck her head in my bag again as I rested it on the arm of the couch. Something about that brush drove her crazy. Was it because there was a spirit trapped inside it? Or was there something particular about this spirit?

I zipped my bag—having learned that lesson already—and placed it on the couch cushion. Saffy leapt off the armrest and sat square on top of it.

"Don't want the brush to get away either, do you, Saffy?"

She purted at me in response, a strange mix of a purr and a chirp, but definitely all Saffy.

Although I'd repeatedly told her the bag was zipped and the brush couldn't go anywhere, Saffy was still sitting on my purse a few hours later when I headed upstairs to get ready for bed. She had only left in order to eat, and she'd raced through dinner to get back to my bag as fast as she could, tail shaking the entire time. My pudgy kitty liked to eat.

As I pulled on my nightshirt, I caught movement out of the corner of my eye.

"Saffy?" I asked despite knowing what I had seen was much too large to be my calico cat.

In the mirror, I could see a young woman's ghost wearing 1960s attire. Her dirty-blond hair was long and kept back with a thin leather headband that crossed her forehead horizontally, a single small braid hanging over it by her ear. She wore a flowy teal tunic and paisley-print bell bottoms that matched the teal shirt but had a variety of other bold colors in the design.

"Boy, that fabric would make some fun throw pillows." The ghost smiled slightly and looked down as she stuck out a leg to admire her pants. I hadn't realized I'd said anything out loud until she reacted.

A long beaded necklace with a peace sign pendant hung from her neck, all of it bright yellow and starkly contrasting with her tunic. She easily would have fit in at the Woodstock Music and Art Festival in 1969. I wondered if she had gone. Gram had made the drive from her hometown of Sunny Valley to the rural farm in Bethel, New York, where it took place with some friends of hers, so it was entirely possible.

Now that the ghost had made an appearance, I had to find out more about her and her possible connection to Ashley, Rich and Daniel, and Ken.

"I was wondering if you would ever show up." Smiling, I pivoted to face the hairbrush ghost.

Gone. She had vanished in the time it took me to turn around.

A small jangly crash in my living room was immediately followed by a loud thump. It wasn't a normal noise at all, although the thump sounded similar to Saffy's ungraceful jump to the floor. But not quite. Something about it was off. It wasn't something I could ignore, especially given what—no, who—I had just seen up here.

Sighing, I headed back downstairs to check on what the commotion was, not looking forward to having to clean my living room again so soon.

As I turned the corner coming down the stairs, I could see Saffy puffed up, her fur standing on end and her back arched as she stared at my purse upended on the living room floor. The brush was out of the bag but stuck on one of its straps. So much for it being zipped closed. The strap didn't seem to bother the hairbrush any as it dragged the bag across the floor. Saffy charged after my bag and the brush, hissing.

Finally, the strap fell free of the brush, and Saffy skidded into my purse. The brush floated above her head in midair as if waiting for something. Saffy growled quietly as I stared at the brush. It was stronger than it had been before. Why now? Was this because the ghost had finally manifested?

I stepped off the final stair, and the brush moved forward at a distance almost equal to my step. I moved forward. So did the brush. This happened repeatedly. The brush was matching my pace a few steps in front of me as if trying to lead me somewhere.

"What do you want to show me?"

The brush pivoted as I took my next step and gave me my answer. *The door.*

I looked down at my bare feet, polka dot pajamas, and pink T-shirt that matched the dots with a large cupcake on the front. Things could be worse than going outside looking like a thirteen-year-old at a slumber party, and at least I hadn't yet applied my face mask, but I did not look forward to the prospect of going outside.

"Oh, please don't make me go outside like this."

The brush didn't listen. It moved closer to the door as I walked, then hovered there waiting for me to catch up.

"Guess we're going outside." With a sigh, I opened the door for the hairbrush and swooped my arm in front of me toward the porch, bowing slightly. "Lead the way."

The brush floated forward and fell down at the threshold as if it had hit an invisible barrier.

"What in the world?"

Saffy trotted over and sniffed the brush, tapping it once for good measure. Seemingly satisfied, she walked away without a care in the world. It was as if she had forgotten she'd been growling at the brush moments before.

The brush didn't seem all that possessed anymore. Just a normal brush once more.

My phone rang, startling me.

"Who could be calling me at this hour?"

Saffy darted into the kitchen before I could even take my first step, likely hoping that she could score more food since I had to go in there to answer the phone.

I checked the caller ID. Gram. Why would she be calling me so late?

"Hi, Gram. Is everything okay?" The question echoed what she had asked me when I called her a few days ago.

"Oh, yes, everything is good with me, dear. Are *you* okay? After our conversation the other day and then once you didn't call me earlier at our usual time, I got worried."

"Oh breadcrumbs! I'm so sorry. I lost track of time today. Barely even realized it was Saturday."

"Bakery keeping you that busy?"

"The bakery's going fine, but I wasn't really there much today. I was kind of on a date." If the time in the park with Ken and Ivy could be considered a date.

"Goddess be! It's about time!" I could picture her throwing her arms into the air.

"Gram! You say that as if I'm some spinster or crazy cat lady."

"You've been well on your way. Do you still have that sassy calico?" She asked me the same question almost every week.

"Saffy? Of course I do. I would have told you otherwise." Saffy looked over her shoulder at me as she sat in front of her food bowl. Although the center was empty, plenty of crunchies were still inside. "No more dinner for you."

Saffy stood up and sat right back down, stressing her demands. She wasn't going anywhere.

"Not going to work, Saffy."

"See?" My grandmother said, a hint of laughter in her voice. "You may have met this man just in time."

"Gra-am . . ."

"So tell me about this man."

I filled her in about Ken. Everything from meeting him at the hospital to talking with him earlier in the park, not yet mentioning the brush. We'd get to that next.

"Well, he sounds like quite a match for you, although your mom would know that better than I would. I know you have that ability, but it doesn't work on yourself, does it?"

"No," I huffed, "and it's frustrating. That's for sure. Do you know how many weddings I've gone to alone?"

"Plenty if you're anything like your mother. So is that all that's been keeping you busy? What happened with that spell you asked me about the other day?"

"That's the other thing. I have a spirit trapped in a hairbrush. The spell didn't work, she's still tied to the brush, but tonight I actually saw her. So whatever I did has made her stronger, I think. All she could do before was move the brush."

"A possessed brush, huh? Can't say I've encountered that."

This was turning into a longer call than I'd expected when answered the phone. I filled my tea kettle and set it to boil. "And somehow it ties into what's going on with my latest match. It's directly interfering. I met Ken because it jumped out of my purse and tripped me."

"Jumped?" I could hear the slight disbelief in Gram's voice.

"Literally. So the brush came from Ashley, and the ghost following Rich—"

"They aren't giving you trouble again, are they?"

"No, but I've been seeing them more than usual over the last few days. I blame the brush for that too. But they've all been pleasant at least. Nothing scary like before. No one's asking for my help. Well, unless you count the brush, but I feel compelled to do this. Like if I do it, it's one step in the right direction for Rich and Ashley."

"Have you thought about burning it to release its hold on the ghost?"

"Ashley had suggested it out of fear, but there's more to it. I don't think that would actually solve their problem. Let me ask you something. So after I saw the spirit, the brush tried to get me to go outside. But it fell at the doorway, and now it feels like just a brush. Why would that happen?" I grabbed a tea mug out of my cabinet along with everything else I needed and began to prep my tea.

"Don't you remember?"

Clearly, I didn't. "Remember what?"

I grabbed the kettle and poured the water into my cup while Gram explained, "Your mom and I put protection spells on all your entrances. Wards on your windows and doors. The spirit wouldn't be able to cross them on its own."

"Those were real?" As I sat down at the table, I thought back to the day I moved in. Mom and Gram had diligently gone to each window and both the front and back door with sage, salt, and water. There'd been more to it than that, but I didn't really pay attention. I just let them do their thing. It made them feel better since I was living alone, and it stopped them from arranging my cabinets the way they wanted. They had done it to my college dorm rooms and all my apartments too. "I thought—"

"Dear, when are you going to get it through your head? All of it is real."

"But, Gram—"

"You, your mom, and I are all witches. And there were plenty who came before me in our family line. How can you deny it at this point? It's in your blood. It's in your ghost-seeing ability. Your matchmaking. Goddess, it's in your food too. Did you think I was joking every time I've called you a kitchen witch? We can all do a bit of spell work. Your mom only has the matchmaking as her something extra. I only know as much about ghosts as I do because of my sister, Goddess bless her soul wherever she may be." Gram didn't know if her sister, Peggy, was alive or dead. "But for some reason," she continued, "you have more latent powers than the rest of us."

"What if I don't want it?" I blew across the top of my mug. "I didn't ask for any of this."

"No, but you've got it. It's not really something you can give back either, so why don't you try embracing it?"

I shrugged, not that she could see me. "I don't know, Gram." All the pointy hat wearing, cauldron bubbling, frog befriending, broomstick flying images I had ever seen in movies and on TV flashed before me. That wasn't me. Then again, I didn't think it was Mom or Gram either. They'd always seemed to be more new-age practitioners than anything else.

Gram sighed. "Look, I got to go. But just try it for a change. Perhaps this inner fight you've had with it is stopping you from seeing something you might otherwise have known. If nothing else, you would have at least remembered to keep your hand on the brush when letting it outside."

"Well, maybe. I guess since I've tried everything else. Thanks, Gram." I took a sip of my tea, positive it had cooled down enough for me to drink.

"Call me if you need me and keep me informed with how it all goes—with the brush and that man. Love you."

She'd hung up before I could reply.

I placed the cordless phone back on the base. Gram was the sole reason I still had a landline. She said cell signals messed with her aura.

Saffy meowed at me, and once I'd turned to face her, she tapped at her bowl for added effect. Judging by what was still in the dish, she hadn't eaten anything during the time I'd been on the phone.

I shook my head. "No more tonight, Saffy. Come on, let's try that again."

Carrying my tea with me, I walked back into the living room toward the brush and picked it up. I'd left the main door open when the phone rang, so I pushed the storm door out and stepped onto the porch, hoping to pick up where we had left off.

But once outside, the brush didn't move. It didn't do anything. For the next twenty minutes, I sat on my porch swing, drinking tea while waiting for the brush to do something. But nothing.

I couldn't wait all night. My tea mug was empty, and I had to be up early.

"We can try this again tomorrow," I told the brush. "Come back inside and please don't make a mess of my living room while I'm asleep."

I put the brush back in my purse and zipped it closed once more. Saffy investigated my bag but walked away and headed upstairs almost immediately. I followed her. Her lack of concern eased my mind a bit about how my living room would fare overnight but did not make me feel any better about where the spirit was. It had to be deep in hiding if Saffy couldn't sense something. I wondered if she wasn't even there anymore or if Mom and Gram's wards had cast it out for good.

I couldn't dwell on it tonight, though, or else I'd spend the whole night awake. Hopefully finding out who had sent Ashley the brush would provide us both some answers.

CHAPTER 17

I rose at my usual four o'clock in the morning after an uninterrupted night's sleep. Saffy was still curled between my knees, no signs of her ever having left during the night. Although I tried to carefully slide out from under her like I did every morning, my leg cramped, and I let out a quick gasp. Saffy popped her head up and glared at me.

"So sorry to have woken you," I said semi-sarcastically as she'd already put her head back down. "But now you can get breakfast earlier."

Gone was my sleepy cat as Saffy's head shot up. She did a full-body stretch, first with her front legs and then her back before launching herself off the bed. Once she checked to make sure I was out of bed, she scampered downstairs and landed heavily on the living room floor with a loud thump. I chuckled. Goofy thing had missed a step.

I rushed through my shower and dressed quickly, then met Saffy at her food bowl, where the cat eyed me critically.

"Sorry, Saf. Was that not fast enough for you?"

She seemingly shook her head before craning her neck to supervise me as I dropped a scoop of food into her bowl. But with food in front of her, all was forgiven. She purred at me and lay down at her bowl to eat.

I turned the kettle on to boil water for my tea, then headed back into the living room to inspect the brush. Unfortunately, I sensed nothing special about it. Part of me was unsurprised, but the other part had hoped for some sort of energy coming off is after a night of rest.

"Hello, good morning," I said, thinking a friendly greeting might draw the spirit out if it were hiding.

Nothing. Not that it had really ever reacted to me personally.

That gave me an idea.

I placed the hairbrush in the middle of the floor. "Ashley."

Nothing.

I paced the floor. "Rich."

Nothing.

The tea kettle whistled.

"Daniel," I said a little louder as I walked past the brush and back into the kitchen. I set my filled tea ball to steep in my travel mug, peering into the living room to see if the brush had reacted to the name of Rich's ghostly grandfather.

Nothing.

"The nineteen-sixties," I shouted while still standing in the kitchen waiting on my tea.

Nothing.

"Woodstock."

Nothing.

"The moon landing."

Nothing.

I pulled the tea ball out of my mug and screwed the top on.

"Kennedy assassination," I said, walking past the brush once more and sliding my shoes on by the door.

Nothing.

"Hippies." I pulled on a light jacket and grabbed my purse, slinging it over my shoulder.

Nothing.

Remembering the spirit's pants from the night before, I shouted, "Paisley!"

Once again, nothing.

I couldn't stand around all morning trying to get the brush to react. Sundays required an extra dozen muffins for each diner to accommodate the after-church crowd. So I grabbed the brush off the floor and plopped it back into my bag.

The walk to work in the crisp air of the predawn hours did its part to finish waking me up. I spent the time talking to the brush, still trying out different things to see if it would respond. And still nothing, although a couple of the town's ghosts looked at me like I was crazy as I passed by. They had never paid me much attention before, and I didn't want them to start now. For the first time, I hoped the brush was just a brush and that the ghosts couldn't sense anything inside it.

Sam was waiting for me at the back door to the kitchen when I arrived. I let us in, and Gina showed up a few minutes later.

"Oh my goodness, Sam. That cake was amazing. Mom loved it." She pulled out her phone and showed us photos of it on the table with other baked treats that hadn't been there when he'd set it up. "My brother, who runs his own bakery, was really impressed by your flowers." It turned out that he had brought the other desserts.

Sam was still beaming with pride from Gina's compliments when Lily walked in a few minutes later, on time as she always was. Bryan rushed in a moment behind her, panting.

"Okay, let's get to work. We have a busy morning. Nothing crazy, just more. More muffins for the diners, more scones for the inn's high tea service, more cookies for those stopping in after church. You know the drill."

"I heard you had another date with the hot doc yesterday," Donna said as I arrived with the muffin delivery. There was already a cup of coffee waiting for me at my spot at the counter.

I rattled off the variety of muffins for the day, and after she was done writing, she looked at me expectantly. I sighed. *Fine.* I'd give her a bit of information to satisfy her. "I wouldn't necessarily call it another date. We ran into each other. He was with his daughter, and they were going to the park. He asked me if I wanted to go along. So I did."

"Did you get something to eat or drink?"

"Well, yeah, we stopped at the bakery first to grab Ivy a cookie and got drinks at Leafs, but—"

"Then it was a date."

I took a small sip of my coffee. It had likely been sitting for a few minutes before I arrived and was already cool enough to drink without burning my tongue. "But we just sat on a park bench and watched his daughter play on the swing set."

"Doesn't matter. There was food involved."

I raised an eyebrow at her. "Is that your definition of a date?"

"Well, there can be more to it than that, but they always have to include food." Donna laughed.

If that were the case, then I needed to talk to Courtney again. I'd promised I would call her and tell her about any date I went on. Plus, I needed to ask her what she thought about this whole dating a dad thing. As much as I liked Donna, she gossiped about everyone—me included—and I didn't want my possibly silly doubts to get spread around the town as easily as the rest of my dating life apparently was.

"Well, food is good," I replied, sliding off the stool. "You might be on to something, but I have to get back to the shop. Thanks for the coffee."

"Have a good one, Joanie. See you tomorrow."

The muffins and scones were in the oven when I returned to the bakery, and my team was filling the first batch of pastries with cream. Chocolate and vanilla were my standards, but today I had experimented with an orange cream as well. I liked having something extra special on Sundays for my customers. Next time, I'd have to try adding the orange to the chocolate cream.

I'd told Sarah to come in an hour later to make up for her being in charge and having so many hours this week. It must have done her some good as she arrived seeming eager to work and almost excited to be put in charge again. All she had needed was a bit of a confidence boost. I'd be sad to lose her someday down the road once she found her calling.

After the baking team had cleaned up the kitchen, Gina left to take a much-deserved early lunch. With her gone and Sarah manning the shop, I stepped into the kitchen with the brush.

Sarah flew through the door. "What are you doing?" She stared at the brush in my hand.

"I need to see something."

"Don't you remember what happened last time?" She crossed her arms. "If things go all witchy again, I am not cleaning this kitchen. You are."

I placed the brush on the counter, roses-side down. "I'm pretty sure nothing's going to happen again."

"Don't press your luck. That was a lot of flour."

I grinned at her and winked. "Trust me."

She rolled her eyes and pushed back through the door to the shop. The door swinging shut cut off any reply she had.

I set out the candlesticks and placed the black and white candles inside them. After lighting the candles, I placed the burnt-out match on the sage to set it to smoke so I could cleanse the room—an idea I was getting way too comfortable with. Then it was time to speak the words my gram had taught me.

I did everything exactly as I had on Thursday afternoon, but the brush failed to react. Drats.

With no time to try again, I quickly cleaned up, storing the supplies in the kitchen closet.

Sarah was looking at me expectantly, one eyebrow raised, when I walked back into the shop with the brush. "It didn't sound like anything crazy happened back there."

"Not this time," I answered, putting the brush in my purse for later. I couldn't deny being slightly disappointed, but at the same time, I was happy to not have another flour disaster on my hands.

She breathed a sigh of relief. "Thank goodness."

I could feel her studying me, and when I looked up, she met my gaze and tilted her head to the side. "Are you sure you're not a witch? I mean, it's cool if you are. To each their own, I say."

Once she got an idea in her head, it was hard for her to let it go. "No, I'm not a witch . . ."

"You said that with less defensiveness and certainty than the other day." She cocked her head to the other side. "You okay?" She waited for me to say more.

Finally, I caved. "Yeah." It had almost come out as a sigh. "I mean, I'm not a witch, but I'm thinking my mom and gram might be? Gram told me what to do with the brush."

Sarah smiled. It was one of those grins that had me questioning everything I had confessed.

"What?"

"I think you just took a step toward accepting your witchiness. I knew I was right."

And maybe she was. But I wasn't going to tell her that.

CHAPTER 18

Once Gina got back, I left, taking the delivery for the inn with me so neither of them would have to do it. Glad I had left my bike here the day before, I loaded up the trailer and rode to my house, where I popped the delivery into the trunk of my car. I hopped into the driver's seat, started the engine, and then drove to the inn.

Fortunately, Billy was in the kitchen again when I arrived, which meant a quick stop was in my future. Just what I needed.

"Heard you've been on a couple of dates recently," he said as I walked in.

Really? Him too? "Who told you?"

He laughed. "Libby. Who else? I hear he's quite a looker."

I rolled my eyes. "At least you aren't calling him hot doc like everyone else."

"Why would I? He's not a doctor."

"Thank you. That's what I said. Anyway, I got to run. Please tell Libby hello for me."

"Will do. She really wants you to stay sometime."

"I know. And I will. I promise." I pushed through the

kitchen door to the outside, then popped my head back in. "Good to see you, Billy. Bye!"

I jogged back to my car and hopped in, then made a three-point turn in the driveway to leave rather than looping around in the parking lot.

That had been one of the longest conversations I'd ever had with Billy, but I still had just enough time to stop for coffee—and a marshmallow rice treat. I guessed at what Ashley might like based on her past choices at the bakery and chose to get her what I was getting, a Moroccan spiced chai tea. Fortunately, Duke was behind the counter taking orders when I got there. He wasn't much of a talker. Gary, the conversationalist, was busy refilling the bag your own coffee beans station at the back of the shop, so I could do no more than give him a quick wave before darting out the door, careful not to spill anything.

I arrived at Ashley's house right on time. She must have been waiting for me as she stepped out onto her porch before I could turn off my car. I unlocked the car door as she approached.

"Morning," she said, plopping into the passenger seat.

"How are you?" I held out her cup of tea, and she accepted it with a murmur of thanks.

She immediately took a sip, something I had yet to do because of the temperature. "Mm . . . this is delightful. Chai?"

I nodded. "Moroccan spice."

"I never would have chosen it for myself, but I'll definitely be getting it again. Thank you."

I knew she'd like it. "Ready to go?"

She placed her tea into the open cupholder in the center console. "You bet," she said along with the snap of her seatbelt latching.

"Let's do this."

Our forty-five-minute drive took us to a beautiful but secluded area over the river and into the lower mountains. I learned early on in college that cities weren't my thing—and my college wasn't even in what some would call a big city—but in this rural of an area, I didn't think I'd see enough people on a regular basis for me to be comfortable living out here. Small towns were more my thing.

We turned off the county highway at a small sign that listed the address of a home down a dirt road and finally arrived at a log cabin a few minutes later. It looked a little run-down. Some chinking missing between logs and a cracked window pane were the worst I could see from the front. Smoke rose from the chimney, though, and a hunter-green hatchback was parked out front, so someone was home.

Ashley and I got out of my car and quietly approached the front door. I knocked, and less than a minute later, a woman with jet-black hair in a messy bun opened the door partway and peered through the opening.

"Hello? What do you want? I don't want no solicitors."

"We aren't solicitors, I promise." I held up a hand palms out as if solemnly swearing to tell the whole truth and nothing but the truth,

"Well, what are you doing here? I'm a ways off the main road for you to be having car trouble and looking for help."

Wow, was this woman suspicious of people knocking on her door. In this day and age, though, I couldn't blame her. I had heard crazy things about fake door-to-door salespeople when I lived in the city my last year of college.

"We're not having car trouble either," I assured her, trying to give her a friendly smile. I pulled the silver-plated hairbrush out of my purse. Do you recognize this?

"No." She started to close the door.

It wouldn't shut all the way. She and I both looked down. Ashley's foot had blocked it from closing.

"Please. It was mailed to me from this address. It was in a box with a bunch of other stuff."

The woman opened the door back up, revealing more of herself. "Now, the box I remember. Didn't realize my address was on it."

Ashley barraged her with questions. "Why did you send it to me? How did you have my address? Do I know you? Do you know me?"

The woman shooed us backward as she stepped out onto her stoop and closed the door. "Name's Millie."

Ashley and I introduced ourselves. At least Millie was acting less suspicious of us now.

"I bought the place a couple months back. I like my space, and when this place went up for sale, I had to go for it." Millie looked up at the front façade. "Needs a bit of a fixing up, but I'll get that taken care of before it gets cold again. Working on the inside now. I already cleared out some furniture that was left behind, and now I'm taking it room by room."

"Found that box I sent you in a hallway closet in the back" —she stuck her thumb out and motioned over her shoulder —"under a bunch of stuff. Lots of random junk. Your name and address were already on it. All I did was mail it. Looked like family heirlooms or something. Wanted to do right by whoever owned the place last and get it to you. Least I could do.

"Sorry if I scared you. Bet you felt a bit like I did when you both showed up just now. I hope you weren't looking for someone. I'm not it." She shrugged. "Don't know what happened to the previous owner."

Ashley sighed. I could see she was visibly disappointed.

"Millie"—she looked up at me—"thank you for your time. You've helped a lot."

"Yes, thank you. Might not have been the answers I wanted, but at least I have answers now," Ashley added.

"Yes, well, have a good day now," Millie said, her hand already on the doorknob.

We backed up two steps before we turned around and walked to the car.

Once we got in, Ashley slumped in her seat. I drove away, and she remained quiet for several minutes before speaking.

"I don't understand," she began. "Who would know me and where I live?"

"I don't know. What about the other things in the box? Are you sure none of them are yours?"

"I don't even recognize those things."

"What about your parents? Could it be their stuff?"

"It's not my dad's. It's a lot of women's stuff. Like the hairbrush. An empty perfume bottle. A beaded makeup clutch. Definitely not my mom's taste either. Even when she was younger."

After a few more minutes, she spoke again. "Could this have something to do with my father, my real one?" She looked at me, clarifying, "My dad isn't my father."

That was news to me, but I'd only been in town for four years. That gossip had likely come and gone years before.

I glanced at her from the corner of my eye, keeping most of my attention on the road. "Do you know anything about him?"

"Only that I have one." She laughed, then grew serious again. "Really, that's all I know. Mom was so secretive about who he was. I don't even know if he was from town, but he'd have to be, or at least, he came to it. My mom didn't go anywhere. Born here. Raised here. Died here. I'm pretty sure her one big trip was her honeymoon with my . . . step-dad."

"He's your dad, Ashley, don't let this get to you. Biological or not, he raised you and loved you as his own."

She grew quiet once more and remained that way until we were on the edge of town. "Thanks, Joanie. For all of this. But can I ask you something?"

"Sure thing."

"Why are you doing this? Why go through all the trouble? It's not your problem."

"Well," I began, trying to think of the right words that wouldn't make me sound crazy, "I guess I got caught up in the mystery of it all. After living with that brush for a few days, I want to get down to the bottom of it. And something's seemed to be weighing on you lately, and if I can help with that, I want to. You deserve to be happy." Wanting to avoid sounding too much like a sap, I added, "A haunted brush. Who would have thought?"

Ashley laughed, and this time the smile afterward stayed on her face. "I know, right? I wouldn't believe it if it weren't happening to me. Sounds like something straight out of a book or movie. People don't get haunted brushes delivered to their doorsteps in real life. Next thing you'll tell me is you've seen its ghost."

I giggled—a little too loudly—as we pulled up to the front of her house. I didn't think she'd noticed the awkwardness behind it. "Yeah, that would be something, wouldn't it?"

"Yeah." She unbuckled her seatbelt and pushed open the car door. "Bye, Joanie. Thanks again."

"See you around."

I waited until she was back inside before pulling away.

After the dead end, I needed to figure out my next move.

CHAPTER 19

I had hoped we'd get answers, but instead, I was ending my day with Ashley much sooner than I'd planned. I headed back to the bakery to work. It felt like I hadn't done enough of that this weekend.

As expected, Sarah and Gina had it all under control.

"I didn't think you'd be back so soon," Sarah said. "That was, what, not even four hours?"

"And that includes making the inn's delivery." I glanced up at Gina. She looked dead on her feet. She wasn't used to working such a long day. "G, do you want to head home? I can take over for the rest of the day."

"You sure?"

"Absolutely. Thanks for stepping up and covering for me today."

"Thanks. I think I'm going to go take a nap." She shuffled into the kitchen, mumbling goodbye. She'd perk up a bit once she got outside.

I turned to Sarah. "How did things go here?"

"Chelsea and David want to schedule a meeting to go over designs for their wedding cake, but beyond that, it was a fairly standard Sunday. Probably a little—" She put a hand on her mouth, stopping herself from saying the next word, *quiet*. We tried to not use that word. It could go from quiet to crazy in no time at all. Instead, she changed the topic. "Did you know they want it mermaid themed?"

"I didn't, but that's cute. I'll draw some stuff up for it today if it stays like this. Hey, I wanted to run something by you."

"Sure. What's up?" She cocked her head to the side.

"What are your thoughts about coming on full time? This isn't your first week coming close to hitting enough hours, and I might need the help if I keep having weeks like this one. Plus, now with Lauren stepping back to one shift a week for the next month, there's plenty of time to pick up if you want it. You might as well get the benefits."

"Like, real health benefits? I could use those. Yes. Yes, I'll go to full time."

"Great, I'll get the paperwork in order tonight and tomorrow."

A customer walked in then, and we carried on with our day, but I kept catching Sarah eyeing me as we worked. When we had our next lull, I said, "Out with it."

"Did you sort out the matchmaking thing between Rich and Ashley?"

"Not yet." I sighed.

"Here's what I don't get."

"What's that?"

She pointed to my bag under the counter. "What does the brush have to do with it?"

"Why do you think it has something to do with them? I'm not saying you're wrong. I'm curious how you picked up on that."

"Well, Ashley and Rich are cute together. It's obvious to

anyone in town who's seen them that they like each other, and it doesn't seem like there were problems until that brush appeared. I mean, she probably didn't have it for long before giving it to you."

"A week, but you have a point, and I'm working on it. That's what I've been trying to do the last few days." I needed time to think. "Hey, why don't you go home early. You've worked enough this week."

"Rethinking that full-time offer already, huh?"

We both laughed.

"You've earned it. And I'm sure you had other stuff to do. It wasn't really a planned thing this week."

That's all the convincing it took. She rushed into the kitchen closet and grabbed her things before heading out the door. "Thanks, Joanie. I'll see you tomorrow."

The rest of the day passed by without incident, and by the time I left for home, I had been able to sketch three designs for Chelsea and David's wedding cake to run by them next weekend.

The next morning, I stepped into Olde Templeton Diner with my two dozen muffins to waiting customers. I looked at Walter and Paul, then cast a questioning glance to Donna. "I'm not late, am I?"

Donna shrugged drastically, bringing her hands up to ear height. "They were waiting for me to unlock the door this morning. Although they're usually my first customers on Monday mornings, this was early, even for them."

"We're here for the muffins. What did you bring us today?" Walter asked as Donna waited by her specials board to write down my answer.

I rattled off the four flavors. They'd been in the regular rotation lately, and I'd have to introduce something new soon.

"So you really like the muffins, huh?" I asked the two men.

"We get one every day. Donna even saves two to warm up for us on Tuesday when you're closed," Walter answered.

"But there's something about the Monday muffins that gets our week started on a good note," Paul said before taking a sip of his coffee.

"A double dose considering we eat them on Tuesday too." Walter clinked his coffee mug with Paul's.

I looked at the two men. They'd been coming to the diner every day since I opened up and who knew how long before that. "Say, you've both been in the village for years, right?"

They looked at one another then at me. "Ever since we were kids," Paul answered.

"So you know everyone?" I asked.

"Pretty much," they said in unison.

"How about Ashley O'Donnell and her parents?"

"Sure do," Walter answered while Paul nodded. "My wife, Martie, used to mind Ashley's mom back when we were in high school."

"What do you know about her dad?"

I could feel Paul's gaze scrutinizing me. "Her dad or the man who swept in from somewhere when her parents were split up and made Missy fawn all over him only to disappear, leaving her with child?"

"He's a good man going back to Missy and raising Ashley as his own," Walter commented. "Not everyone could do it. But he loves that little girl."

Donna brought out their grilled muffins with butter already melting on them. "She's not so little now, Walter.

She's twenty-some-odd years old! Be right back." She turned and disappeared into the kitchen once more.

I pulled my ponytail tighter. "So her biological father wasn't someone from Heartwood Hollow? Just some mysterious drifter?"

Both men nodded while chewing on their bites of muffin.

"Do you remember anything about him? A name or where he stayed?"

Paul cleared his throat and took another swig of coffee. "What was that style of the mid-nineties? Combat boots. Flannel. Ripped jeans."

"Grunge?" I prompted.

"Must be," Paul agreed. "Wore dark sunglasses too. Gave off that bad-boy vibe."

Walter nodded. "Yeah, that's him. He was here for a while. Had to have stayed with someone in town. He certainly wasn't at the local motel." Before I could ask how he knew that, he answered, "I did maintenance for the whole building, and I would've seen 'im."

"So could he have been someone's son or brother? A cousin? A nephew?"

Walter shrugged. "Guess anything's possible, but we never saw him with anyone else."

"And we never saw him again after he left," Paul added.

Donna walked back out of the kitchen and dropped two heaping plates of food in front of the men. Scrambled eggs, sausage, and home fries for Walter. Two fried eggs, home fries, and corned beef hash for Paul.

I'd taken up enough of their time. "Thanks, you two. Stop by the shop sometime. Pick up something for Martha and Nancy."

The men nodded their goodbyes, mouths already full of food.

"See you later, Donna," I said, waving toward the kitchen as I walked to the door.

I peered into my purse at the brush as I stepped away from the diner. "I think Ashley was on to something when she thought you could be related to her biological dad. You'd have the answers for me, wouldn't you?" I sighed. What was I doing still talking to this brush?

Thoroughly perplexed, I biked back to the bakery. This brush haunting and how it tied to everything was more complex than any multi-layered cake I had ever been tasked with making. And I had created several complicated cakes over the years.

The morning rush came and went. Mondays were always busy. Maybe Walter and Paul were on to something about my Monday muffins. They flew off the shelves each week, followed by the scones. We'd yet to run out prior to noon, but in the early days of the bakery, we had come close. Today almost came close enough to worry me about my supply—I blamed school being out for the week-long April vacation— but I believed we'd be fine with the extra my team had made this morning well into the shop's open hours. Even still, we were down to our last dozen by the time I had to make my late-morning deliveries.

With boxes packed and prepped by Sam, who was putting extra hours in during his week off from school, I loaded up my car. I'd driven it to work today because I had a cake delivery, and no matter the size of the cake, it made me feel better to secure it with the straps I had installed in my trunk.

First up was a small cake to the photo studio for a little boy who had turned one over the weekend. The little boy,

Jacoby, was close to my heart as he was the second child of the first couple I matched after moving to Heartwood Hollow. I'd delighted in creating the humongous cupcake-shaped vanilla cake with bright-blue frosting and fondant polka dots, knowing he'd destroy it all within moments as part of the photo shoot. His mom promised me pictures. I'd put them next to the photos of his sister doing the same thing a year and a half ago.

Then I dropped another dozen muffins off to Donna, who had forgotten about school break and ordered her usual amount. On most days, when the muffins were gone, they were gone, but she hated to disappoint customers, especially on Mondays. She hadn't even set aside muffins for Walter and Paul to have tomorrow yet. She bumped up her order for the rest of the week.

Next was the inn. Libby greeted me at the door to the kitchen as she opened it for me. I slid past her with my boxes, set them on the counter, and began to unpack the first.

"I've missed you these last few days. It's been so busy here."

"I don't think I've ever heard Billy speak so much at once until the other day."

Libby laughed as she opened the second box. "I may have told him he needed to get the scoop on this new man of yours."

"He did seem more interested than I would have expected him to be," I replied, chuckling.

"Mm-hm . . ." Libby started. "But you know me. He didn't get enough. So how are things with you and your new man?"

I trusted Libby to not spill anything I told her, other than to Billy. She liked to know everything going on but wasn't a telling secrets kind of person.

"I wouldn't call him my man—"

"But you want him to be," Libby interjected. She stole one of the cookies out of the box, pointed it at me with a wink, and took a bite.

"It's still all so new, Libby. I wouldn't go that far yet. I don't want to rush into anything, and neither does he, especially since he has his daughter to consider."

"Why? Was the divorce messy?"

"Not from what he's told me"—I eyed her—"which is very little."

"Okay, okay." She put her hands up. "Point taken. Not your story to tell."

"That and I really don't know. Besides, we could end up just friends and then it doesn't matter." I finished loading the first two tea trays and broke down the box.

"You'll need to find someone eventually. You're not getting any younger. And who knows? Maybe it will be him. From what I've heard, your two dates have gone well. When's the third?"

I wasn't about to go into my "you don't need a man to be happy" speech with Libby, who had been happily married for several years. "We haven't talked about it. And I wouldn't call the second one a date, really." Even though Donna classified it as one, I still wasn't convinced. But I needed to change the subject before this conversation stayed all about me and my love life or lack thereof.

"Libby, you've lived here all your life, right?"

"Sure have. Why?"

"Do you happen to remember someone who stayed awhile in town in the mid-nineties? Mysterious bad-boy type?"

Libby screwed her lips to the side. "Hmm . . . now that you mention it, it's possible? Slightly longer dirty-blond hair, sunglasses. Oh, he was hot. I was thirteen at the time, and he was the first older-boy crush I had. He had to have been eight, maybe ten years older than me. Was around that whole summer."

"Do you have a name or know where he stayed?"

She shook her head. "No name, but he was definitely staying in town."

"How do you know that?"

She looked at me as if I had two heads. "Isn't it obvious? He walked everywhere."

Of course. "Thanks, Libby. That helps." It was more than I had before, at least.

"What's this all about?" She put her hands on her hips.

"I'm helping a friend with something."

"Ashley?"

I probably shouldn't have been surprised. "How did you guess?" Perhaps I could get a little more out of her that she didn't realize she knew.

"He was with Missy, her mom, a lot. She was having problems with her husband, they'd gotten married right out of high school and were having some growing pains. They split for a time right when he came around, but he was gone once summer ended."

I eyed her, a sly grin on my face. "You know a lot for having been thirteen."

Libby shrugged. "It was the first big town scandal I was aware of."

"Gotcha." Thirteen was a big year in the scheme of growing up. For me, that was when the ghosts started to ask for help.

"Well, I have to be going," I told Libby, breaking up the last box for her.

"Are you sure you can't stay?" She seemed disappointed.

"I promise I will soon. It's been too long since I've had one of your tea services."

She wrapped me in one of the hugs she was famous for. "I had to try. And bring that man of yours when you do."

She wasn't letting my hesitancy sway her. I turned my gaze to the ceiling, half rolling my eyes as I patted her on the middle of her back. It was all I could do since she had pinned my arms to my side with the hug. "We'll see."

CHAPTER 20

After a bustling Monday afternoon, I was ready to start my evening. Since I still had my car from my earlier deliveries, I drove to the grocery store to stock up on things for home. Saffy needed cat food, and I much preferred to drive on days I had to buy that. I didn't like lugging the eleven-pound bag home on foot. Although I regularly lugged much larger bags of flour or sugar from the bakery's cellar storage, it was awkward to carry with the rest of the groceries.

I strolled down the produce aisle looking for inspiration for something new for the bakery—I loved trying new combinations, and Tuesdays were my usual days to experiment. When I glanced up from the pears I was contemplating, Rich was at the other end of the aisle heading my way. He was alone. Completely alone. Daniel was nowhere to be seen.

I placed my hand on the purse to see if I could feel a reaction from the hairbrush inside. Nothing yet.

Waving to catch his attention, I met him halfway, stopping in front of the sweet potatoes.

He cracked a smile. "Should I be surprised that we've run into one another again?"

"We can call this one pure coincidence." I chuckled but hoped he didn't think I was following him. Pointing to the bag in my cart, I continued, "I needed cat food."

"I didn't know you had a cat."

"Yep. She's a calico."

"Quite the attitude, those have. My mom always had cats when I was growing up. She hasn't gotten another one since the last passed away a couple years ago, though. One was a money cat. Her name was Zoe."

"That's what my gram calls Saffy." I thought people my age didn't use the term.

"She bring you good luck like they say they do?"

"I'd like to think so, but I didn't think you believed in that sort of thing."

He gave me his megawatt smile. "I didn't think you did either." He had a point. "So is Saffy short for anything? It's not a name one usually hears for a cat."

"Yeah. Saffron."

"That's a spice, right? How come that one? Not so much used in baking, I would think. I'd have guessed *sugar* or *cinnamon* for you."

"It is a spice, although you'd be surprised what baked goods it can appear in. I got her my junior year in college after I moved into an apartment. I had a class on savory pastries and one of the units was on saffron. Long story short, she stole my container of it, and that's how she got the name."

"Cats are quite the characters, aren't they?"

It was nice to see Rich so happy and normal-Rich-like. Since first noticing his grandfather's ghost with him, he hadn't quite seemed himself.

"They really are." So far, the brush hadn't reacted to being near Rich. Beyond my having seen the spirit the night when the brush tried to lead me outside, I hadn't seen it react since the last time Daniel was around.

Over Rich's shoulder, I spotted Ashley turning the corner to come down the aisle. "Oh, it's Ashley." I waved as we made eye contact.

Rich flashed a megawatt smile, and he spun around to watch her approach. I pressed my hand into my purse even harder. Still nothing, not even a little. I wondered if they needed to be closer for the brush to react.

"Hey, you two. How are you both?" she asked once she reached us.

After exchanging pleasantries, Ashley placed a hand on my arm. "Thank you for all your help yesterday."

"Don't mention it. And I haven't given up on either mystery."

"Mystery?" Rich asked, still smiling, his eyebrows raised.

"Joanie's helping me out with something that might have to do with my biological father. Maybe I'll even find out who he is by the time it's all over," Ashley answered, twirling a lock of her hair around her index finger.

"Oh, wow, that's great. Very kind of you, Joanie," Rich said to me.

I nodded. "Happy to help."

Ashley smiled sweetly at Rich. "So what are you up to for your week off?"

I started to drift away from the conversation as Rich answered. After standing next to the sweet potatoes for so long, I had decided to include them in my Tuesday baking experiment. Muffins sounded good. I glanced around, searching for something I could combine with the sweet potatoes.

"So, since we can both stay out late, do you want to go to dinner tonight?" Rich asked.

With that question, I was interested in the conversation again, if only to listen to Ashley's answer. The tingling in my toes grew stronger, and the sensation worked all the way to my stomach, creating a flying-butterflies situation. It happened whenever my matches first met, and now it confirmed my belief in their being perfect for one another.

"You know what? Yes. Definitely. I could use a night out." She smiled and dipped her head, looking up at him through her long eyelashes. "When?"

"Well, how much longer do you need here?"

Before she could answer, I excused myself. They didn't need me hanging around anymore. "It was lovely chatting with you both. Enjoy your dinner. You both already know this, but I think you two are perfect for one another." I grinned, happy with how well things were going.

"Have a good night, Joanie," they said at the same time, then looked at one another and laughed.

I chuckled. "See? You prove my point right there. Bye, you two." I turned my cart to head through the fruit display, still pressing my hand against the purse. Nothing. Absolutely nothing. I checked back over my shoulder at Ashley and Rich. They were still chatting and laughing. Still no Daniel either.

What could have made both the brush spirit and Daniel leave? I wondered if the moon had something to do with it. What day was it? They said the moon's phases affected people. Was it the same for ghosts? I'd have to ask Gram what she thought about that, but part of me believed that maybe, just maybe, everything had righted itself on its own.

Needing to get home to Saffy, I continued on my way. Finally I spotted it. My second ingredient. Blueberries!

CHAPTER 21

Saffy greeted me at the door when I got home, my arms full of groceries. Once again, I was trying to juggle everything so I wouldn't have to make more than one trip to the car. The cat food under my arm was complicating things. "I sure wish you could actually help me with these or at least be able to get the door."

Saffy purted at me, her nostrils flaring. She smelled something better than her dinner and hadn't yet figured out what it was. Worried I was about to drop her food and send crunchies everywhere, I rushed into the kitchen. She followed me, still sniffing the air. Usually, she'd have beaten me in here by a mile because groceries meant new food for her.

"Saffy, off the table," I chided as she leaped up to find the source of the smell. She glared at me as she jumped back down. That look, however, was nothing compared to the one she gave me as I removed the rotisserie chicken from one of the bags and placed it on the counter next to the stove.

"None for you. You'll spoil your dinner, and it's still early for that. After you finish your meal."

I swear she huffed as she spun around and strutted to her food bowl, her tail swishing.

I looked up, half rolling my eyes. "Okay. Fine. I'll feed you now." I was such a pushover. "But you're still not getting chicken yet. It's Monday. You know what that means." I warmed up her canned food that I'd opened last night, and she lay down in front of her bowl to eat.

Leaving out the veggies to cook as part of dinner, I put the rest of my groceries away. Then I set the oven to preheat, rinsed everything, and put the carrots and green beans into their own baking dishes, adding maple syrup over the carrots and tossing the green beans with olive oil before seasoning them with salt and adding slivered almonds on top. While I waited for the oven to tell me it was ready, I peeled potatoes then cut them into chunks and set them in a pot of water to boil.

Saffy watched me the whole time I prepped dinner. Once she finished eating, of course. She was hoping I'd cave and give her chicken early, and I was keeping an eye on her so she wouldn't try to pull a fast one. During our first Thanksgiving together, she ran away with a turkey drumstick and hid under my bed with it. I had to coax her out with the one thing she liked more than anything else. Catnip. Once she was no longer near the drumstick, I had to push it out with a broom. Saffy ended up with it anyway. I couldn't serve it with holes all over it, but at least by giving the drumstick meat to her in a dish, I didn't have to worry about her eating the skin or choking on the bone in her human-food frenzy.

A knock at the front door broke both Saffy and me from our stare down. We went to see who it was. It could only be one person as most people defaulted to my doorbell. This person, however, knew how much Saffy disliked the loud bell sound. I stood on my toes and looked through the peephole. Saffy hopped to her spot in front of the window.

"Right on time, huh, Saf." I opened the door to reveal one of my older gentleman neighbors. Holding the door open for him as he crossed the threshold, I asked, "Matt, did you burn your TV dinner again?"

"Naw, you know I only use that as an excuse to see you."

I quirked a grin. "And get my cooking." Matt had lost his wife six years ago and now lived alone. Soon after I moved in, we struck up a friendship. I cooked for him at least once a week and regularly sent him home with leftovers.

Matt removed his cap and sweater vest, then ran a hand through his gray hair. "I can't help it if your cooking is as good as your baking."

"You flatter me." Taking his things, I hung up his vest on my coat tree, and put his cap on top of it. "Well, I'm sorry to tell you I bought an already cooked chicken for tonight, but I am making the sides. The mashed potatoes are almost done, and green beans and maple-glazed carrots are in the oven."

He followed me into the kitchen.

"And since you're here, I could actually use you. I'm trying out a new muffin recipe for the bakery."

"Now you have my attention—and my stomach."

"Go on and set the table. You've got to earn it. You know that." I cleaned the scraps of potato peel from the table so he could lay out place settings, and within a few minutes, I was dishing up dinner to an eagerly awaiting Matt.

Once he was settled, I cut a few pieces of chicken and crumbled it in between my fingers. Saffy, who had returned to the kitchen to supervise the rest of the cooking process, trotted over to her bowl where I gave her the chicken bits.

"Happy now?"

She dunked her head into the bowl and meowed loudly as she ate. Yes, she was thrilled.

I shook my head at her as I turned and sat down to dinner with Matt, who had watched the entire exchange with a broad smile. We ate in pleasurable silence for a few moments before I realized that he could probably help me with more than just my muffin recipe.

"Can I ask you something?"

Matt nodded. "Of course. I'm pretty sure we got over needing permission for such things after the first time you cooked me dinner."

"What do you know of Ashley O'Donnell's family?"

"Not much, to tell you the truth. Good folks, Ashley's grandparents. Her mom's parents, anyway. They were three years behind me in school."

"What about her dad?" I hoped he could shed some light on that mystery.

"Only what the gossips said. How much of it's true, I'm not sure." He shook his fork at me in a conversational but slightly serious manner. "Don't know who her father is, if that's what you're asking. Not my business."

He mashed some of his carrots in with his potatoes and took a bite. "Now, if my Henrietta were still here, she'd talk your ear off. Woman was the gossipiest hen in the coop."

"Sounds like quite the woman." I said that whenever he talked about her. The stories he'd told me about their life together warmed my heart. They were full of fun activities and lots of travel to faraway places.

"That she was. I sure do miss my bird."

I had to press my luck and ask about something else that could be considered gossip. He seemed about the same age as Daniel would have been if he was still alive. "So what do you know about Rich Johnson's family?"

"Are you up to your matchmaking again?" He pointed his fork at me again before spearing a piece of the chicken.

"Possibly." I couldn't help but give him a wry smile. If he wanted to believe that was the reason I was asking, that was fine by me.

His smile matched mine, and he shook his head, chuckling. "Just like my Henny. She would have loved you."

"And I have no doubt the feeling would have been mutual."

Matt cleared his throat. "Well, now, I can tell you all about his family, and it's not gossip since I know it firsthand."

I sat up straighter, ready to listen to anything he had to tell me. Was this the break I needed?

"Rich's family was one of three Black families in the neighborhood back then. This is back in the fifties and sixties, mind you. I was born in forty-seven and so was Daniel, Rich's granddad. We met in school and became the best of friends. Stayed that way into high school."

He took a bite of the green beans, then washed it down with a sip of milk. "I always felt he was proving himself so he could go somewhere, do something great with his life. Danny was the receiver to my quarterback. We had most of our classes together, but he was smarter than I was. We hung out a lot off the field and out of class too. Didn't care what they said. S'why I never liked gossip."

"What did they say?"

"Oh, I won't repeat any of it. It was the time we lived in— a white boy being best friends with a Black boy. I'm sure you can fill in the blanks. We didn't care, though."

"Good, I'm glad you didn't let that get between you." It would probably be good for him to talk with Rich. Maybe together they could work through some of Rich's concerns about Ashley. As his grandfather's good friend, Matt might have some idea of what Daniel had gone through and could offer advice as best as he could.

"Well, now, I wish it could say it all ended happily, but it didn't. Something happened, and whatever it was ruined his life."

My brow furrowed. "What happened?"

Matt shook his head and gave me a sad smile. "He never said. All I ever got was that 'she turned him down.' It changed him. Changed everything. He quit the football team midway through the season. His grades took a dive. And he almost didn't graduate."

He sighed. "It was like he'd lost the joy he'd had before. After graduating, I got him a job at my father's car dealership. It was the least I could do. A year or so later, he married Mae, Rich's grandmother. It was a nice small ceremony. Nothing grand like these days, and the cake was made by his mama. I was one of a handful of white men to go. The others had also been on the football team."

I stood up and cleared my plate from the table, then did the same for Matt. "Do you think he was happy once he got married?" I wondered if what Bev had felt growing up was true.

"Oh, I'm sure there were times he was. Especially once his kids were born. Little Beverly was the apple of his eye. Rich, too, once he came along. But like I said, he had been one of three Black families at the time, and once he lost that drive, I think he settled. Don't get me wrong, Mae was a great girl, but she apparently couldn't hold a candle to this 'she' he mentioned."

"Do you know who it was, the girl?"

"Sadly, after all these years, I never learned who she was. He never mentioned a girl at all when we were in school. Knowing how people were with him and me, I can only assume this she was white girl. Must have been quite the gal to have had that effect on him. I never had the heart to ask him. And years later, why would I have brought it up when he had buried those feelings long ago? But sometimes I still wonder what really happened and who that girl was, if she's still around."

She was around, all right, but not in the way he thought. I couldn't tell him that, though. And if Daniel's onetime best friend didn't know who the hairbrush ghost was, would I ever find out?

CHAPTER 22

Matt left after I made three half-dozen batches of muffins in which I had to perfect the blueberry ratio to the sweet potato batter. He ate one from each batch while he was here, but I sent him home with nine more, plus a heaping of leftover chicken and mashed potatoes. We had done a number on the green beans and carrots, so he didn't get much of those. I'd kept some for myself since I needed some for my lunch so I wouldn't have to go out and get something on my day off. After the busyness of the last several days, I was looking forward to staying home.

I tidied up the kitchen before settling down in the living room to read a book and drink a cup of nighttime tea. Saffy lay on my feet over the blanket I had wrapped myself in. I liked to be cozy as I read.

A couple chapters into my novel, something rattled then slid across the floor. I'd become familiar with the noise and knew what it belonged to. Strange, I would have sworn I'd left my purse zipped to prevent this sort of thing from happening.

Saffy's head popped up. Once she located the noise, she

jumped off the couch and scampered across the floor, tail shaking.

I looked down as the brush levitated, then it floated over to me, landing at my feet. Saffy jumped up and tapped at the brush with a paw, sniffing it. Then something unexpected happened. She rubbed her face on it. I took a sip of tea and continued to watch the scene before me unfold. Saffy began to purr. She wasn't an unhappy cat, but purring was a rarity.

Was the brush trying to apologize for all the trouble it had caused, or was it gearing up for something bigger? I hoped it was apologizing. I didn't want to clean up another mess.

But when the motion light at my back door switched on, I doubted the brush's intentions. The light rarely ever came on since my backyard was fenced. Wondering what could have tripped the detector if not something connected to the brush, which Saffy was still lying next to, I ventured into the kitchen. Before I reached the window over the kitchen sink, the light turned off. Now I couldn't see anything. Thinking it was an animal just passing through, I turned to leave, but the next moment, I heard what sounded like a *yip* crossed with a *yoo-hoo*. I flipped the switch by the door, bathing the backyard in light, and looked out the window set into the door.

I was greeted by the full moon of my neighbor George, who was bent over lifting up one of my garden gnomes. He placed it back on the flower bed and stood up, his white hair a beacon on his head. I focused on that as I opened my door and stepped outside.

"George, is everything all right? What are you doing out here?"

George began to turn around, and I quickly covered my eyes before I could see anything else.

"My hot tub is missing. Have you seen it? I can't find it anywhere."

"George, it's Joanie, your backyard neighbor. You're in my yard, darling." And *darling* he truly was. Somewhere in his late sixties or early seventies, he was such a sweet old man. He got confused sometimes, more now than when I moved in. This wasn't the first time I'd found him in my yard, but it was the first time he wasn't wearing anything. "Have you tried looking for it in your yard?"

"I misplaced it, dear." It's what he always called me when he got this way. "Will you help me look?"

"Come on, why don't I walk you back to your yard. We can look for it on the way."

I walked up to him, my eyes averted, and spun him around so his back was to me. Holding on to his shoulders, I walked him toward his yard. My fenced backyard had two gates. One led out the side onto the sidewalk. The second gate led to George's fenced-in yard. Years ago, when his kids were actual children, they had been friends with the kids who lived in what was now my house. George and the other kids' father installed the backyard gate so the kids could easily play with one another without ever leaving one of their yards. I could have had the gate removed, my realtor had even suggested it, but I had been so enchanted by the story that I couldn't bear to replace it with regular fencing.

Unsurprisingly, the gate leading to George's backyard was swaying gently in the breeze, the latch rattling slightly. I pushed it all the way open and directed George through as the back screen door of his house opened.

"Dad? Oh gosh, Dad, what did I tell you about wandering around naked? No one wants to see that." The man in his mid-thirties made eye contact with me. "Joanie, I'm sorry about that."

"Nathan, have you seen my hot tub?" George asked.

"Yeah, it's on the deck, Dad. Hang on. I'll be right down."

George clapped his hands with excitement as Nathan ducked back into their house. Moments later, he hurried downstairs with a bath towel. He handed it to his father.

"Wrap up. We'll go in the hot tub in a few minutes."

I lifted my hands off his shoulders and stepped back. George did as his son asked.

"How about you go put on some swim trunks, and I'll be right behind you," Nathan suggested.

George trotted off without a word to either of us, but he looked back with a big grin on his face as he reached the bottom step leading up to the deck. Then he ripped the towel off himself and slung it over his shoulder.

I covered my eyes and averted my gaze once more as George climbed the stairs and walked into his house.

"Thanks for bringing him home, Joanie. I'm sorry if you're now blinded by what you saw or have it burned into your retinas. You really shouldn't have to witness"—he made a circular waving motion with his arm outstretched toward his back door—"that. Are you sure you don't want me to replace the gate with a non-gated section of fence?"

"Oh, no. You don't have to trouble yourself. It's all right. Besides, I'd rather have him sneaking into my backyard where it's safe than to have him escape out into your front yard and down the street. It really is okay. Your dad's a sweet man, I don't mind him dropping by occasionally." I chuckled. "I didn't realize there would be a full moon tonight, that's all."

That reminded me, I needed to ask Gram about spirits and the moon. I looked up. It wasn't full, but it was close.

"Thanks, Joanie. I really appreciate it. He's not always like this, as you know. He overdid it a bit today. That's when he's at his worst."

"Well, no harm done. You and your dad have a good night. Enjoy the hot tub."

"You too. And if you ever want to use it, please, feel free. That gate swings both ways."

I nodded, unsure how to respond to Nathan beyond that. As the youngest of three, single, and living only about a half hour away in Snowhaven in an apartment, he'd moved in over a year back when his dad first showed signs of not being able to live on his own. Nathan had gained a short commute to work but ditched the rent and gave the rest of his family some peace of mind about George's living situation. When Nathan worked, George visited the senior center, a division of the town nursing home. So far, the arrangement seemed to be working out for everyone.

I waved over my shoulder at him as we went our separate ways. Once I made it back into the kitchen, I turned the outside light off. It wouldn't go off again until something tripped the motion detector. Hopefully it would stay off for the rest of the night. I wanted to get back to my reading, and I didn't need to see any more full moons until the real one a few nights from now.

I paused in the doorway between my kitchen and living room to watch as the hairbrush stroked Saffy from head to tail, over and over. Saffy had flopped onto her side, a position I only saw her in after catnip. What was going on with that brush? I had no idea but didn't care as long as this peace continued. It was nice to not worry about how I'd find my living room whenever I left the two alone in here.

I quietly approached and sat on the couch beside them, then carefully slid my legs back under the blanket. Saffy lazily stood up and then settled into the crook of my legs, stretching out on her opposite side. The brush continued to pet her as I picked my book back up and got lost in the story once more.

CHAPTER 23

Shortly before three in the morning, I awoke. It wasn't too unusual, given that I had to be at the bakery most mornings by four thirty to start the day, but Tuesdays were my one day off a week. All I wanted to do was sleep in, but that wasn't going to happen. I stretched freely and realized Saffy wasn't in between my knees like she usually was. A quick tap above my head at the top of the pillow confirmed she wasn't in her second spot either. Moving my legs around my bed, I couldn't feel my cat anywhere.

I rubbed my eyes and looked around. It was still plenty dark, but the nearly full moon brightened my room enough for me to tell that Saffy wasn't on my bed at all. So where was she?

"Saffy?" Sitting up, I clicked on my nightstand light and jumped back so quickly my head smacked the headboard. "Sh . . . ugar!"

Inches away at the side of my bed, the hairbrush ghost stood over me.

"You nearly scared the cookie crumbs out of me." This was why I didn't want to help ghosts when I was a teen. I never knew when they were going to pop up. "What are you doing? Are you okay?"

The ghost didn't react. This was going to be harder than I thought if she wasn't going to answer me. I scrubbed at my face with the heels of my palms. Still in her teal tunic, paisley bell bottoms, headband, and peace sign necklace, she continued to study me. I looked her up and down, peering over the edge of the bed. She was barefoot.

"Do you understand me?"

She kept staring, cocking her head a little to the side. Nearby, the hairbrush rattled. How had it ended up in my room? I had left it in my purse downstairs after it was through petting Saffy before I went to bed. Or maybe Saffy had been done with it. There was a fine line between good pets and too many pets with her.

"Can you speak?"

More rattling from the brush. Wherever it was, I couldn't see it.

Saffy hit the floor with a thud. She had to have been on my dresser next to me. It was the one other thing she fit on in the room that could have resulted in such a thump when she landed.

I might not have been able to see the brush, but she could.

"Saffy, leave it alone."

With what I swore was a humph, Saffy jumped onto my bed and sat by my feet. She'd barely reacted to seeing the ghost standing next to me as she rested her head over the edge of my mattress, if at all. I wondered if my cat couldn't see the ghost but still sensed the brush the way she had been able to all along.

"Can you do anything?" I asked the spirit.

Her face pinched with determination. The brush rattled some more.

"So all you can do is move the brush a bit. Did you wear yourself out petting Saffy earlier tonight?"

Saffy turned toward me as she heard her name but stopped to stare at the ghost. So maybe she could see her after all.

The brush levitated like it had several hours ago. This was the third time I had seen it, but I wanted to see something else.

"Okay, that's better." I had to give the ghost credit. I didn't want her to leave in frustration or blink out because she was trying too hard to do something. At least this time, she wouldn't be hitting any wards in my bedroom unless she tried to go out the window.

The brush glided onto my bed and fell by my feet. Saffy, who hadn't taken her eyes off the spirit since spotting it, jumped two feet high and landed a foot away from where she had been. She crept back toward the brush and, once she felt she was close enough, lifted her paw.

"Saffy, I said leave it." The last thing I wanted now right was for Saffy to cause the ghost to leave by interfering with the brush.

I turned back to the ghost. Her face was peaceful once more now that the brush was still.

"How about a name? I can't keep talking to someone no one else can see and not give you a name. Then it can be like I'm talking to you as an imaginary friend instead of a hairbrush or the thin air."

The ghost raised an eyebrow.

"I know, I know. It sounds silly to me too, but think of it this way: my gram says names have power. Perhaps having one will give you a bit more." She nodded. "But since you can't tell me yours, I'm going to have to guess."

I studied the ghost. Beyond the clothes, she looked young.

Around my age, if that. It didn't mean that she died in her twenties, though. She easily could have been that age when she was happiest. Gram explained to me that ghosts often reverted back to an age in which they were comfortable, healthy, happy—or at least that's what her sister, Peggy, had told her. I had never been good with determining someone's age, but if the ghost was around twenty-five in the late sixties, then she was born in the mid-forties to sometime in the early fifties. What names were popular then?

"Well, one of Gram's sisters was Peggy. How about that?"

The ghost shook her head.

"No? Okay. Well, Gram's name is Carol."

Another shake of her head.

"Barbara? That was her other sister."

She pulled her head back slightly and turned her head to give me a bit of side eye.

"Okay, not that either. Sandra?"

She scrunched up her nose a bit.

We continued like that for several minutes. It seemed like she had a problem with each one. I was quickly running out of names that I thought were common in those decades. After going through the names of my family and all the ladies in Gram's social circle that I could remember, I turned to current events of the time. Beyond knowing the major events of the decade, like the moon landing, Woodstock, and the JFK assassination, my knowledge of prominent nineteen-sixties women wasn't that vast.

"What about Rosa?" I finally asked.

The ghost considered this a moment, then smiled.

Based on her reaction, I didn't believe it was her real name, but it was one we could work with. "Rosa? Do you like the name?"

She nodded.

I looked up at the ceiling in gratitude. It finally felt like we were getting somewhere. Even Saffy was comfortable again. She had settled down between my knees once more, putting her head down and closing her eyes.

"Great. It's decided. Rosa. I have to admit, I chose it because of the roses on your brush." As soon as it left my mouth, I cursed myself and slapped myself in the face. "Drats, I totally should have thought of it for Rosa Parks. She's a way better reason to have given you that name. You seem like you would have supported what she did, the whole civil rights movement too."

She nodded again, enthusiastically this time.

"There, so, Rosa, now that your name's settled, can you help me with whatever is going on with Ashley and Rich?"

The brush rattled like crazy, sending Saffy into a tizzy. It spun in circles, getting closer and closer to the edge of my bed. It teetered for a moment, then fell with a hard smack against the wood. Saffy went after it.

"Saffy, leave Rosa's brush alone."

She jumped back onto my bed and glared at me before circling my knees and lying down once more.

I looked back to where Rosa was standing, but she wasn't there anymore.

She'd vanished.

Again.

CHAPTER 24

Some point after Rosa disappeared, I managed to fall back to sleep. I didn't remain that way for long.

A pounding on my back door and the shouting of my drew me from sleep. Although someone coming to my back door like this was out of the norm—in fact, it was a first—it was Heartwood Hollow, so I wasn't worried. So much so that I tried to ignore it and rolled to my side, rethinking my back-yard gate that led to the sidewalk now I knew people could get in that way.

"Joanie. Joanie!" the female voice yelled again. I groaned. It wouldn't have been so loud if I didn't insist on sleeping with my window partially open each night, no matter the weather. I'd woken up with snow on my floor before.

I groggily pulled myself out of bed, waking Saffy in the process. Somehow she hadn't been bothered by the noise. I guess she was tired from Rosa's visit too. Usually my move-ment would be her cue to run downstairs for breakfast, but now that she was awake, she could definitely hear the commotion. I assumed she was freaked out by it as she stayed rooted to her spot. Probably for the best. Since the back door opened into the kitchen, the banging would be loudest there.

I shuffled to the window a few feet away and pushed it all the way up, then did the same with the screen to stick my head out. In the haze of recent sleep, I couldn't place the familiar voice.

The long blond hair was my first clue. The second was the bright-yellow nail polish that I could see from twelve feet above her.

"Joanie. Joanie!"

Hearing the voice once more confirmed it.

"Ashley, what are you doing?" I called.

"Oh my goodness." She brought a hand up to cover her slack jaw. "Did I wake you? I figured you'd be an early riser with having the bakery and all."

"It's the one day I can sleep in as late as I want." I leaned my head against the window frame. Despite my schedule, I wasn't an early bird. More like a reformed night owl. My walking or biking to the bakery each morning was as much about waking me up as it was staying in shape.

"I'm so sorry, Joanie, but I need to talk to you. Can I come in?"

I could tell something was wrong—beyond the fact she stood at my back door banging to get in. This sort of thing wasn't Ashley's style. Sure, she'd breeze into the bakery all disheveled if something was bothering her, but she'd never try to barge into someone's house without a good reason. "Yeah, yeah. Give me a minute. I'll be right down."

I closed the screen and window. Had something happened during her date with Rich? Given the situation with the ghosts, I figured whatever she had to tell me was big.

I shuffled into my bathroom, splashed water on my face, then pulled my hair back.

"Saffy, it's okay. It's Ashley," I told her as I struggled to put on a pair of leggings as I crossed the bedroom to get to the hallway. She picked her head up but stayed lying down, eyeing me. "I'm going downstairs. Do you want breakfast?"

Those were the magic words. She stood up, stretched, then hopped off the bed. She met me at the doorway, and we walked downstairs together. This wasn't usual Saffy behavior. She'd have scampered ahead of me and been in the kitchen before I reached the bottom step.

"You're being a bit of a fraidy-cat, you know. I told you it's just Ashley. You'd like her. She pets cats for fun."

I unlocked the door and let Ashley in.

"Thanks, Joanie. I really am sorry to wake you."

"Tea?" I offered.

She stood there awkwardly. "Yes, please."

Giving her a reassuring smile, I said, "Have a seat. Won't take long." I set my teapot on the stove to boil, noting the time on the clock. A little after seven. Better than nothing.

Saffy sat in front of her bowl, waiting for me to feed her, flicking her tail. She hated to be kept waiting. I normally fed her first thing when we woke up, but this morning had already proven itself to be anything but normal. I switched out her empty bowl for a full one. She lay down and shoved her face into the bowl. Although she was hungry, her position and speed of her eating suggested she was still tired.

Right before the water hit boiling point, I removed the kettle from the stove and poured two cups of tea. Something with caffeine for me and chamomile for Ashley. I tended to have that at night, but her nerves needed it now.

Ashley had been sitting at the table, silent, politely waiting for me to get settled before speaking. At least she didn't have a tail to flick in impatience like Saffy. I set a cup of tea in front of her and one at my seat along with two spoons and a squeeze bottle of local honey. I didn't use sugar to sweeten my tea, but if I was going to start having people over regularly, I'd have to consider getting packets or a sugar bowl. All I had was a five-pound bag of it in the cupboard. I walked to the fridge and returned with my milk bottle. After stirring in some honey, I unscrewed the milk cap and poured some into my cup. Whoops. Preferring this tea without it, I hadn't meant to do that.

"Milk or honey?"

She didn't answer me, but that seemed to be her cue to begin talking. "I don't get it. I thought it was all going well." So I was right. Something had happened on her date. "We went to a wine and paint night at the art studio then to dinner at Nick and Etta's. We laughed, we drank, we painted. But then it all went wrong."

"What happened?" I pushed the milk and honey toward her.

Taking the honey, she squeezed the bottle a bit too hard, a large glob of it dropping into her cup. It was a bit much even for me, and I loved the stuff. She took a sip and hid a face, too polite to admit that she had likely ruined her tea with the extra sweetness. "Paint night was going splendidly. Now, I'm not the best painter, but that's what makes it fun, right? So we're drinking wine and painting, chatting in between Mona's instructions. When I drink, I loosen up. I gesture— sometimes wildly." She demonstrated, moving her arms in broad sweeping patterns. "Well, one of those times, I was holding my paintbrush, and I flung paint onto Rich's canvas."

"That's a minor accident, though. How does that ruin a date?" I sipped from my cup, then remembered I had leftover muffins from last night. I stood and walked to my cupboard. "Muffin?"

"Oh, yes, please."

I took two out of the container and set each on its own plate, then returned to the table with them and handed hers to her.

"Thank you." She took a small bite of her muffin and continued. "I apologized profusely, and we both laughed it off. Somehow, he turned that splotch of paint into something that worked by the time we were done. His looked better than mine!"

She pulled out her phone and showed me a photo of the two of them next to one another, holding their paintings of a pair of birch trees and flowers. They were smiling ear to ear. It looked like they had a wonderful time.

"So what happened after that?" I listened to the soft pitter-patter of feet as Saffy left to go to the living room. I'd likely find her curled up in her spot in the morning sun whenever I finished up in here.

"We walked back to our cars with our canvases, laughing the whole way. I almost dropped mine. He had me doubled over and in tears with the stories he was telling me. I didn't know he was so funny! The wine helped, I'm sure, but every-thing was fine. We walked to Nick and Etta's. We each had another glass of wine and had just finished our appetizer when he brought up my ruining his painting, and not in some joking way."

Ashley sighed. "Call me shocked since he had already agreed that it looked good. I apologized again, but it wasn't good enough, because all of a sudden, I'm being accused of purposely flinging paint onto his canvas. I tried to keep it down, people were looking at us, but him on the other hand . . . It was like he was trying to sabotage what had been a fun date by starting the fight."

Needing time to think of what to say, I sank my teeth into

my muffin. If I were a betting person, I'd wager that Daniel had accompanied Rich on this part of the date and goaded him much like I had seen that day in the hospital cafeteria.

"And then, to top it off," Ashley continued, "he flailed his arms and knocked into the poor waiter for the table next to us while he was carrying a tray full of food. Pasta and meatballs fell all over them both. I felt wicked terrible for the waiter, but Rich kinda deserved it."

She shrugged. "And although he's the one who ended up covered in food, I feel like such a fool because I basically sat there and let him behave that way. I should have walked out when he first said I did it on purpose. Can't say I was expecting that from him."

"It doesn't sound like him." Maybe that's what happened when you had a ghost getting involved. I wondered if Gram could teach me over the phone how to put a ward on a person, do kind of what she and Mom had done when the ghosts were getting too much for me.

"You doing okay?" I asked when her silence stretched to several moments.

"Yeah, I think I just need a few more minutes. Finish my muffin."

"Not the tea?" I unsuccessfully tried to hide a grin.

"You caught me," she said through slight laughter. "I like sweet things, I think I've proven that with how often I'm in your bakery, but that was a bit much, even for me."

At that moment, the doorbell rang. So much for Saffy's nap in the sun.

I had a good idea who it was. "Excuse me."

Ashley nodded and, without thinking, took another sip of tea. She was less successful in hiding her reaction to the taste that time. She chased it with a bite of muffin and smiled.

I entered the living room as the doorbell rang a second time. Saffy was standing at full attention, her face pressed up against the glass, growling. She did that no matter who was at the door after the bell would ring. My friends. The mailman. Various delivery drivers. Everyone.

"Who is it, Saffy?" I peered through the peephole. Suspicions confirmed, I opened the door, annoyed with myself for having left the brush upstairs. I would have loved to see if it would react with everyone here. It was a little too late to go grab it now.

Behind Rich stood Daniel, a solemn look across his face. I wished I knew what he was thinking. No doubt Rich had come to talk about his date. At least I'd get a fuller picture with his side of the story.

As if to go warn Ashley, Saffy took off for the kitchen.

Smiling, I asked, "Rich, how can I help you?" loudly enough for Ashley to hear me since Saffy couldn't tell her. Hopefully she'd come say hello and they could work this out.

"Joanie, I need to talk to you," he started, not returning my smile. "You're the one person I can talk to about this. It's Ashley."

"Come on in, Rich," I said, emphasizing his name while looking squarely at Daniel. He didn't take the hint and tried following his grandson into my house.

Blocked. Apparently, those wards were good for something.

Rich sat on my couch. Since Ashley hadn't come out, I didn't know whether to tell him she was in the other room, so instead, I asked, "Tea?"

"Yes, thanks." Finally he gave me a small smile.

"All right. I'll be back in a minute."

I walked into the kitchen and set the tea water to boil once more. Saffy was sitting in the chair next to Ashley, who was petting her under the chin, one of her favorite spots. Saffy had found her new best friend and was rewarding her with a loud purr. When Saffy saw me, she jumped from the chair and sashayed out of the kitchen, looking pleased with herself, tail up and her head held high.

"So Rich is in your living room?"

I nodded.

"Has he come here to talk about the date?"

"That's my guess. Do you want to come talk to him?"

"No. I don't think I'm ready, especially if he's still mad about it. I don't know if he's ever going to get it. I like him. I can see us together. But it's like he's creating hurdles to jump when he doesn't need to. I have some things to think about." She lifted her muffin. "Mind if I take this to go?"

"Sure thing. It will work out, you'll see." I wasn't sure how, but it would. I had yet to be wrong about a match, no matter the circumstance, and my toes still tingled.

"Hope so." Ashley stood and put her jacket on. "Anyway, I'll see myself out. Thanks for listening."

"Hey, before you go, why'd you go to my back door?"

"It's funny. I was walking by, every intention of going to your front door, but then the gate popped open, almost like an invitation. I realize now it was rude. Sorry."

I waved off her concern. "It's all right." Her explanation didn't surprise me. Much like blue lights at my bakery, it seemed my yard had a mind of its own. I doubted I'd need to replace the gate after all. It wouldn't let just anyone inside.

Ashley exited the kitchen through my back door with a quick wave over her shoulder.

I headed back into the living room. Saffy was sitting on the couch, one paw on Rich, who was bent over, elbows propped on his knees and head in his hands. Whatever had happened—and I knew they both had more to tell me—was really weighing on him.

I set the tray down on the coffee table in front of him. "Here you go."

"Ashley's in the kitchen, isn't she? I heard her voice."

I wasn't going to lie. "Was. She just left."

"She hates me, doesn't she? I'd hate me. I was awful last night."

"Oh, I wouldn't say she hates you." I nudged the tray closer. "But I think she's feeling a little hurt and confused. What happened?"

"Hasn't she already told you everything?"

"Sure. From her side. I want to hear it from you."

He ran a hand through his close-cropped hair. "I mean, I don't know where it started to go wrong. We had been having fun at paint night. She was talking with her hands and flung paint on my canvas in the process. She actually got paint on my shirt, too, but didn't even notice that. I laughed it off, though. We were having fun, and besides, I had a jacket to hide it." He added milk to his tea, then stirred it before draining half his cup.

"But the more I thought about it while we were at the restaurant, the more I began to believe she meant to do it. She's never talked with her hands like that. Then I got mad and threw my arms up, and I ended up covered in tomato sauce. I cooled off real quick after that, but the damage was done."

Saffy had inched closer to Rich to the point where she was now half in his lap as he scratched behind her ear. She hadn't met Rich or Ashley before, but she was eating up the attention. Ken would be jealous. This wasn't how she behaved toward strangers. If I didn't know her, I'd have thought she was a therapy cat.

Rich took a long sip of his tea. "I'm conflicted."

I leaned forward. "How so?"

"It's just—" He sighed. "There's a part of me that feels like she sabotaged this date to make me feel like a fool. But that's not her. I recognize that . . . now. In the moment, not so much. I don't know what came over me. I've never been that type of guy, although I guess I've proven I can be. She deserves better than that. Than me. Especially after that stunt. And the thing is, my painting actually does look good. I was planning to give to my mom for her birthday. Not sure if I'd be able to look at it whenever I'm there after what happened."

"I really think you should try to talk to her."

"Yeah. I know, but I don't think I'm ready." Rich gave Saffy one last scratch behind her ear and stood. He slid on his jacket, then straightened it by pulling the front down on both sides simultaneously. "Thanks for letting me vent. I don't know if I feel all that better, but I'm glad to have gotten some of it off my chest." He nodded at me, then walked out the front door.

Daniel stood up to follow him. After looking at us through the window, he had moved to the porch swing to wait. No doubt he had been the what—or who—that had come over Rich. Hopefully the ghost wouldn't erase all the progress his grandson had made.

I headed into the kitchen to make a fresh cup of tea. Before it had time to steep all the way, I brought it back to the living room and placed it on the coffee table next to Rich's empty cup. I flopped onto the couch, spreading out my arms and legs and leaning my head back. It had been a long morning already, and I had only been up for an hour. Saffy scooted closer to me and laid her head on my thigh. It had been a long morning for her too.

Several moments later, when I knew the tea would be cool enough, I leaned forward to grab the cup. Before I could, the doorbell rang, sending Saffy scurrying off the couch, growling.

Now, who could that be?

CHAPTER 25

Groaning slightly, I stood and shuffled to the door, wondering where my quiet morning had gone. My book was begging to be finished, and I needed to find out how it ended.

I peeked out the peephole, then opened the door for my second round of visitors.

"Ken, Ivy. Good morning." Thank goodness I wasn't still in my pajama pants. On a normal day, I would have been.

"Morning Joanie!" Ivy sang. I instantly sensed this kid was a morning person. Part of me envied her. Even as a child, I was a night owl. My sole reason for getting up early was the bakery.

"Hi. Is this a bad time?" Ken asked. His brows were furrowed, his mouth drawn into a tense line.

"No . . . no, of course not. Come on in." I stepped back, pulling the door open.

Ken stepped inside, his intense gaze boring into me with concern but not for me. Lacking any concern whatsoever, Ivy bounded after him. She spotted Saffy sitting in the middle of the floor and squealed.

"Kitty!" She rushed toward an unprepared Saffy, who shot off like a rocket and hightailed it up the stairs.

Ivy tried to follow, but Ken called her back.

"Saffy's afraid around kids. You'll need to be quiet if you want her to come to you," I explained doubting that Saffy had ever seen a kid so close before. Although she seemed curious about them every Halloween, but she saw them from a safe distance through the safety of a window. Even then, she tired of them and their trampling up to the door after the first hour. The only time she could have interacted with any was during the first few months of her life before she came to live with me.

Ivy stamped her foot and crossed her arms, putting her chin down toward her chest. Was this how all kids reacted to disappointment? No, I'd seen plenty of disappointed kids in the bakery when they were told they couldn't get one more treat. I was beginning to believe Ken had understated how spoiled Ivy was, but what did I know?

"Ivy, why don't you go play in the backyard?" Ken suggested. "That is okay, right?" he asked me after a moment.

It seemed to me he wanted a moment alone, and if so, that was probably the best place for her. And Saffy. "Oh, sure, it's fine. I don't have much out there. Nothing she can hurt herself on, if that's what you're worried about." I hoped George wouldn't go looking for his hot tub again. As Ivy bounded outside, I remembered that just because it was my day off didn't mean it was anyone else's. I breathed a sigh of relief knowing George and his bare bum would be at the senior center.

Ken slumped into the couch.

"Can I get you tea? Perhaps something for stress relief? Don't take this the wrong way, but you look like you need it."

"That would be great, thanks."

I dashed toward the stove. The water in the kettle was still warm and was boiling within a minute. The chamomile was getting a lot of use today.

"What's going on?" I asked as I set the tea tray down in front of him.

"I have to meet with my lawyer about Ivy."

"Is everything okay?"

Ken scrubbed at his face. "Her mom is suing me for custody. Can you believe it? It's been four years since our divorce."

"Wow, I'm sorry." I placed my hand on his shoulder. "Are you worried that she'd actually win?"

"Don't courts favor the mom?"

"That's what I've always heard, but you have to have a strong case since you've had her this long. You gave me the short version the other day, do you want to fill in some of the blanks? It might help in figuring out what points to make with your lawyer. Is it the same one as before?"

"No, but that one is sending over his files. This one is a family friend, though, so he's aware of the situation. So remember how I said we got a divorce because she wasn't ready to be a parent? Well, she's ready now."

"What's changed?"

"She's met someone and is pregnant. She wants Ivy back, says she'll complete the perfect picture." He held out his arms and made a framing motion with his hands, extending his thumbs and index fingers. "She can think that if she wants, but what it boils down to is she's angry we moved because it's a few hours farther away from her. Not like she ever made the effort to see her when we were closer. She's not getting my daughter. It's not happening. Simple as that."

"Do you not think she's ready for kids in general?"

"She might be more so than when Ivy was born, but she's

done nothing to prove it. She's flighty. Always has been. When she got pregnant, I wanted to settle down. Get married. Her parents insisted on marriage, anyway. But Kelly didn't understand the concept of settling."

Ken took a sip of the tea. "She didn't know what she wanted to do. She bounced around at various part-time jobs that she could ditch at the drop of a hat if a better—or more fun—opportunity came around. Even after having Ivy, she wanted to travel the world and live out of a backpack. That doesn't work so well with a kid in tow, not for her anyway. She always wanted to be able to go on the trips her single, childless friends were going on. Sure, I figured a weekend away here and there wouldn't hurt if that's what she needed to keep her happy, but not these week-long-plus escapades out of state. Even out of the country! I put my foot down when she said she was going to Iceland for a week with two-weeks' notice—like being a mom was some sort of nine-to-five office job. She left anyway."

"How?" I couldn't believe Ken would pay for her to go jaunting around the world especially if he didn't want her to go. More than that, it boggled my mind how anyone could just leave their kid. Though that wasn't just due to Kelly and Ivy.

"Trust fund. Got access when she graduated from high school." He took another sip of his tea and sighed. "It was more than the travel too. She never did her share of the chores from cooking to cleaning. I thought it would get better. We were young. I thought she'd grow up when Ivy was born. But even then, I did almost all of the feeding and changing. She was always good at playing with Ivy and making her laugh, though. She was definitely the fun parent."

He shrugged. "How could I be? I was too busy doing

everything else to be fun. I put myself through college while working two part-time jobs and raising Ivy.

"Wow." I couldn't think of anything else to say. It was impressive. He had to be one of the hardest working people I knew, and I hadn't even known him long.

"She asked for the divorce after coming home from Iceland. She admitted she wasn't the best parent and said I could have custody. There was no fight. And I didn't want to stress out Ivy by having one. So when she didn't move out right away, I didn't say anything. That first night after the divorce was final, she still expected me to cook for her. She still expected Saturday brunch a few days later. And I did it for a while to keep the peace, but I began to resent it and finally asked her to leave after a few months."

Saffy came out of her hiding place upstairs and made her way to the couch where Ken sat, tightly gripping his knees. She headbutted him and lay facing him. I wasn't sure if this was her accepting him or her resuming today's role as a therapy cat.

"So what did she do?"

Upon another headbutt, Ken began to pet Saffy. "She did her traveling, backpacked Europe, met numerous men, and had the time of her life, I'm sure. I never heard from her, but she always sent gifts home for Ivy. Big ones. Somehow, she continues to be the fun parent."

The more he pet Saffy, and the more she purred, the more the tension left Ken's body. He seemed looser, and the color had returned to the knuckles on his hand that still held on to a knee.

"Meanwhile, I graduated toward the top of my class and got a full ride for my master's program. I worked through that, too, to afford our small apartment."

"What about the trust fund Ivy's mom has?"

"I can't touch it, and she's only ever used it to fund her travels and buy whatever fun toys or cute clothes she's wanted for Ivy. I have to give her credit on that part. She's made sure Ivy's dressed well. I don't have an eye for any of that. Anything I ever got her came from the consignment shop."

"Oh." What else were you supposed to say to that?

"I graduated with my master's degree back in December. It took me a little longer than I would have liked, but that's the life of a working parent who's going to school. I applied for this job back in January. Got it at the end of February, but I took it on the contingency of finding a house. I've always liked the houses in this area, and I was so done with apartment living. And, more than anything, I wanted Ivy to have a backyard to play in. It was the one thing I wanted to be able to give her that Kelly never had. Luckily they were willing to wait for me, and fortunately finding a house here all fell into place. So here I am."

"Funny how that works out sometimes."

He smiled at me, his gaze soft. "Yeah. A lot of things around here are like that, it seems."

I could feel myself blushing, a slight heat rising in my cheeks. He was talking about me, I knew that. Flirting back was a foreign concept to me, but I had to do something before it got awkward. Not knowing what else to say or do, I returned the smile.

Ken had baggage. What single parent didn't? What person didn't? I saw ghosts. That was quite the baggage. But I hadn't realized his baggage contained all that it did. Ken and Ivy were a package deal, no doubt—a father and his child, a dad who was looking out for his daughter. But I hadn't factored in his ex until now, hadn't considered the idea of dealing with custody battles, shared or alternating weekends and holidays, the mom's side of the family, this new relationship of hers, or her future child too. Everything with the mom would affect Ivy, which would, in turn, affect Ken and his life, including his relationships.

It was a lot to take in, and it wasn't even my life.

Ken looked down at his watch. "Hey, I got to go. I hate to do this, but would it be okay if I left Ivy here with you while I go talk to my lawyer? It should only be about an hour."

"Oh—"

"If you can't, um, I'm sure I can find someone else. Lichelle was busy, and—"

"No, no. Don't be silly." I waved my hand, dismissing his worry. "There'd be no time for that. You have to get going. I don't mind. Really, I don't. Ivy and I have been getting along fine. You go on."

Ken breathed a heavy sigh of relief. "Thank you."

He stood up, barely interrupting Saffy's nap despite her using his leg as a pillow. She settled back down as soon as her head hit the couch cushion. "I'm going to tell Ivy I'm heading out for a bit. Don't want her to get worried by coming in to find me gone."

"I don't want that either." I wouldn't know what to do. The meltdowns in the bakery were few and far between, but they were nothing a sweet treat couldn't handle. I guess I'd give Ivy a muffin, but if Ken telling her he was leaving would prevent an issue, I was all for it.

Ken strode to the back door and opened it to step outside. "Ivy, I need to go out for an hour. You're going to stay here with Joanie while I'm gone. Be good, okay?"

"Okay, Daddy!" she called. I watched her from the window. She seemed completely enthralled with something in the yard. Probably an anthill or some type of bug. I'd never found my backyard that interesting before. Part of me hoped she'd stay that way for the next hour.

Ken pivoted and walked back inside, and I saw him to the front door.

He took one of my hands and, giving it a small squeeze, kissed me on the cheek. "Thanks again, Joanie."

My cheeks flooded with heat. "Don't mention it. It's really no trouble."

He bounded down the steps and hopped into his car. I gave him a small wave as he pulled away and began to drive down the street.

I could handle this.

Ivy was a good kid. At seven years old, she wasn't some baby who needed her diaper changed or a toddler I'd have to chase around my house to keep her from getting into things she shouldn't. I wasn't ready for any of that. Besides, it was only for an hour. Ken would be back before lunchtime. I wouldn't even need to feed her.

This would be easy.

Right?

CHAPTER 26

The door from outside to my kitchen banged shut as Ken turned at the end of the road. It was like a switch had flipped, and Ivy had transformed from a quiet and agreeable girl to anything but. She marched into the living room. Saffy's head shot up as soon as she heard the noise, and she scooted upstairs out of precaution.

If Ivy had spotted my cat, she didn't mention it. She stood in the center of the room, slightly hunched over, arms stiff at her sides. "I want a cookie!"

"I don't keep cookies in the house, Ivy. Sorry."

She glared at me.

Hoping she'd catch the humor in my statement I tried lightening the mood. "It's hard enough trying not to eat them all in the bakery."

"I want a cookie," she demanded, stomping her foot for emphasis.

So much for not having to feed her. "I have muffins. Do you want one of those?"

"Okay," she mumbled, pouting. She trudged behind me into the kitchen, then slumped into a chair to wait.

I pulled one of the blueberry sweet potato muffins from my cupboard. "Do you like these as is or cut in half with butter like how Olde Templeton Diner makes them?"

Ivy stuck her hand out. "Whole." I placed the muffin on a small plate, then gave it to her. She placed the plate on the table and picked up the muffin. My muffins weren't tiny. This one was about half the size of her face. Ivy ripped the muffin top off and set it down, then brought the rest of it to her mouth. She took a big bite, then stopped mid-chew.

At first I thought she might have been choking. I hadn't seen her swallow. Then her tongue moved. I could tell she was working something around her mouth. Her tongue kept pressing against her cheeks. A sour expression crossed her face, and she leaned forward. She slowly forced the chewed muffin out of her mouth, letting it drop back onto the plate with a squishy plop.

That was never a good sign. I didn't need to have children to know that.

"I hate raisins," she stated darkly.

"Oh, honey, those aren't raisins," I said softly, hoping gentleness wouldn't escalate the brewing storm. "They're blueberries."

"You're lying," she snapped, jumping off her seat. She stomped around the kitchen table. "They're raisins, and they're gross. I want cookies!"

"I don't have any cookies, Ivy, I'm sorry."

"Make me cookies. I want cookies." She circled the table once more, and when she had a clear path, she stormed out the back door screaming, "I want cookies," over and over.

I rushed to the door, which was wide open. "Ivy, please stop shouting. I can make some cookies."

The wailing continued. "I want cookies. Make me cookies."

Was this sort of reaction normal for a seven-year-old? How was I to know? I needed to calm Ivy down, but I had no idea what to do except give in to her demands. Weren't you not supposed to do that, though? I didn't care. To me, there was no other option.

Telling her I was making them didn't work. What if she stayed screaming the whole time? She'd hate me, and Ken would realize that I was terrible with kids and shouldn't be allowed to watch them. He'd lose interest in me when he saw how badly I handled things. Why did I ever think I could be trusted with someone's child? I shouldn't have said yes.

With Ivy still melting down, I grabbed a bowl from my lower cupboard, then started gathering ingredients. I took the bowl to the door. "See, Ivy? I'm getting things ready to make cookies!"

No change, just more yelling and stomp-pacing back and forth across the yard.

I kept the back door open as I hurried to measure and mix the ingredients for my spiced snickerdoodle cookies. They were the most recent cookie I'd experimented with at home, so I still had everything I needed for them. The whole time, I listened to Ivy freak out. Was this a crash-course in parenting? There was more to it than this—way more—but was this what I had to look forward to when I someday had my own? I glanced at the clock. Not even twenty minutes had passed since Ken had left my house. What if he got delayed and was gone longer than an hour? Ivy couldn't possibly scream for that long, could she?

I dashed back to the door with the mixing bowl in my right arm and the spatula I was using to mix everything in my left. I scooped up some batter to show Ivy. "See, Ivy? It's almost ready to go in the oven."

It was like she couldn't even hear me over her own

yelling. My neighbors were going to hate me, and the whole town would soon learn of my failure with taking care of children. Thank goodness most of them would be at work now. I'd really be done for if it was the weekend.

"Joanie! Joanie!" a voice called.

I looked for its source, hoping it wasn't Ken back early. I needed to at least calm Ivy down before he could return.

Nathan waved at me from an open window at the back of his house. "Joanie, do you need help?"

"I need something!" I shouted back at him, nodding my head in exaggerated motions.

He held up an index finger. "Be right down."

I put the mixing bowl on the counter next to me and watched as he rushed down the steps from his deck and crossed his yard. We met at the gate between our yards, and I filled him in on the situation, everything from Ken leaving Ivy with me for the hour to her wanting cookies and freaking out over the non-raisins in the muffins.

"What do I do? I'm making her cookies now, but telling her that did nothing to calm her down." I scrubbed my face with my hands, likely getting some combination of flour, sugar, spices, and butter all over me. Oh well. "She's getting what she wants. Why is she still freaking out?"

Nathan patted me on the back and shook his head. "That's just the way they are sometimes."

We reached Ivy, who had resorted to screaming while standing still once I entered the yard. How did she have a voice left? I would have lost mine a long time ago.

Nathan kneeled, getting on her level. Why hadn't I thought of that? I'd seen parents do it tons of times at the shop. I couldn't hear what he was saying, but Ivy stopped screaming and was calming down. Forget all the talk of my being a witch this past week and the so-called spells trying to get the spirit free from the hairbrush. What Nathan was doing was *real* magic.

After mere moments, Ivy was fully calm and had taken a toy out of her pocket. She played with it as if nothing had ever happened, as if she hadn't been screaming for the past twenty-five minutes.

Nathan stood up and brushed off his knees.

I stared at him, mouth slightly ajar. "Thank you."

"Oh, it's no problem."

"What did you say?"

"It's not so much what I said as how I said it. I made her feel heard. Said you were making cookies and"—he smiled—"probably needed supervision."

"You were great. But how did you know what to do?"

"Both my siblings have children. I get to hang out with them sometimes. I'm the cool uncle." He chuckled and shined his knuckles on his button-down. "But, seriously, kids are a lot like old people and vice versa. Since moving back in with Dad, I've realized the older he gets, the younger he acts. You've seen him. It's like handling a child some-times. So I guess you can say I've had practice with him too. Just not in the conventional sense." He grabbed at the back of his neck, and I noticed the slight blush creeping up toward his ears.

"I don't know," he continued, "but to me, it seems like kids and old people can both start to feel a bit like puppets after a while."

I cocked my head to the side, waiting for him to elaborate.

"They're pulled this way and that, all based on the deci-sions of others. It's unsurprising that they try to put their foot down every now and then, especially when things don't go the way they planned."

Mulling the comparison over in my head, I said, "I can see

that. I really am so grateful you were home to help. Why are you home? I thought you'd be at work today."

"My dad has a doctor's appointment. I'm working from home so I can bring him there in a couple of hours. He's at the senior center now so I can actually get some work done."

I placed my hand on his upper arm but removed it quickly when I realized—again—that I still had stuff on my hands. His blush expanded, covering his ears completely.

"Sorry. I really was making cookies for her."

"Anything good?"

"Spiced snickerdoodle. I can bring some over later if you want." Ivy was once again exploring the spot in the backyard she had been studying earlier before Ken left. "I owe you. You really saved me."

"Eh, don't mention it. You helped me out the other night with my dad and the hot tub, so let's call it even. Although I wouldn't say no to cookies."

"I'll wrap some up for you once they've cooled down."

Nathan rubbed at his neck again. "Okay, I should be getting back to work. We have a computer log-in that counts our activity time and keeps us honest."

"Oh, sure, sure. Thanks again, I would have been lost without you."

Nathan smiled. "Bye, Joanie," he said to me quietly before adding, "Bye, Ivy," loudly enough so she could hear.

"Bye-bye, Nate!" she called, an enormous smile across her face.

I hoped Ivy wouldn't start screaming again as soon as he was gone.

He walked back through the gate and up into his house. As I watched, I felt a small tug on my shirt. I looked down. Ivy stared back up at me, her hand still holding part of my shirt. Sugar cubes, although I had changed into leggings, I was still in my baggy pajama shirt. Wow, was I a sight.

I smiled, grateful for her seemingly calm demeanor. "What's up, Ivy?"

"Nate said I could supervise you making cookies."

"You sure can." So far so good. Nathan was a genius. "How about we go inside, and I can show you what I've already done."

"Okay!" She skipped along in front of me as we headed into the house.

I closed the back door and took up my bowl and spatula once more. "See, Ivy?" I showed her the cookie batter. She'd already pushed a chair over to the counter to stand on. She wasn't short, and although my counters were a bit taller than average, she now towered over the countertop.

"Now we need to form the batter into balls so they bake into cookies. How big do you want your cookies to be?"

Ivy spread her arms out wide. "This big."

I giggled, hoping she'd realize I was having fun and not trying to put down her idea. I didn't want to send her back into tantrum mode. "That would be humongous! I don't even think my oven's that big. Why don't we try something"—I spread my fingers wide on one hand and pointed to it with the other—"this size?"

Ivy's eyes grew big. "Okay!"

"Do you want to help?"

"Yes!" She started bobbing up and down as if she knew she shouldn't be jumping on the chair. I had a feeling she'd done this before.

I reached into one of my drawers and pulled out two scoops, then handed one to Ivy. "So here's how I do it." I lowered the utensil into the bowl and pulled out a complete scoopful of dough. "Then I press this button here"—I pressed the little lever-like button above the upper right corner of the parchment paper-covered pan and flipped the scoop over, releasing the dough—"and drop it onto the pan."

I pointed to the empty spot in the upper left corner. "Do you want to try putting a scoop right here?"

Ivy nodded and, sticking her tongue out at the corner of her mouth, slowly gathered a scoopful of batter and carefully, as if it was precious cargo—and to a seven-year-old, it easily could have been—dropped it into place.

We made a pan of six dough balls that would be at least five inches wide once they spread out during baking. Our second pan consisted of smaller ones to make cookies about three inches wide. Those were the ones I planned to package up and bring to Nathan as a thank you.

Sliding the pans into the oven, I glanced at the clock. It had been fifty minutes since Ken left us alone together and twenty since Ivy calmed down from her solo screaming match. If Ken was right with his estimation, he'd be back in ten minutes.

I set the oven timer for twelve minutes, hoping that Ken would be here by the time the cookies were done. I wasn't sure if I could deal with another one of Ivy's meltdowns only this time with her on a sugar high.

Ivy moved her chair from the counter to in front of the oven as I stepped away. She plopped herself down and brought her knees up to her chest, wrapping her arms around them. She set her chin down on her knees and stared at the balls of dough through the glass oven window.

I smiled. I remembered doing the same thing as a kid.

Okay, maybe I could handle this after all.

CHAPTER 27

en returned right on time as the cookies came out of the oven. Ivy had been standing behind me as I pulled out the pans and placed them on the stovetop, but she bounded to the front door as soon as she heard the doorbell. I quickly placed one of the larger cookies onto a cooling rack and followed her. It would make that one slightly crispier than the rest, but I wanted to make sure she could try a cookie before she left. Ivy threw open the door as I entered the living room. Even though I knew it would be Ken, a small part of me had to make sure Ivy wasn't opening the door for some stranger.

"Hi, Daddy!" She jumped into his arms.

He enveloped her in a big bear hug as she hung from his shoulders. "Hey, kiddo. Wow, you're getting big." He set her back down on the floor after several moments. "It sure smells good in here!"

"We made cookies!" Ivy grabbed him by his hand and pulled him behind her into the kitchen. I followed them, then walked around the table to get behind Ivy to help show off our final product.

"You two did all this?" Ken's mouth opened in feigned shock.

Ivy nodded, a huge grin on her face.

"It was nothing we couldn't handle, right, Ivy?" Thank goodness for Nathan's saving the day or else this hour would have turned out terribly.

"She tried to feed me raisins—yuck!" She stuck out her tongue in disgust.

Ken glanced in my direction, and I mouthed *blueberries* over Ivy's head. A small smirk formed on his face. "She did! Well, I bet these cookies made up for that, didn't they?"

I grabbed the cookie I had put onto the cooling rack. "Ivy, why don't you take this into the living room and eat. If you're quiet, maybe, just maybe, you can get my cat, Saffy, to come out and say hello." She'd been in hiding since Ivy's tantrum.

She nodded, then thrust out one hand, and I set the cookie into it. Her mouth dropped open as she gazed in wonder at it. It covered her hand and more. She placed her other hand over the top of the cookie as if to protect it, then tiptoed out the kitchen.

I lifted the rest of the cookies one by one off the pans with my spatula and set them on cooling racks. I grabbed two of the smaller ones and handed one to Ken. "How did things go? You're seeming calmer now."

Ken drew a deep breath, then released it with a smile on his face. "I feel calmer."

I reached for his forearm and gave it a quick squeeze, leaving my hand there when done. "That's great. So everything's going to be okay?"

"I'm still going to have to go to court if the judge decides to modify our agreement, but my ex doesn't have much of a leg to stand on. Her being the mom is basically it. Everything else is in my favor, from her willingly handing over custody four years ago with no conditions, to her not having a stable job, to her history of bouncing from one place to another. Sure, Kelly might settle down a bit now that she's pregnant, but the courts aren't likely to reverse our arrangement because of all I've done to improve our lives. Sure, we've moved, but that change, although substantial, improved Ivy's living conditions. Plus, Kelly doesn't pay child support or anything like that. So my lawyer's confident it will all be okay."

"I'm really glad to hear that." I dropped hold of his forearm and tucked a stray strand of hair behind my ear. It once again reminded me I was still in pajamas. My hair wasn't fully done up for the day, only loosely tied back from before unlocking the door for Ashley.

Ken took a bite of his cookie. "These really are good. It's definitely the baker, not just the bakery."

I smiled. Sometimes there was nothing better than home-made cookies straight out of the oven. "Ivy really did help, you know. She scooped the batter and put the dough balls onto the pan." I scooted past him and opened my refrigerator.

"I'm glad to hear it. She's been on a bit of a baking kick since getting here. I wonder why that could be . . ." He gave me a weighted stare before breaking out into another grin.

Nothing went better with warm cookies than milk. I pulled out the jug I had in there and held it up. "Want some?"

"Oh, yes, please."

Glancing back at Ivy and not wanting to bother her since she looked settled, I took two glasses out of my cupboard and poured Ken and me milk. I handed him a glass. "She sat and watched them bake in the oven. I didn't realize she could be still for that long."

"She's a bundle of energy. I'm well aware she can be a handful at times." He took a long sip of milk, draining the glass of half its contents. "I really am sorry for unloading on you earlier. I didn't realize how much I needed to talk about what was happening, I guess. And I'm sorry for springing Ivy on you and your cat without warning."

"Oh, don't worry about it. I'm glad to have been able to help, and Saffy will be fine as soon as it's quiet." Though there were no promises on her ever liking Ivy . . . if Ivy came over again. I grabbed a quart-sized plastic bag out of a kitchen drawer and began to load it with Ivy's hand-sized cookies. "Hey, I don't mean to be rude, but I actually have somewhere I need to be. I'm sorry, it's not that I want you to go—it's really not—but I still need to get ready and everything."

"That's fine. I've already taken up enough of your time today."

Handing him the bag, I gave him a half grin. I truly did feel bad for kicking him out, but something Nathan had said when we were in the back yard had given me an idea. Now I needed to see if it would work. My match between Rich and Ashley depended on it. If it worked, I'd have two reasons to be thankful for having Nathan as a neighbor today.

"No, it's all right. It's not like I asked you if you had plans before barging in here earlier." He laughed and held up the bag I'd given him. "Should I be paying you for these?"

His levity made me feel better.

"On the house." I spread my arms wide—bending them at the elbows so my forearms would point toward the ceiling, my hands palms up—and spun in a circle. "Literally, this time."

He threw his head back in a bark of laughter, then straightened to face me. "How about we actually plan the next time we get together. Dinner soon?"

"I'd like that."

We ran through one another's schedules as we walked out

into the living room, where Ivy sat quietly eating her cookie. Or what was left of it. More than half of it was gone. Despite the silence, there was no sign of my calico cat.

She smiled wide at her dad and then at me. Hopefully all was forgiven for earlier. I gently bumping my arm against Ken's. "I apologize in advance for her sugar high."

"Oh, it's nothing I haven't seen before. But after the high comes the crash. That should allow me to get some more unpacking done. The house is still a mess."

I thought about the two boxes hiding in my guestroom closet that had yet to be fully unpacked after my three-plus years in the house. I was pretty sure I hadn't unpacked them when I first moved into town either. "Well, that takes time. You'll get there," I told him . . . and myself.

"Come on, kiddo. Let's get going. Say goodbye to Joanie."

Ivy jumped up off the couch, then popped the last big bite of cookie into her mouth. "Bye, Joanie!" Crumbs tumbled from her mouth as she ran to the door.

Ken nodded toward the mess on the floor. "Sorry about that."

"Don't worry about it." I opened the door to show them both out.

Ivy hopped down the steps of the porch and down the short path to the sidewalk. "Come on, Daddy!"

Ken pivoted quickly on his heels to face me. We were the same height with me standing in the house and him on the porch. I hadn't realized how much green he had in his eyes before.

"Let me know about dinner," he said. "You can pick the place this time."

I nodded as he leaned forward and kissed my cheek before turning and following his daughter to the car.

Hand on my cheek where his lips had been, I closed the

door and headed to the window to wave as they drove away. Saffy appeared out of nowhere and jumped up into her spot.

"Had to make sure they were both leaving?"

She turned to me, and I would have sworn she nodded as if having understood my question. But then she sneezed, and I noticed the cobweb hanging from her whiskers.

"Hiding under my bed again?" I really had to clean under there. "Don't worry, you'll have the whole house to yourself soon enough. I'm heading out in a few."

It was time to put my idea into action.

<h1 style="text-align:center">CHAPTER 28</h1>

First things first. I had to get changed. I couldn't believe that many people had seen me in my pajama shirt. My leggings weren't much better, but at least they were my cupcake pants. I rushed up the stairs and quickly undressed, then hopped in the shower once I realized I still had dried batter on the side of my face and likely in my hair.

As I stepped out of the bathroom, wrapped in a towel and heading for my dresser, I called for Saffy. She'd followed me upstairs, but now I didn't see her anywhere. Was she hiding again? Poor thing. Ivy must have really freaked her out. I'd assumed she'd be fine once she saw them leave.

"Saffy? It's okay, she's gone now."

A scratching from nearby on the wood floor was my only reply.

A moment later, she pulled herself out from under my bed. Saffy glanced at me, her head low with humiliation at my having witnessed her difficulty in getting out. She was no longer a kitten who could slide under there with ease. The sides of the bed frame were about four inches off the floor, but under the bed was slightly taller, the box spring halfway recessed into the frame. Saffy had to crawl to get under there and couldn't stand up straight at any point once she was. Her pudginess didn't help things either. Saffy rubbed up against my legs, then jumped onto the bed.

"I'm sorry Ivy scared you. She's seven, and judging by her reaction, I'd say she doesn't have a cat of her own." I dug through my drawers for a sweater to wear. It was a nice day out, but still cool. And at this time of year, the weather could change at any moment. Snow was still a possibility.

Saffy turned counterclockwise three times before lying down, but she kept an eye on me as I pulled out a violet sweater.

"But can you blame her? You are pretty adorable."

Saffy grumbled.

"Don't worry, I don't need your fashion advice today. This isn't a date. Today, I'm hoping to get some answers." She buried her head in her front leg as I threw on my sweater and then stepped into the pair of jeans I had worn yesterday. They always fit better the second day.

I sat on the edge of the bed to put on my socks. "I'll be back later today. Don't wait up." I gave her a quick scratch behind her ears before heading downstairs.

I grabbed my purse off the couch, then dug inside it to make sure I still had my keys, turning to find them on the side table as I did. But the hairbrush wasn't in there. My whole plan would have been ruined if I had shown up without it.

As I jogged up the stairs, my footfalls heavy, I called to Saffy to tell her it was me, so she wouldn't think Ivy had returned to find her. Saffy was staring at me with wide eyes once I reached my bedroom. "I said it was just me. Do you know where the brush disappeared to after last night?"

She glanced down.

"Oh, that's right. I didn't pick it back up after it fell. Thanks." I walked around to the other side of the bed, but it was nowhere to be seen. I dropped onto my hands and knees and peered under the bed.

At the center of my headboard along the wall, the brush lay flat.

"What, were you both hiding under here or something?" I tried reaching for it, but I kept getting blocked when the bedframe hit my shoulder. A hushed snort of laughter came from above me, and I looked up. Saffy's head hung over the side of the bed. I'd swear she was laughing at me. That was what I got for thinking she was pudgy earlier.

I rotated my body so I could slide my leg under instead. Although I had a little trouble with the low clearance of the bed frame, I caught the brush with my foot and then dragged it against the wall until I could easily pick it up. Held out for inspection, it seemed no worse for the wear.

Downstairs, I plopped it into my purse, zipping it closed before I grabbed a jacket. With that on and the bag over my shoulder, it was time to go.

I felt a bit silly driving such a short distance to Ashley's house, but I wasn't going to let the possibility of her not wanting to go for a walk keep this experiment from happening.

I left my car running as I knocked on her door.

"Joanie? What are you doing here?"

"Get in the car. I have an idea. You're coming with me to the park."

"Oh, um, okay. Let me just throw my shoes and a coat on."

Nodding, I turned back the way I'd come. "I'll meet you in the car."

A few minutes later, my passenger door opened, and Ashley slid onto the seat. "What's this all about?"

I handed Ashley my phone. "Can you type in Rich's number?"

"Okay . . ." she said, drawing out the second syllable as she dug out her phone and pulled up her contact list. After keying in the number, she handed the phone back to me. "There you go."

"Don't say anything," I said as I pressed call before setting the phone on speaker and putting it in its dashboard holder. "I'm calling him in case he wouldn't pick up for you yet."

Ashley frowned but nodded sharply once.

I threw the car into gear and drove away from the house.

On the third ring, Rich answered. "Hello?"

"Hey, Rich, it's Joanie."

"What's up?" His voice sounded tentative.

"Can you meet me in the park by the playground?"

"When?"

"Now. I'm in my car on my way there."

"Oh, um, okay."

I smiled at how his answer matched Ashley's from a few minutes ago. They really were right for one another.

"Great! See you in a few." I ended the call before he could say anything else. We'd already made it to the park entrance. I pulled into the little lot.

Ashley and I took the short path to the playground and sat in a bench two over from where Ken and I had watched Ivy play a few days before.

Ashley pivoted to face me, bringing her closer leg up onto the bench. "Joanie, what is this all about?"

"I'm testing a theory about the hairbrush."

Ashley's face paled slightly. "Do you have it with you?"

"I've pretty much carried it with me since you gave it to me. I had it at the cabin the other day too. Are you okay?" I placed a hand on hers, resting on her lap. "You look frightened."

"It's just the more I think about it, the more it freaks me out. A haunted hairbrush, I mean, really?" I nodded, fully understanding her disbelief. "And we still don't know how it's tied to me. What do you hope it's going to do here of all places?"

"I'd rather not tell you and risk influencing the experiment. We'll find out when Rich gets here."

She shrugged and drew her lips to the side. "I guess that makes sense."

"Oh, look. There he is." I pointed behind her, then waved to catch his attention. Daniel followed behind him several feet away, his feet dragging.

Rich's arm rose in response, and he smiled until he caught sight of Ashley sitting next to me. His steps faltered, and his gait slowed, allowing Daniel to catch up to him, and his wide grin fell to one of politeness. He stuck his hands in the front pockets of his jeans. Daniel mirrored the behavior, placing his hands in his pleated trouser pockets. After the hairbrush spirit's return, I was not surprised to see him tagging along.

"Joanie, how are you?" Rich nodded. "Ashley, I didn't realize that you would be here too."

"Is that a problem?" Ashley asked, the barest of edges lacing her tone.

"Not at all, actually," Rich replied. He looked down and dug his foot into the grass in front of him at the side of the path. "I wanted to apologize for my behavior last night."

Ashley's features softened, but she said nothing.

"It was uncalled for," Rich continued, "and I'm sorry. I

shouldn't have accused you of purposely trying to ruin my painting. God, it sounds stupid just saying it, doesn't it?"

Ashley giggled. "Slightly. Or not stupid, but just immature. What are we, in kindergarten?"

"Sometimes it feels like I teach it," Rich chuckled, and Ashley's giggle turned into a genuine laugh.

"I bet. The things I hear about at the junior high. We really are no better, are we? And I'm sorry too. I shouldn't have gotten so offended." She reached out and touched his forearm. Daniel's gaze hardened, but he made no other movement.

"But you had every right to be," Rich said, smiling at where her hand touched him. "Don't apologize for how you feel."

"Thanks," she dropped her hold and pushed a lock of hair behind her ear.

"And the thing is, the painting actually turned out great. If anything, you did me a favor. My mom is going to love it."

She raised an eyebrow. "You're giving it to your mom?"

"Yeah, as a birthday present." He pulled a hand from his pocket and ran it through his hair. Their mirrored behavior made me smile. It was one of those unconscious things people did when around those they liked. "And I'm sorry about dinner. I was a jerk. I deserved to have that food dumped on me."

"But your clothes!"

"Eh, I didn't like that shirt anyway," he answered, waving it off.

Without either of them noticing, I slipped the hairbrush out of my bag. The moment it hit open air, the reconciliation that had been going so well turned sour.

"But if you hadn't talked with your hands," Rich began.

I stopped paying attention to what he was saying to stare

at Daniel. At first he glanced at the brush, but then something else caught his attention. He looked over my shoulder, a forlorn expression falling across his face.

Turning, I saw Rosa, then quickly looked back at Daniel. He looked pained, as if seeing this young woman physically hurt him. But what did this almost-elderly man have to do with a girl in her twenties? I did the math. They would have been almost the same age in the sixties. He had to have known who she was when they were alive, but how?

Rosa wasn't paying any attention to Daniel or me, however. She stared sadly at Ashley, her mouth turned down, bottom lip sticking out slightly. It was as if we didn't even exist. Was she even aware of us? Of me? Or could she only see Ashley? Who was she to her?

Ashley's raised voice drew my attention back to their escalating conversation. She was standing, facing Rich. "I told you, I start to talk with my hands when I'm drinking. What happened to all of this 'I'm sorry' business? Was that an act? I thought you were a nice guy, Rich."

"You're puppets!" I shouted, thrilled with my discovery. Thank you, Nathan!

Both Ashley and Rich stopped arguing and pivoted toward me. Even Daniel refocused his gaze on me, dropping his hand from Rich's shoulder. When had he grabbed on to him? I glanced behind me. Rosa was gone. I wondered if I had scared her.

"What?" Ashley and Rich asked in unison.

"This isn't your fight."

"I don't follow," Rich said.

"You're only fighting and bringing your issues into it because of their issues." I dropped the brush back into my purse and zipped it close.

It was like a switch had flipped.

Rich blinked rapidly and shook his head. "Wow. God, there I go screwing it all up again. I'm sorry, Ashley."

Ashley held the side of her head, rubbing it as if she was trying to massage away a headache. "I'm not much better, I guess." She smiled at him sheepishly. "Apology accepted."

"I don't know what came over me," Rich confessed.

"Same here," Ashley agreed. "It's so weird. I would have sworn just a little bit ago that I was over what happened last night. But all of a sudden, I wasn't."

"I could have said the exact thing."

Ashley turned back to look at me. "Joanie, what were you saying about us being puppets?"

"I can't explain exactly." I sighed, then stood up. "But it has to do with the thing you gave me. You're involved in it too, Rich. And I don't mean to be vague, but so does Daniel."

Rich straightened and jerked his head back as if dodging something in front of his face. "Daniel? Who's Daniel. Wait. You mean my grandfather? Is that why you asked my mom about him the other day?"

"Yes." I pulled my jacket down in the back where it had gotten bunched up from sitting.

"But he's dead."

"I'm well aware. Believe me." I suspected my secret would be revealed as a result of this pairing. I'd soon deal with it when the time came. "Now, come on. Let's head to my car, the both of you. We have to track down some answers."

"Answers?" Rich sounded skeptical. I couldn't fault him for that.

"I'll explain once we get there."

"But where are we going?"

I spun on my heels and walked backward a few steps, responding, "We're going on a road trip."

Rich opened his mouth to say something, but Ashley stopped him before he could get anything out.

I turned around, knowing they'd follow if I acted like I was confident in what I was doing. And I was. Sort of.

"Just trust her." I cast a glance over my shoulder and saw Ashley link her arm around Rich's. "She has yet to steer me wrong."

I appreciated her faith in me. In reality, I wasn't certain where this trip would lead by the time we were done, but I hoped it would help.

CHAPTER 29

As we hopped in the car, Rich and Ashley both taking seats in the back, I found myself grateful for having been woken up early on my day off after all. I couldn't keep taking time away from the bakery, even with Sarah agreeing to go full time. But there was still plenty of time remaining to take this trip today. Thank goodness for school break giving Rich and Ashley the time off too.

For the entire forty-five-minute drive, the two of them talked, having a normal conversation that sounded much like any other couple still getting to know one another. It was cute and full of laughter. I chimed in occasionally, but overall, I was happy to let them have their time, and even happier Daniel hadn't decided to reappear and come along for the ride. He had clearly recognized Rosa. Perhaps he needed the time to process seeing her again. But who was she?

I turned down a familiar dirt road, and Ashley realized where we were heading.

"Why are we going back to the cabin?"

I glanced at her in the rear-view mirror and smiled. She and Rich were holding hands.

"You've been here before?" Rich asked. He craned his neck as he looked out the window at the tall pines. There wasn't much else to see as I slowly drove over the uneven terrain.

"Yeah, on Sunday," Ashley replied. "I received a box from this address in the mail. It might have something to do with my biological dad."

"Is this what Joanie was helping you with?"

Ashley nodded. "She drove me out here."

I pulled up to the cabin. Millie's car was out back, and smoke rose from the chimney.

"Looks like she's home." I would have been disappointed if she wasn't. It was a long drive to turn up empty.

We got out of the car, our doors slamming one after the other in rapid succession. Millie had to have heard us with that much noise. Now I needed to figure out what I would say. She probably wouldn't believe the truth, not that I'd told all of it to Ashley and Rich yet either. I had to come up with something quickly though. It wasn't a long walk to her door, and I was leading the way. Behind me, Rich and Ashley held hands, and still no Daniel. Two things in my favor. Hopefully things would go well here too.

I knocked.

A few moments later, Millie opened the door more than she had the first time. "Joanie, right?" I nodded as she asked, "What are you two doing back here?" before turning her attention to Rich. "I don't know you."

"Name's Rich." He gave her one of his megawatt smiles, instantly putting her at ease. It was his own special superpower.

She nodded. "Pleasure."

"Millie, we had a question for you. What have you been doing with all the stuff you've been clearing out as you go through your house?" I hoped she wouldn't say she tossed it all. That would be as bad as her not having been here when we arrived.

"S'all in the garage out back minus some of the awful furniture. That I trashed. Wasn't good enough to be saved or donated anywhere. Why?"

"Um, I think the box you sent me may have come from my dad, my biological dad." Ashley stepped forward. "I never met him. I don't even know his name." Guess I didn't need to think of something to say after all.

Millie's face softened. "Well, I wish I could give you a name. I didn't grow up knowing my daddy either, and I understand how that can be. Bought the house from a bank, not a person. Haven't found anything with a name on it other than that box I sent you. But let me go grab the key to the shed. Go see if you can find anything in there to help you." She shuffled away, leaving the three of us on the stoop to wait.

"Not the most welcoming person, is she?" Rich mumbled.

Ashley shushed him quietly but smiled behind the finger she had brought to her lips. "Well, we did drop in without warning, and this is more than we got last time."

Millie returned a minute later. She dropped the key into my hand. "Shed's immediately out back. It's practically attached to the house. Gonna move it when I'm sure mud season is finally over. Give the logs a bit more room to breathe in the back corner. They stay too wet with the shed there. Just holler when you're done, and I'll grab the key from you. Good luck."

She closed the door, and we turned on our heels to step down from the stoop and walk around the log cabin. The shed was one of those prefab plastic things meant to look like it had vinyl siding and real windows. One of the bigger ones, we would fit comfortably as we searched. I inserted the key into the padlock holding the two doors together. The lock sprung open, and I slid it out from one of the door latches and let them both swing wide open, keeping the lock and key in the other door so I wouldn't lose it.

Three-quarters of it was full almost to the top. No way were we all going to fit inside the shed. "So I guess I'll hand each of you a box and we can sort out here?"

"We'll probably be able to see better, anyway. Not like those sheds have lights," Ashley replied, her gaze taking in the stacks of boxes, nothing labeled as far I could see.

"What are we looking for anyway?" Rich asked.

"Everything, I guess," Ashley answered. "We don't really know what could help us. Stuff with a name, obviously, but don't dismiss anything without looking through it first."

I was glad I had taken her along and not made the trip on my own. She seemed better equipped to handle this than I was. I never liked going through boxes. It was why I still had two mostly packed boxes in my closet. I didn't want to deal with them. If it weren't for my fear that Mom and Gram would have gone through them if I didn't, there would still be a bunch more hidden away at my house.

We searched for a good two hours, coming up empty. Nothing with a name, and nothing more than what looked like random objects that one would collect throughout a lifetime—random magnets, mismatched coffee mugs, partially burned candles, and more.

I opened the next box, then took out a toy Ferris wheel and a stuffed clown as I tried to see what else was in the box. The next item was a shadow box with a small toy, several ride tickets, and what looked like rings you'd try to get over glass bottles. Lifting the shadow box and putting it aside, I spotted a milk bottle with a logo and the words *Astoria Fair.* I pulled it out and placed it next to me, revealing a refrigerator magnet about the size of my hand. It contained a landscape of the fair, a Ferris wheel to the side that matched the toy I had removed from the box first with *Astoria Fair* in red letters below it.

"Hey, look at this," I called.

Rich and Ashley stopped looking through their respective boxes and came up behind me to look over my shoulder.

"What did you find?" Ashley asked.

"This whole box is nothing but stuff relating to this amusement park. I haven't come across anything else this cohesive, have you?"

I handed Ashley the milk bottle and Rich the magnet.

"Hey, I remember going to this as a kid." Rich studied the magnet. "That Ferris wheel seemed a lot taller when I was little."

"Mom and Dad took me here every summer growing up. Let me see." Ashley held her hand out for the magnet. Rich handed it to her. "Oh, yeah. That Ferris wheel seemed wicked high back then." Ashley handed both things to me.

I placed the milk bottle and magnet back into the box. "What happened to it?"

"Um, I'm sure parts of it are still there, but it closed down years ago. Before you ever got here," Ashley replied.

"We were probably what, fifteen or so?" Rich asked.

Ashley nodded. "Something like that."

I'd only grown up a few hours away and had never heard of this place. It couldn't have been that big of a fair. Then again, several fairs were closer to me growing up.

Ashley tugged at her ponytail. "Do you think it's important, Joanie?"

"To us? Could be. To whoever lived here? Yeah." I showed

them both the shadow box. "You don't make these if it's not. Where could we find out more about it?"

"Like I said, it closed down years ago. It's not like we can go and ask someone working there."

"Astoria isn't too far from here. We could check out their library," Rich suggested. "They should have microfilm of the newspapers from when it was open. No doubt there were articles that talked about it."

Ashley gave Rich a look of approval, a short *huh* escaping her lips as she gazed at him. I was impressed too, but I didn't need to give him the validation like Ashley did.

He shrugged big, his shoulders reaching his ears. "It's nothing. I had to learn this stuff for my job. Have to be able to help students figure out where to research. I teach history. It's not *all* available on the internet. You have to know how to look elsewhere. Books. Interviews. Newspapers."

We stood staring at him, but Ashley had a grin on her face and was making lovey-dovey eyes. Clearly smitten. The tingle in my toes spread to my knees. This was a good sign, one I was thrilled to have after their bad date.

Rich's grin turned sheepish. "Sorry. I get a bit passionate about research."

"Oh, nothing to apologize for. You're really smart, you know." Ashley batted her eyelashes. "I like it."

Rich's megawatt smile reappeared, his face almost glowing from the compliment.

"So, to the library?" I interrupted. "We need to put all of this back before we can leave."

"You can keep that box if you feel it's important to ya," Millie said, making us all jump. I didn't realize she had come out of her house, never mind into the backyard. "Sorry, didn't mean to scare you all. Here, let me help you put some of that away." She reached down and picked up a box near Rich's leg.

"Thank you," Ashley and I said simultaneously for different reasons. I appreciated the extra help in moving all the boxes and was sure Ashley was happy to have something possibly related to her dad even if she didn't understand how yet.

Working together, it took twenty minutes to get everything back into the shed.

After we were done, Millie locked the shed and pocketed the key. She walked us to the front yard and saw us to my car. "Good luck to you," she said as Ashley slid into the back seat next to Rich, her car door still open. "Hope you find the information about your dad that you're looking for."

"Thanks again. It really means so much to me." Ashley buckled in, and Millie shut the car door for her.

I stuck out my hand. "Thanks for everything, Millie. I'm sorry to have shown up unannounced again."

She eyed me, taking my hand. "You're an odd one."

I cocked my head.

"Don't get me wrong, I like ya, but I can't figure you out all the way. Can't quite see how you fit into all this, but somehow you'll make it work. Like ya got your own stuff going on that you're dealing with too. Something"—she zigzagged her hand in front of me starting at my head and going down to my midsection—"extra. Good luck with that."

I didn't quite know how to respond to that. Could she tell that I saw ghosts? "Um, thanks. I'm starting to feel that you have something a bit extra going on too."

"Nailed it. S'why I like my own space away from people. I don't think you're on the same path as me, but they may cross again someday. Merry part, Joanie. Blessed be."

Millie walked away, leaving me standing outside my car looking at her retreating back, staring until she had walked inside her cabin. Gram regularly used similar phrases when saying goodbye to her friends. I could remember it from as far back as my memories went. I wondered if Millie knew Gram or my mom. How big could the witch community in the Fiddlefern Fjord region be?

"Hey, are you ever getting in the car?" Rich called. "The library isn't going to stay open forever. They sometimes take different hours when school isn't in session."

I shook the thoughts from my head and slid into the driver's seat. "Yeah, sorry about that. Ready to go?"

Rich looked more excited than I had ever seen him before. "To the library!"

CHAPTER 30

We passed the ruins of the fair on our half-hour drive to Astoria from Millie's cabin. All three of us silently gazed out the window at the skeletons of rides gone by and an abandoned caretaker's cottage standing outside the gate. It was a shame the town hadn't done anything with the space. The fairgrounds looked like it stretched far back into the woods. It would have made a lovely park.

Astoria's library sat in the center of town. The brick building had white columns out front flanking the large central door, reminding me of Town Hall in Heartwood Hollow.

The three of us walked to the front desk.

"Hello," the librarian there greeted us. An older man, he wore a plaid button-down with a solid sweater vest over it. He spoke softly, but I didn't think it had anything to do with the stereotype of libraries needing to be quiet.

After we all said hello, Ashley and I let Rich take the lead. He looked like he was in his natural habitat. "We're here to do some research on the fair the town used to have. I'm hoping you have some newspapers on microfilm that we might be able to look at."

"Oh, sure, sure. We have the town gazette going back since it was founded. Some of it's even been digitized and made text searchable, but that's mostly all the new editions. We try to do them as they come in now." He lifted a flap on the counter that allowed him to pass through to where we were standing. "We rely on volunteers to help us go backward to get the earlier years. I'm sure you understand."

Rich nodded. "Oh, of course. One of my students is interning at our library at home to help them do the same."

"Oh, good, good. Follow me." He glanced to the woman still working behind the counter. "Gloria, I'm going to get these fine young people set up on the microfilm readers."

"All right, Theo." Gloria looked up at us and smiled politely. "Welcome."

Theo led us through what appeared to be a reading room to an elevator. He pressed the down button, and once the doors opened, we stepped in and waited as Theo inserted a key and pressed a button reading L0. After a second, I felt the expected pull of the elevator beginning its descent. "We don't let patrons use the elevator regularly. It gets stoved up a lot, and one time Audrey got stuck on it for two hours, and good golly, did she put up a fuss after that. So now we use it if we have materials we need to cart, but my back's acting up a bit, so I'm cheating." He chuckled. "There's a staircase on the opposite side of the floor that will bring you back up when you're done."

I didn't know who Audrey was, but I likely would have been fussy if I'd gotten stuck like that. Now I was worried we would be. Those sorts of stories weren't ones I wanted to hear while in an elevator known to break down. When the doors opened several long moments later, a wave of relief hit me. I'd be grateful to take the stairs later.

The room featured a dozen or so empty corrals used for individual study, tables for spreading out materials or working with others, and rows of vertical archival boxes that I assumed housed magazines, documents, or other paper materials. The random things I remembered from the annual tour of the campus museum at college amused me. At the college I graduated from, those types of boxes held thousands of menus from all over the world. They had been fun to peruse for inspiration.

We wound our way through the corrals and several rows of boxes until we reached these three large machines, each at their own tables. They were boxy, with a computer screen above a light box with some sort of magnifying lens attached.

"Here we are," Theo said. "Now do you all know how to work one of these, or do I need to show you how?"

"Show us," Ashley and I said in unison. Rich said nothing. I bet he'd used these plenty of times. He probably could have taught us as easily as Theo could.

Theo set each of us up at a station, then disappeared into an area of filing cabinets. He returned with three tiny boxes. He handed Rich one, and Rich got right to work, pulling out the film and loading it into the machine in front of him. Theo took his time showing Ashley and me what to do before undoing it all and having us try it for ourselves. It took me a few tries to feed the start of the film, but I thought the way it all wound through the machine on spools at such a rapid pace was neat. If only I could read it that quickly. After several minutes and a few successful attempts in a row, Theo deemed Ashley and me worthy to start our research.

"All your films are ten years apart. I figured that would

make it easier for you all to know what to grab next. That will keep you busy for a while, especially when the paper was daily. It's twice a week now. You likely won't need to worry about looking at mid-October through mid-April. The fair operated seasonally, so that should help you some." He ticked his head toward Rich as he looked at Ashley and me. "Ask him if you get stuck on the machines. He knows what he's doing."

With that, Theo shuffled away back toward the elevator.

We scanned microfilm for what felt like forever. This was so not my thing. Ashley's only a bit more so, driven by the hope of finding answers that were hard coming. We got slower and slower as time passed. Rich seemed unfazed by the wealth of information before him.

"Hey, that's my grandfather!" Rich exclaimed after some time.

Both Ashley and I popped our heads up. Was this what we had been looking for, or was it a happy coincidence?

"Really?" Ashley asked.

"Yeah, come look. I mean, he's younger looking than I ever saw him, but it's him." He laughed. "Can't mistake that mustache."

Ashley and I jumped up from our seats, glad for any distraction. I motioned for Ashley to go first.

She bent forward to look at the screen. "That's really neat, Rich. What a find. Do you know who he's with?"

"No idea. Never seen her." The *her* piqued my interest. "Obviously, it's not my grandma. Must have been before they got together." He lifted the side of the box and read off the date. "Nineteen sixty-five. Yeah, that's over a year before they got married."

Ashley stepped away from the machine, allowing me to see. She returned to her station and resumed scanning the films. She still wanted to find information about her dad. I couldn't blame her. I would have wanted to in her situation.

But this photo was everything.

I knew the girl.

Rosa.

CHAPTER 31

I stared at the grainy black-and-white photo. It was Rosa, all right. She was even wearing the same paisley pants I saw her ghost in whenever she appeared. "Rich, would you mind making me a copy of this?"

"Sure, I was going to ask for one for myself. Why do you want a copy?"

"They're only described as two teens in the caption. I want to ask around back home and see if anyone knows her. Are you sure you don't?"

"Positive."

"And you don't know her either, Ashley?"

"Should I?" she asked, already focused on her machine once more.

Rosa had to be the "she" Matthew told me about at dinner. How could she not?

"Ashley, this woman owned the brush."

That caught her attention. She stood and walked back over. "How do you know that?"

It was time to come clean. "I've seen her."

"What, around town? Why didn't you ask for her name? That probably would have saved us a lot of time today."

I shook my head. "Not like that."

Ashley nodded in understanding. Rich looked at me questioningly, an eyebrow raised, his arms crossed in front of him.

I sighed. It was now or never. "I've seen her ghost. She's haunting the brush—trapped is probably more like it."

"Wait, so you're telling me you see ghosts?" Rich tightened his folded arms and lowered his head, studying me.

"Yes."

Ashley nodded emphatically. "After living a week with that hairbrush, I believe it. Rich, that thing moves on its own."

"Thanks, Ashley." I appreciated her support. It wasn't easy to admit, but telling them wasn't as hard as I had expected it to be. "Rich, I see your grandfather too. He follows you. Still has that same mustache as in the picture, but he wears pleated pants and a plaid-ish suit coat."

"You could have seen that in one of the photos at my mom's house."

"True, but that photo I saw was of him and your mom when they were dressed up. He wasn't wearing the outfit he does now."

"Okay, let's say I need a bit more convincing. Who else do you see? Anyone I would know?"

I ran through my mental list of ghosts I'd seen regularly about town. "Well, there's the man who walks his dachshund in a trench coat, fedora, and thick black-rimmed glasses."

Both Ashley's and Rich's mouths dropped open.

"What? Who is he?"

"Arthur Miller. He used to be the football coach at the high school. He died at least ten years ago. That dog a couple years before that. He took her everywhere, even to away games, and couldn't bear to get another dog after she died," Rich explained.

"Huh." Well, now I at least could say hello to him by name. That would surprise him, I bet.

"So," Ashley began, "how do you think these two relate? This girl and Rich's grandfather?"

"Just look at the photo"—I pointed at the two of them smiling wide, his arm around her back. I hadn't been the greatest with history in school, but even I knew that wouldn't have been considered an everyday occurrence back in the sixties—"they're facing the camera, but their eyes are trained on one another. They loved one another."

Both Rich and Ashley leaned in close to the screen, their heads barely touching one another.

I continued, "Daniel recognized the hairbrush that day we ran into each other outside the general store, and today he saw Rosa in the park. You should have seen the longing on his face as he watched her."

"Rosa? I thought you said you didn't know what her name is," Rich said with a trace of skepticism, turning to study me. I was sure he was looking for any reason to doubt what I said I could do. It wasn't easy to accept. It took me long enough to.

"I don't, but I wanted to call her something. It's for the roses on the brush."

"But who is she?" Ashley asked, straightening and pivoting on her heels to face me.

"Beats me, but I think the only way we'll find out is if I can free her from the hairbrush."

"You mean *we*," Ashley corrected, waving her arm between her and me. "I'm in. I still need answers about why this brush was sent to me."

"And I'm in too," Rich said, standing. "If this is related to my grandfather, I owe it to him to help you figure things out."

I gave each of them a genuine smile. It felt good to have them be willing to help after what I'd told them. Perhaps it was a sign I should open up more. Come clean to Sarah for starters. Maybe if I told her about the ghosts, she'd lay off the whole witch thing. I'd have to tell Courtney too.

"Thanks, guys. It's possible your combined energies will be able to help. I don't think I'm enough on my own. I've tried a few times to draw her out alone without luck. You two could be exactly what I need"—I pointed at the picture—"what they need."

In the distance, the elevator beeped. I glanced at the wall where a large clock hung. "That will be Theo coming to get us. I didn't realize how late it had gotten."

Several moments later, he shuffled into view. "Find what you were looking for?"

"I think so," Rich stated. "Could we make two copies of this photograph? Coincidentally, I found a picture of my grandfather at the fair while doing research."

"Huh." Theo whistled. "Guess you were meant to find it. Sure, I can get those copies made. Hang on." He pressed a few buttons on the film reader, and a printer I hadn't realized was nearby flared to life, slowly spitting out two sheets of paper.

I retrieved the pages. The copies of the grainy photo weren't the greatest, but you could still tell who the individuals were. I hoped someone would recognize Rosa when I showed the photo around town as I made deliveries.

"Thank you so much, Theo. You've been a big help," I said once I'd returned to the group.

Theo had already begun to extract the film from my machine, rewinding it onto the spool. "Oh, it's no bother. Now, I don't mean to kick you out, but we're closing soon, so I figured I'd help you get things back in order."

I smiled and thanked him again as he moved to Ashley's machine. Rich, as expected, didn't need help with his.

Films put away and machines off, the four of us made our way back to the elevator. So much for the stairs, but fortunately we made it up in one piece. I paid Gloria for the two copies we made before Theo escorted us to the front door. "Come back if you need anything else."

Rich shook Theo's hand. "You have a good night, Theo. Take care."

Ashley followed suit, then I did the same.

We piled into my car. I started the engine and then pulled away from the curb. We were mostly quiet as I drove the hour home. Both of them nodded off in the back seat with Ashley's head resting on Rich's shoulder. They really were a cute couple.

Back in Heartwood Hollow, I drove to the park and pulled up next to Rich's car.

Rich gently shook Ashley awake. "Come on, we're home."

Ashley sat up straight, wiping the sleep from her eyes.

Rich opened his door. "I can take Ashley home, Joanie."

"Okay, sure. So my place tomorrow? We can order a pizza and try to figure out this whole Rosa thing."

Ashley nodded.

"Sounds good," Rich added. He stepped out of the car and jogged around the back to open Ashley's door for her.

She stepped outside, then opened the front passenger side door. "See you tomorrow," Ashley said as she leaned in to grab the box with the fair memorabilia inside it. "And thanks."

I hoped with the three of us working together, we'd be able to put this mystery to bed once and for all.

CHAPTER 32

Wednesday morning started as normal, meeting my bakers and making my two rounds of deliveries. The one difference today was that I had the photo of Rosa and Daniel with me, hoping that I would run into someone who could tell me Rosa's real name.

I beat Walter and Paul to the Olde Templeton Diner, but they weren't looking to score Wednesday muffins like they were Monday muffins. I chatted with Donna for several minutes over a cup of coffee. She recognized Daniel for having sold her first car to her, but she had no idea who Rosa was. She couldn't even confirm if she had lived in Heartwood Hollow. Donna made it her business to know everyone. Maybe she hadn't been like that when she was younger, but I had to consider the possibility that Rosa wasn't from here. My task would get a lot more difficult if that was the case.

Eventually I had to leave without talking to Walter and Paul, and I walked back into the bakery feeling disheartened, my feet dragging.

"Everything okay, Joanie?" Sam asked as he wiped his

brow with his forearm, a tray full of whoopie pie halves fresh from the oven in front of him.

"Yeah, just trying to figure some things out."

"Anything I can help with?"

"Not unless you can tell me who this girl might be." I pulled the photo from the front pocket of my apron and showed it to him. Lily and Gina, both in the process of frosting cupcakes, put down their piping bags and walked over to glance at the picture. Bryan finished cutting his scones to shape, then did the same. All four shook their heads. I hadn't really expected them to know, considering they were all years younger than I was.

"You should leave the photo out on the counter with a sign that asks if anyone knows her. One of your customers might have an answer for you," Sam suggested.

"That's a great idea, Sam, thanks."

We made quick work of what was left in the kitchen, then stocked the shop's cases. My crew started in on a second round of treats as I waited for Sarah and prepped the shop for opening.

Sam popped his head back in. "I hope you find her."

"Thanks, Sam."

He gave me a quick wave and ducked back into the kitchen.

I removed the photocopy from my apron, then walked behind the counter and grabbed a marker from the drawer beneath the register. The marker squeaked with each large red letter I wrote beneath the square image. *Do you know me?* I tossed the marker back into the drawer and slid the picture underneath a clear protective sheet we had covering the checkout portion of the counter, where I typically displayed business cards for some of the local establishments and my partner businesses. They could live with being partially covered for the day, or however long it took for me to find out Rosa's real identity.

Sarah waltzed in a few minutes later, a smile on her face. "Good morning, Joanie. How was your day off?"

"Busy, and I didn't get anything I had originally planned done." I didn't tell her that my original plans had been to finish the book I was reading and stay under my blanket on the couch all day. I chuckled to myself. Wow, had my day gone off the rails. But it hopefully had brought me one step closer to both figuring out how to free Rosa and bring Rich and Ashley together. Seeing them yesterday, out from under the influence of spirits, had only deepened my resolve to see them happily matched.

"What's this?" Sarah pointed to the photo. "Is someone missing? That's a pretty old photo to use, though, isn't it? Unless it's one of those cold case type things you hear about on TV."

I addressed her questions out of order. "It is an old photo. From nineteen sixty-five. But it's the only one I have. I have no clue who she is, and that's what I'm trying to find out." I tapped on Daniel. "This is Rich's grandfather."

"Why am I not surprised this has something to do with that match of yours?"

"I can't help it. I like to get involved."

Sarah rolled her eyes at my response. "I'll say. And, let me guess, this witchy hairbrush stuff is somehow related to all of this too."

I tightened my lips into a thin line, sucking them in slightly, as I avoided her stare in an attempt to look innocent.

She sighed. "Well, no one can accuse you of not going the extra mile to see things through."

"Tell me about it. I drove all the way to Astoria yesterday with Rich and Ashley to figure things out. We found this picture in an old newspaper while we were at the library there."

"Wow. And I hadn't even meant that literally, but you do that too. If I ever get in trouble, I'm turning to you for help." She ducked into the kitchen to put away her bag.

"So do you know who the girl in the photo is?" I asked when she returned.

She tied a purple apron around her waist. "Can't say I do, sorry."

"It's okay. I didn't expect you to, but I'm hoping someone who walks in does. She could have been their classmate or neighbor or"—I shrugged—"even their grandmother, since we're talking about Rich's grandfather being with her."

"It's a definite possibility. We get everyone through this bakery at one point or another. There's probably not one person in Heartwood Hollow who hasn't stopped by at least once. I'm telling you, it's the magic you bake into your food."

I laughed. "Speaking of food, did you know Donna has to save Monday muffins for Walter and Paul to eat on Tuesdays? They can't go without them."

Sarah threw her head back. "Those two are too cute. I swear, they've been old since I was a little kid. Always together causing trouble."

"Probably been that way for decades."

We had a good chuckle over that as we settled into our morning. The next couple of hours flew by as customers dropped in to pick up their orders or to grab their usual after not having it the day before. Most noticed the photograph I had on the counter, but none could tell me who Rosa was.

After the boxes for the late-morning deliveries had been packaged, I slid the photo out from under the protective cover. I needed to make sure I covered my bases and asked everyone I ran into while on my route.

First up was the yoga studio for cheat day.

I placed the box of five dozen cookies on the side table that waited for me, a few oranges and apples on a bowl to the side.

"Hey, Kimmy, do you happen to know who this is?"

She took the photo from my hands and studied it, bending side to side. "Certainly not the best quality, is it?"

I shook my head and explained where I had gotten it, playing it off as doing a favor for Rich since I saw so many people throughout the day.

"Let me ask the girls as you finish setting up." She took the paper and walked around to the different gaggles of women, some putting on jackets, others taking them off, some waiting for me to get the cookies out of the box before they could descend on the table and revel in cheat day.

A few minutes later, I backed away from the table. Kimmy approached me, announcing "Have at it" to the awaiting ladies As they *oohed* and *aahed* over the spread, she turned to me, a frown across her usually serene face. "No one knows her. Christina thinks she recognizes her as having lived on her street years ago, but she can't be sure since she was a kid at the time."

"Thanks. It was worth a shot. I'm not giving up."

She handed the photo back to me. "You seem really invested in this for it not being anyone related to you."

"I like a good mystery. And they looked so happy, you know? I'd like to find out more for Rich's sake."

"You two aren't—" she waggled two fingers at me, a sly grin having already replaced her frown.

"Goodness, no." I laughed. "He's a friend. Besides, he and Ashley have been hitting it off lately."

"Oh, that's right. But I heard about what happened at paint night."

I brushed it aside, dismissing it with a wave of my hand. "That was just a silly accident with a paint splotch. You know how the town talks. No, things are good between them."

Her grin blossomed into a full smile. "I'm glad. I've always liked Ashley. She comes in occasionally for a class, but she's not a regular. My sister babysat her when she was little."

"Oh, nice." I looked at the clock on the studio wall. "It was nice chatting with you, but I need to get to the inn. Thanks for asking the girls about the photo." She said goodbye, and I scurried out the back door, tossing the cookie box into the recycling bin as I walked down the stairs. I hopped onto my bike and rode off toward the inn.

Libby was waiting for me as I pulled my bike off to the side of the driveway. "Cheat day?"

I nodded. It was her go-to question whenever I was right on time. She preferred I be early whenever possible.

"Come on, I'll help you with the boxes." She bounded down the inn's front steps and met me at my bike. She took the top box from my stack and led the way into the kitchen. I set the box down on the counter next to the awaiting tea trays.

"I threw in a few ginger scones today too," I said as I popped the tape securing the box. "Had to make a batch for Rachael."

"Still suffering from morning sickness, huh?"

"Yeah. Mark says it's really bad. My ginger treats have been the only things she can reliably keep down."

"Poor thing. My sister ended up in the hospital she had it so bad."

If I ever had kids, morning sickness was not something I was looking forward to.

After we arranged all the scones and teacakes, I pulled the photocopy of Daniel and Rosa from my apron. "Can I ask you something?"

"Sure can. What's up?"

I handed her the picture. "Do you know who this is?" I pointed to Rosa, then shifted my finger to Daniel. "This is Rich's grandfather."

"Didn't think I'd need my glasses to take the delivery today." Libby chuckled and held the paper up close to her face, adjusting the distance slightly. "Ah, there. You know? She does look familiar."

"Really?" Hope of a solid lead blossomed in my chest.

"Oh, sure. I never forget a face." Her smile slipped, and hope that had barely taken root inside me wilted. "Names, on the other hand. I don't remember her name, but she lived here in town. Died a while back, I think."

"Thanks, Libby."

She handed the picture back to me. "Sorry I can't be of more help. Are you staying today?"

I shook my head. "Can't. Need to get this photo back to the bakery. I'm hoping someone will see it on the counter and be able to tell me who she is."

"Smart idea. Okay, some other time, then." She pointed at me in a semi-fake scolding manner. "Soon, though."

"I promise. Tell Billy I said hello."

"I will. He liked talking to you the other day."

"Likewise," I replied, stepping backward toward the door. "I'll see you Friday."

When I got back to the bakery, I let Sarah take her lunch since she was going to be running the bakery in the afternoon by herself. It was her week to take the slow shift and close.

We worked in tandem for another two-and-a-half hours when she got back, the first hour after lunch always being a slight uptick before the usual drop off. Needing all the time I could get before Rich and Ashley came over, I'd skipped lunch to leave even earlier than normal.

"Any plans for this afternoon?" Sarah asked as I took off my apron. "Seeing hot doc perhaps?"

"Oh, I doubt it. He's with Ivy keeping her busy since school's out this week."

"Things still going okay between the two of you?"

I shrugged. "I guess so. No real change."

"One of you needs to make a move."

My eyes widened. "Me? Make a move? Oh, no. It's been years. This is new, and I need practice still."

Sarah shook her head at me. "That's the thing about practice. You don't get it if you don't do it."

"I don't want to jump into a relationship. I wouldn't be jumping into a relationship either if I was him. He's got Ivy to think about." Plus, there was the whole ghost-seeing thing on my end, which complicated matters more. But as much as I knew I'd have to tell her eventually, I wasn't ready for that any more than I was a relationship.

I ducked into the kitchen to hang up my apron, then came back out to grab my purse. As I walked back around the counter, I pointed at the picture of Daniel and Rosa under the plastic protector once more.

"Just in case, I'm going to leave this here today. If anyone recognizes her, call me. I'll come back right away."

She nodded. "Sure thing. Have a good afternoon, Joanie. See you in the morning."

CHAPTER 33

I grabbed a late lunch at Leafs and Grounds, my usual sandwich and bag of chips, snagging two marshmallow rice treats in the process. When I saw how busy it was, I regretted not taking the photo with me so I could have asked everyone if they recognized Rosa. I could only hope I had left it at the bakery for a reason. Though if everything went well tonight, I wouldn't need the photo anymore anyway.

After lunch, I hurried to the town library. The librarians here knew me well. I came here weekly to get something new to read.

Emily greeted me with a wide smile. "Need something new already? Oh, wait, yesterday was your day off. Of course you do."

"Usually, you'd be right. But yesterday ended up being so busy, I didn't read at all. Not even a page."

"Happens to the best of us."

I turned away from the desk. As often as I was here, I hadn't explored the whole place. I primarily stuck to the cookbooks and the fiction section. Now, I didn't know where to go.

"Need help finding something?"

Usually I wouldn't mind exploring, but I was on a time crunch. "Reference section?"

Emily pointed me in the right direction, and I'd taken two steps before she stopped me. I pivoted to face her. "Before you leave today, I want to talk to you about a small cake for Pete's birthday next week. He's turning forty."

"Oh sure, sure. We can do that." I waited a beat to see if she'd say anything more, but she waved me off.

"Not now. Later. Go do your thing."

I perused the shelves for a while, not fully sure what I was looking for, but finally found a couple books on Wiccan practices and beliefs and two more on the history of witchcraft. With the town's rumors about me, I felt a little weird grabbing the books off the shelves. If anyone saw me, I'd be adding fuel to the fire.

Then I headed straight to the fantasy shelves and picked up a new release and a book whose cover caught my eye to add to the top of my pile. I hoped I could hide the reference books amongst a couple of my usual reads.

"So, what were you thinking about for this cake?" I asked as I set the books down on the counter for Emily to check out, thinking I could distract her with this conversation from noticing my pile further. She probably wouldn't have said say anything if she did—as one of Ashley's roommates, she may have already known something about what was going on—but I didn't want to risk it.

It seemed to do the trick as Emily chatted away about flavors and potential designs on the cake, only for her to say she trusted my judgment by the time my books were placed into one of the loaner tote bags. "The new release is due back in a week, but you have two weeks on the rest."

"Great, thanks." I slung the bag over my shoulder. "See

you next week when I return these. You can let me know if there are any last-minute changes to the cake then." I already knew I was going to assign this cake to Sam. He was going to enjoy the freedom of making this cake with so few guidelines. I really wanted to see him do well, and I planned to provide him with any opportunity I could for him to do it.

As I reached the house, Saffy's head popped into the window. Even without my car to alert her to my arrival, she somehow always knew when I was home. She pulled the rest of herself onto the windowsill and watched with interest as I came up the walkway. With the wards around the house, I doubted it had anything to do with Rosa inside the brush.

Saffy disappeared as I reached the porch but was there to greet me at the end of the couch once I'd opened the door. I dropped my bags onto the couch, and she dove for them, surprising me by sticking her head into the tote from the library. She grumbled as she wiggled backward out of the bag, then gave me a look full of her usual sass.

"They're books, Saf. What did you think they were?"

She glanced back at the library tote, the image of the three little kittens eating pie at a table while wearing mittens on full display. Now I understood.

"Sorry, I know it looks like it could be from the pet store, but it's not. That's a picture from a nursery rhyme. It's a kids' story. And that's people food. It's not real." As if not wanting to believe me, she tilted her head as she studied the bag. "Besides, see the mittens? You'd never eat like that." She was not the type of cat to wear anything, never mind mittens. It had been hard enough keeping the cone on her when she got fixed after I got her. Now my gram's cat, Sterling, on the other hand . . . it was as if he preferred clothes.

Saffy gave the bag one last look and then scurried into the kitchen. Pointing out the mittens must have done the trick.

Or maybe it was just the mention of food reminding her that she usually got a snack first thing when I got home, if not dinner right away.

"It's not time yet, you silly thing. I'm home early. It's Wednesday." My telling her that was in vain. Those facts didn't matter to her and her perpetually empty belly. I followed Saffy into the kitchen, where she was already sitting by her food bowl. She'd realize it wasn't time soon enough. Saffy continued to stare at me as I made my myself a cup of tea, a chai with a delightful spicy kick.

"Okay . . . you can have your snack now."

As the tea steeped, I got her snack ready, Saffy supervising the whole time. The timing worked out perfectly. My tea was ready by the time she got settled, allowing me to return to the living room. I sat on the couch and pulled the reference books out of the tote bag, spreading them in front of me on the coffee table. I grabbed the first one and perused the index, searching for a keyword that might clue me in to whether this book would have something to free Rosa from the brush. After doing the same with the next four, I came up with a game plan. It was a time-consuming one—I'd have to read them all. I cracked open the first book to start at the introduction and settled in for a different type of reading than I was used to.

Fortunately, the first book wasn't long, a basic primer on the history of witchcraft. I finished it in an hour and a half. The second was much of the same. I hadn't really been expecting to find a real spell book on the library's shelves, but I had been hoping for a bit more help. It was clear after reading the introductions to the other two books that they wouldn't have what I needed either, but I'd still read them to gain more insight into Mom and Gram's beliefs. Gram was right. It was time to at least be open-minded about it all.

CHAPTER 34

A couple hours later, Rich and Ashley arrived. I could hear their laughter as I went to let them in, glad they seemed to be back on track after our adventure yesterday. Maybe that's all they had needed—to be told what was happening. Would Daniel and Rosa back off now? Though as I pulled the door open and stepped back to allow them in, I noticed Daniel standing a few feet away, so I wasn't sure how likely backing off would be.

Stifling giggles, Rich walked in carrying two boxes of pizza and a smaller box. "After yesterday, we thought we owed this to you, so we grabbed it ahead of time."

"That and he's hungry," Ashley added, following him into the house with two bottles of soda.

"You can set those down on the kitchen counter," I said, my eyes still fixed on Daniel. As he stepped onto my porch, an idea struck me. Maybe it was good he had come. Once I knew the others were out of earshot, I invited him in. "You might actually be able to help. But leave Ashley and Rich alone. Don't make me regret this."

That's all it took for him to cross the wards protecting the entryway. Daniel walked into the living room, giving me a polite, grateful smile. He shuffled toward the kitchen, where I could hear the clinking of plates and cups being removed from my cupboard.

"Hope you don't mind we helped ourselves. I told you he was hungry," Ashley said with a laugh as I reached the kitchen. Her eyes sparkled as she glanced at Rich.

He was removing two slices of pepperoni pizza from the top box. "We weren't sure what you liked, so the other is half cheese, half veggie."

"I like *all* pizza. Just no anchovies." I looked back at Ashley. "It's totally fine. If you want something other than soda, I can make tea. There's also milk in the fridge."

As I waited for Ashley to grab her pizza, I prepped Saffy's dinner. She had scampered away when the doorbell rang. Since Ivy's visit, she had been gun-shy about the door, and because she'd been curled up on my legs, she wasn't watching to see who it was from her spot. So she took no chances at a repeat encounter. Having heard me open her canned food from wherever she was, however, it didn't take long for her sprint into the kitchen. Saffy slid across the floor as she rushed toward her bowl, seemingly no longer worried over our guests. Either she recognized their voices from the other day or only cared that neither of the voices belonged to Ivy. Totally focused on her food as I brought it to her dish, she didn't even pay attention to Daniel a few feet away. As soon as the food hit her dish, she shoved her face inside.

"Does she always do that?" Ashley asked.

I chuckled at Saffy who was happily growling at nothing as she chewed, face hovering over her food. "Only if she's really hungry."

"I don't think I've ever heard a cat make that noise." Rich furrowed his brows in concern. "Is she okay?"

"Just extremely satisfied. It's probably more of a purr without the rumbles than anything."

He nodded slowly, likely questioning the normalcy of my cat. Little did he know, I'd been doing the same since first getting her.

I sat down, joining Rich and Ashley at the table. We chatted about nothing in particular and ate our fill of pizza and breadsticks, which had been in the smaller box. They had driven to a small place halfway between town and Snowhaven a half hour away. It wasn't the closest pizza place, we had two in town with another opening soon, but it was so worth it.

The entire time, Daniel leaned against the refrigerator, the closest he could get to Rich without being on top of him. I was thrilled to see my latest matched couple getting along despite Daniel's close proximity. Although he watched with us all with interest, he didn't interfere. Had he finally accepted the two of them together and gotten over whatever hang up he had that was causing Rich to lash out and Ashley to go on the defense?

There was only one way to be sure.

As Rich and Ashley cleaned up after dinner, I brought Rosa's hairbrush out from my bag, then grabbed the supplies I had first used to try to bring her forth at the bakery. At least if things went poorly this time, there would be no industrial mixer to turn on or fan to blow around a tipped bag of flour.

Ashley stilled when I placed the hairbrush at the center of the table. I doubted she'd fully moved past the idea of it haunting her while she had it, but in spite of that, she was here to try to solve the mystery and help Rosa out. That's what mattered.

Rich reached over and squeezed her hand. "It will be okay. It's just a brush. A brush with a ghost attached to it, but a brush nonetheless." He glanced over at me as I consolidated the remaining few slices of pizza into one box. "That's how you'd describe it, right?"

I nodded. "Close enough." I flanked the brush with the two candlesticks and their partially burned candles.

"What are these for, Joanie?" Ashley asked, the hint of fear I expected replaced by curiosity.

I explained as I took out the sage and lit a matchstick, then blew it out to place the smoking end on the dried herb. I walked around the kitchen, explaining how the smoke would cleanse the space of negative energies.

Daniel kept a watchful eye on me as I approached. I wondered if the sage would somehow banish him from the kitchen or force him to flee, but as I drew closer, we both realized that wouldn't be the case. He shrugged as I blew the smoke over his head, smiling slightly. I took his still being here as a positive sign.

Sage burned and room cleansed, I sat back down and held my hands out to my sides. Without any prompting beyond that, Rich and Ashley joined hands with one another, and each took one of mine. Daniel inched closer to the circle toward his grandson, then placed his hands on Rich's shoulders. At that moment Saffy headbutted me, but instead of walking away, she sat by me, tickling my leg with her whiskers. She had to have felt the energy shifting in the room like I could.

I called Rosa forth using the words Gram had told me, the same ones that had sent us on such a catastrophically messy path in the bakery a week ago. Within moments, the brush began to spin, faster and faster. Rosa's form blinked into existence, but like a bad connection with a Wi-Fi signal, her image jumped and stalled, frozen as if paused on screen. I glanced at Rich and Ashley. I wasn't sure if they could see her. Their expressions told me nothing, so I assumed no. Surely, they'd have more of a reaction if suddenly they, too, could see a ghost.

Daniel could see her, though, and understood what was happening. His hands clamped on to Rich's shoulders, and his face scrunched up, his eyes squinting. It was as if he was trying to add his energy to the circle.

But it was working. With Daniel's energy, Rosa's frozen form flared to life, and she moved about on the table, trapped by the circle our arms created. She saw Daniel, and her face lit up with love and delight.

And then horror.

My gaze shot to Daniel. Now he was the one winking out, pouring too much energy into the spell. I feared that if he gave much more, we would lose him. For good. And although that was part of my end goal—for him and Rosa both, if they wanted that—what would happen if it happened now? Would Rosa be free? Would Rich and Ashley be happy? Or would his leaving like this cause a rift between them all that couldn't be closed?

Nothing Gram had told me about had prepared me for this possibility. Daniel was running out of time, and I didn't know what to do.

CHAPTER 35

I fumbled for an idea to save Daniel. There had to be something, but what?

"This is not the way," an unfamiliar voice spoke, but I knew who it was. *Rosa.*

She smiled at me, then turned to Daniel as she lifted the hairbrush, anchoring herself to it once more.

Ashley gasped and pulled her hands away from both Rich and me, breaking the circle.

The brush dropped to the table with a loud thud, sending Saffy running out the door into the living room.

My gaze shot to Daniel, whose form was solidifying now. Withdrawing his hands from his grandson, he backpedaled to lean against the refrigerator once more, then stood there, panting. How close had we come to losing him?

"You saw that, right?" Ashley cried out, tears welling in her eyes.

"That was amazing!" Rich said at the same time, not realizing Ashley's distress.

I thought Ashley was scared, but then she spoke again with excitement in her voice. "Did you see her?"

I nodded. "It actually worked for a minute. She was free."

Rich rubbed at his shoulder. I wasn't surprised given how hard Daniel had been holding on to him. People didn't need to see something to feel it, even if they didn't quite understand it. "What happened? Why didn't it work?"

"I think your grandfather was about to sacrifice himself to save her. She refused to let that happen, so she picked the brush up and reattached herself to it."

"There really is someone in the brush," Ashley said in awe as if truly believing it for the first time. She held her arms out to her sides and shook her hands up and down, waiting for us to grab them again. "We need to save her."

"I don't think that's a good idea."

"Why not?" Rich asked, now doing shoulder circles.

"It takes a while for the energies to level out. And neither Rosa nor Daniel are strong enough for another attempt right now."

"I don't want to put either of them in jeopardy," Ashley said, growing quiet.

Rich nodded. "Can we try again tomorrow?"

"Let's give it another day to be on the safe side. Friday? Unless you two already have plans." I felt bad for suggesting such a popular date night. They looked at one another and smiled. "You do. I'm sure I can get Sarah to cover me on Saturday if you want to—"

"We can shift our night around," Ashley said.

"Friday's fine," Rich agreed.

I smiled at the pair, wondering how this match managed to work itself out despite its supernatural issues. It had not been a normal match since the beginning, but my tingling toes and fluttery stomach told me everything would be fine.

At that moment, the doorbell rang, which was followed by a *thump* as Saffy took off from wherever she had been.

"Friday it is, then," I confirmed as I made my way to the living room, passing Daniel, who was still catching his breath. Giving him a sympathetic smile, I hoped he would be okay.

My focus on Daniel prevented me from seeing that Saffy had not run away when the doorbell rang but instead had run toward the kitchen and had stopped in the doorway. "Saffy!" I yelped as I stumble-stepped over her. She seemed unfazed as she circled around and led me to the door.

I peered through the peephole. Ken.

"Saw him through the window, didn't you?" She looked up at me, front paws shifting, making it look like she was shaking with laughter. "At least you aren't afraid when you see who's coming."

I opened the door. "Hey, how are you." Looked him up and down, I smiled wide at the familiar sight in his hands.

"Hi, Joanie. Sorry to just show up unannounced again. Ivy and I made these today for you to thank you for watching her yesterday morning." He handed me a plate full of brownies.

"Yum! They're even the kind where each of them is its own brownie, edges and all."

Ken shrugged. "I told you Ivy likes to bake. Really, I think she likes to eat what she makes, but I'm all about encouraging her in doing something she enjoys, especially when I can have some too. But these are all yours."

"Well, thank you. Do you want to come in, or do you have to get home to Ivy?"

"She's playing with one of her new friends down the street, so I can come in for a bit." He stepped inside.

"Rich and Ashley are here. They were helping me with something after pizza night. There's some left if you haven't eaten."

"I never turn down pizza. I swear I'm still a grad student. Free food and I'm there." He followed me into the kitchen.

Saffy darted in front of us, no doubt hoping for more food. Wasn't going to happen.

Rich and Ashley looked up as he entered. It seemed like they had been having a good chat for the few minutes while I'd been gone, no ill aftereffects from the attempt to free Rosa. They both smiled at him. He nodded politely.

I set the plate of brownies on the counter. "Looks like we have some dessert." I took the plastic wrap off the plate and picked it back up to offer one to everyone. That's when I noticed Daniel. He was standing ramrod straight, glaring at Ken. It would have been intimidating if he had been alive, but even with Daniel dead, I didn't want to be the subject of that ire.

Then Daniel disappeared. He winked out the same way he had the day Ken met Rich and me outside the general store. Hadn't he been upset then too?

Rich and Ashley each took an offered brownie, but there was no light in either of their eyes. The jovial air had turned tense. I had a sinking feeling about this.

Ken was none the wiser as he busied himself with grabbing a few slices of pizza, one of each kind. But I could tell. Ashley was making a smacking sound with her mouth as she chewed, and Rich was drumming his fingers on the table as he stared at her.

"Do you have to eat like that?" he finally snapped after a few minutes as Ken and I both joined them at the table, me trying to be as normal as possible and Ken chowing down before his plate had even touched the tabletop.

"Well, excuse me," Ashley replied. "This brownie, which is very good by the way, Ken, happens to be rather chewy. It's the way I eat. Deal with it." She ended the *it* with an exaggerated *t* sound.

That got Ken's attention. His gaze darted between the two.

"Not a fan of loud chewing, are ya, Rich?" He smacked his lips in an attempt to be funny.

"Ugh. Not you too." Rich looked up at the ceiling and shook his head.

"Oh, come on. He's just fooling around. Quit being so uptight," Ashley chided. "You don't have to be so proper all the time. No one's watching."

I sank my teeth into the brownie. "Oh, this is good," I said loudly, hoping to draw attention to myself. "Just the right amount of chew. Do thank Ivy for me."

"I will." Ken gave me a tight smile, clearly sensing the brewing foul mood in the room. He finished the last bite of his pizza. Quietly. "I think I should head out. I told Ivy's friend's parents that I'd only be gone for a few minutes. Thank you for the pizza."

"Oh, sure, and thank *you* for the brownies. I'll see you out."

We walked to the door, and as I opened it, he asked, "Are you going to be okay?"

I nodded. "With them? Yes. It's been a long day, and they're disappointed that something didn't work out the way they had hoped. They're having a hard time with it."

He glanced back toward the kitchen. "Okay . . . well, call me if things continue to go south, and don't be afraid to kick them out. They're grown individuals, and they can handle their own problems."

"I will," I told him, knowing that what was happening right now wasn't really their problem at all.

He gave me a quick kiss on the cheek before bounding down the steps and getting in his car.

Rich and Ashley were still making jabs at one another when I stormed into the kitchen.

I slammed my hands on the table. "Stop being puppets!"

That seemed to snap both of them out of a trance. "What?" Ashley rubbed her temple.

"It happened again, didn't it?" Rich asked.

I nodded. "Yeah, in front of Ken this time. I think he was getting worried for me."

"Aww, that's sweet," Ashley started. She paused and glanced up at Rich. "I'm sorry. I didn't even feel like myself when it was happening."

"Same," Rich grew quiet. "You don't actually eat like that, though, do you?"

Ashley threw her head back and barked out a laugh. "No, not at all. I have no idea what possessed me to be so annoying." Her eyes grew wide, and her mouth dropped open. "That's what you mean, isn't it, Joanie? About being puppets?"

"Yes," I answered before pausing to think. "Although you aren't actually being possessed. Think of it as being heavily influenced by them instead."

She nodded slowly and bit her bottom lip. "I see." She wouldn't meet my gaze. The thought of possession had to be making her nervous.

Rich smiled to ease her fear and reached across the table to place his hand on hers. "I say we call it a night." He stood. "All of these activities have me feeling a bit worn out." He glanced to Ashley, then swooped his hand in front of him and bowed. "Can I walk you home?"

"You sure?" I didn't quite understand the mood swing that immediately followed his disappearance, but Daniel was still somehow involved. "Things might go haywire again if your grandfather follows you as you walk together."

Rich nodded with fast deliberate bobs. He seemed confident. "I could feel it happening this time. And now that you've pointed it out again, I'll be better prepared if my mood shifts."

"Same." Ashley stood and walked around the table to Rich. "I trust him. It will be okay. I know it." She placed a hand on his back between his shoulders. He melted into her touch, a lazy smile crossing his face.

I still wasn't sure, but my matchmaker's tingle told me I had to give them the chance. "Well, I'm not going to stop you. You two have a good night. I'll see you on Friday."

They saw themselves out. By the time they had made it to my front door, they were laughing again. All was well.

Rich had been right about one thing, though. These last two days had been exhausting. I was beat, but there was still so much to do I couldn't go to bed now.

CHAPTER 36

My feet dragged all Thursday morning, from the early baking to the deliveries to opening the shop. I had stayed up late into the night—for me, anyway—reading and trying to draw Rosa from the brush on my own. What had she meant by "this is not the way"? Was it only about Daniel's help, or were we going about it the wrong way entirely? Those questions plagued me even once I lay down to sleep, joining Saffy who had given up on me hours before.

I was so tired I almost used my car to make my morning deliveries, but I'd stand no chance of waking up if I did that. I did, however, go and get a cup of coffee to help jumpstart myself. Donna poured me a second cup when I got to her diner. I didn't believe—not fully—but perhaps I needed to start keeping a supply of Monday muffins in the kitchen for times like this. If Walter and Paul claimed it worked for them, maybe there was some truth to it. I shook the thought away but made a note to myself to experiment with coffee-flavored muffins. I'd have to talk to Gary to see if we could strike up a deal.

Thank goodness Sarah had some pep in her step and was

doing all she could to keep my mind focused and alert through conversation as I busied myself with cleaning whenever we didn't have customers in the shop, despite the cleaning crew I'd hired having done a deep clean on Tuesday like they always do. If I stopped or even slowed down, I feared I would fall asleep where I stood.

A hazelnut mocha at lunch seemed to do the trick. I felt much more like myself by the time the afternoon rolled around.

Shortly after lunch, I was wiping down the countertop when the door opened and an older woman stepped into the shop. She was bundled in a few sweaters, and she had wrapped a scarf over her head. A knee-length skirt, stockings, and loafers that were well broken in completed her outfit.

"Hello," Sarah and I greeted simultaneously.

The woman smiled, wrinkles deepening at the corners of her eyes. I didn't recognize her, but I liked her immediately. "Hello, dears. I hear you have a picture in here of a young girl from long ago."

I was instantly on alert by her question. No one had come in to only see the photo. Who was this woman? Was word spreading about Rosa?

"We do indeed. It's right over here on the counter." I placed my hand just below the picture.

She approached slowly, likely unable to go very fast. The door to the shop opened once more, and Sam bounded inside. "Sorry. I had to park all the way down the street. The yoga studio must be running one of their more popular classes right now or something. The back lot is full."

I opened my mouth to answer him, but the woman spoke instead. "That's all right, Sammy. I made it in just fine."

Sam walked up to her and wrapped one of his arms around hers. She shifted her weight to lean on him. "Joanie,

Sarah, this is my grandmother, Gertrude. Nana, this is my boss, Joanie, and Sarah works in the shop."

I could feel my smile all the way to my ears. I knew I liked her. Sam's relation to her cemented that fact. "It is so nice to meet you, Gertrude."

"Please, call me Trudy. Sammy told me all about your mystery woman. I haven't lived in the town proper in some time. I'm over at the nursing home now, but he said I should take a look just in case."

I stepped aside, giving her full access to the photo. Sarah slid it out from under the protective covering and handed it to Sam's awaiting hand to hold for his grandma.

She adjusted the distance of the paper and let out a sigh. "Oh yes, yes. Poor girl. I do remember her." I could have done a dance I was so happy to hear Trudy knew Rosa. But Trudy wasn't smiling. "Her story was just so sad. She lost her first husband shortly after having their son, Nicky, if I remember correctly."

Trudy shook her head slowly, sighing. "She eventually remarried. He was a good man, a soldier who did make it home. They'd known each other before, from school, I think, and he treated that boy like his own."

I leaned against the counter, listening, joining Sarah who was already rapt in the tale. As much as she eschewed Gary's advances, she was such a romantic at heart.

"It took a few years," Trudy continued, "but they finally had a son too. Danny, his name was."

My heart dropped into my stomach learning that Rosa had named her second child after Daniel. Had he helped fill the void left by her first love? Given what I knew, it would have been a big hole.

The question begged to be asked. "What was her name? Do you remember?"

She shook her head. "I can't say I do. I remember the boys because they were kids, and I used to see them around town a lot. My candy shop was a popular stop whenever any of the kids in town had a spare nickel or more." She pointed diagonally across the street and waved her hand a bit. "Store was just over that way."

I smiled sadly, feeling slightly defeated. But I hadn't lost all hope yet. "Do you know where I can find Nicky or Danny?"

She thought a moment before saying, "Nicky was a strange boy. Moved out the first chance he could, and I don't think I saw him again until years later, but only the one time. Danny moved out of town when he started his own family. His wife was such a nice girl. If I remember correctly, he died about five years back. It was in the paper. But I think his son lives here. Saw him at one of the home's group outings. Spitting image of his father. I don't know his name, though. Sorry."

"You have nothing to apologize for. This is more information than I ever expected to have. Thank you so much." I swept my arm down in front of me toward the cases in a displaying motion. "Can I get you anything? On the house for your help and because you're Sam's grandmother. Sam made the cookies today."

"Well, I have to watch my sugar. The perils of making candy for decades, but let's try one of Sammy's new creations."

Sam beamed. He'd brought one of his own recipes in today to try. A lemon shortbread with candied lemon and lavender mixed in. I hadn't done much with florals. They weren't big sellers—too many people feared them tasting like soap—but after today, I'd have to experiment. I could see Libby wanting some for teatime.

"You actually provided me with the inspiration for it, Nana," Sam said. "I remember you candying flower petals when I was a kid. Figured I'd candy some that you'd usually see put into a cookie dry."

I placed two cookies into a white wax paper bag and handed it to Sam. "There's one in there for you too. I know you tried them when they first came out of the oven, but there's something special about getting one from the case."

"Thanks." He looked at his grandmother, adoration in his eyes. "Will you be okay here while I get the car?"

She patted his hand. "Of course, of course."

He dashed off with a quick wave and a "Be right back."

Trudy looked at me. "Sammy's such a good boy. He talks a lot about you when he visits. You've been good for him."

"Sam's one of my favorites, but shh"—I put my finger up to my lips—"don't tell anyone else."

Sarah fake scoffed but quickly agreed. "He's a good kid."

"I'm glad you said that, Sarah, since I'm hoping he'll take a shop shift when the summer starts." I turned back to Trudy. "But don't tell him that. I want to surprise him."

Trudy made a motion of zipping her lips as Sam bounded back in. "Found a spot right at the corner." He wrapped his arm around one of his grandmother's, and he guided her away from the counter and toward the door. "Bye, thanks for the cookies!"

"Bye," Sarah and I said in unison.

"Have a great rest of your day, and thanks again," I added.

I slumped back against the rear counter as the door clicked shut.

"Oh, you were so close," Sarah lamented.

I opened my mouth to answer, but a woman with her young daughter came in, effectively ending our conversation. The afternoon stayed busy as people already in the weekend mood came in looking for treats. It happened every Thursday. People were such creatures of habit, especially in this town.

Throughout the hubbub of the rest of the day, my mind kept circling back to one thought. I had been given just enough information to know where to look next for some answers.

Ken walked in shortly before closing. Sarah was back in the kitchen straightening up and prepping what she could for the morning, laying out bowls, restocking dry goods, making sure all the pans were on the drying rack.

He gave me a soft, unsure smile as I greeted him. "Everything go okay after I left last night?"

I nodded. "Oh sure. I told them to stop acting like children, and they snapped out of it. Things were good by the time they left, laughing hand in hand."

His eyes brightened, and his smile grew. The shop seemed to get sunnier as a result, but the actual sun had nothing to do with it. The day had been mostly overcast. Once again the bakery seemed to respond to someone's mood.

"Oh, good. I'm glad to hear it. I was worried," he confessed.

The man's concern was enough to make me go doughy inside. "Is that all that brings you here?"

"Well, I promised Ivy I'd get her something since she didn't eat all the brownies yesterday. She tried one to see how they turned out. She was thrilled you liked them, by the way."

I chided myself for not thinking to grab one this morning for breakfast. It would have helped with a quick surge of energy. "Sure thing. I *think* I have something she'd like." Giving him a cheesy grin, I ducked down to reach into the case, then pulled out a black and white cookie.

I popped back up from the case, ready to put the cookie in a paper bag for him to take home, but froze when I saw how round Ken's eyes had gone as he stared at the photo under the protective covering. I hadn't even realized Ken had come up to the counter.

"Why do you have a picture of my grandmother?"

My mouth dropped open. "Your grandmother? You're Danny's son? You mean you're from here?"

"The next town over. I thought I had mentioned it. But how do you know my dad? And how do you know my grand-mother?" He cocked his head and studied me, tension rising as his shoulders stiffened. "You've only lived here for four years, right? They've both been dead longer than that. Where did you get this picture?"

"Thereabouts," I started, then explained the situation as best as I could, all the way to Gertrude's visit to the shop earlier. Of course, it wasn't the total explanation. I'd left out anything referring to ghosts or the hairbrush being haunted.

"So is that why you had Rich and Ashley over last night?"

"Yeah, it was a decompression session after a long day of research on Tuesday."

The tension eased out of his shoulders, his posture loos-ening as he shifted his weight to one foot. The smile was back on his face. A single dimple had formed on one cheek.

Finally I'd have the answer I now needed to know for myself as much as Ashley or Rich. Having seen her, talked to her, witnessed what she did to save Daniel, I was invested. "So what's her name?"

"Mary Catherine Dawson—Grandma Kate to me."

Why hadn't I thought of guessing classic names when she had come to me in my room that night? "What about her maiden name?"

"Um. I can't recall. Her name was Coogan before she married my granddad. But that was her first husband's name. She didn't really talk much about . . . before."

"Thanks, that's really helpful. I can't wait to tell Rich we discovered the mystery woman with his grandfather."

He continued to look at the photocopy of the photo. "I have other pictures if you want to see them, if you think he'd be interested in them. They're still packed up, but it would give me a reason to go through what's in that box. It's all stuff from my dad. You could come over tonight, and we could get Chinese. I haven't tried the place in town. Ivy's not a fan, so it would be a while before I'd be able to get it on my own." He smiled and batted his eyelashes, leaning over the counter toward me. "You'd be doing me a favor if nothing else. I haven't had Chinese in so long."

"Well, when you put it that way." I laughed before growing more serious. "That would be great. I'd love to stop by and see them. I feel like I have a personal stake in this now that I've been helping them with it for the last week."

"A good mystery really takes you over, doesn't it?"

I nodded.

At that moment, Sarah came back through the kitchen door, apron off, sweater on, and bag slung over her shoulder. "Hi, Ken, good to see you. Joanie, it's after closing. Everything's all set in the kitchen. See you tomorrow."

"Sure thing. Ken was just telling me about his Grandma Kate," I said, tapping on the photo.

Her eyes grew wide. "Really? What a small world! I'm glad that mystery's solved."

If she only knew.

"Have a good one, you two." She pulled open the shop door and stepped outside, leaving Ken and me alone in the shop.

"I'll let you finish up what you need to do here. Head over to my house when you're able. I'll find the box, and we'll order when you get there." He motioned for a pen. I reached behind me and grabbed our order pad. I handed it to him, then pulled a pen from the jar next to the register and gave it to him. He jotted down his address before sliding the pad back across the counter to me. "Here. See you later." He leaned over the counter and kissed me quickly on the cheek, then left the shop.

<h1 style="text-align:center">CHAPTER 38</h1>

I knocked on the door of Ken's house, a cute Cape Cod style with a central chimney. Rapid footfalls approached from inside, and I was not at all surprised when Ivy opened the door for me. She had likely run from wherever she'd been like she had done the other day at my house.

"Hi, Joanie! Come on in. Daddy's making me dinner since I don't like Chinese food." She stuck out her tongue as she scrunched up her face. She reached her hand out for me, and I took it.

"What are you having?" I asked as she pulled me inside into the living room.

"Mac and cheese! I love mac and cheese. Daddy puts hot dogs in it." She hopped her way into the kitchen, still leading me by the hand.

Ken was standing over the stove, stirring a pot of water with macaroni in it. "Hey. Just give me a minute as I strain these and get Ivy situated." He turned off the burner and carried the pot to the awaiting colander in the sink. Steam rose as he poured the macaroni before clanking the colander twice to shake off the excess water and pouring the pasta back into the pot. He'd already cut up hotdogs, which were on another burner with a lid on them. After stirring the cheese packet and a drop of milk into the macaroni, he threw in the hot dog coins. It was a meal I'd had many times during my childhood, and I almost found myself asking if I could have some for nostalgia's sake.

"Grab the bowl, Ivy, and I'll scoop some in for you."

She dropped my hand and did as asked.

"More," she said, and Ken added one more spoonful to her dish before she sat down at the table.

Ken washed his hands. "There. Will you be all set in here?"

Ivy grumbled a reply through a full mouth. I assumed she'd said yes as Ken placed his hand at the small of my back and guided me into the living room through the open doorway.

"I have two boxes from my dad that look promising. Both contain a few photo albums, but I have no idea what's in any of them." He pointed to the boxes in front of the plain gray couch. "Sorry there's not a lot in here. We ordered a real coffee table and a loveseat now that we have a space that can fit them, but they won't be here until next week."

"Don't even worry about it," I said as I sat down behind the first box.

"I have the menu to the Chinese food place right next to you."

"Already know what I want." I passed it over to him.

"Creature of habit?" He raised an eyebrow.

As I removed the first album from the box, I gave him what I hoped was a flirtatious smile. "I know what I like." I would have sworn he blushed a bit, so it seemed to have been successful. Once he figured out what he wanted, he called in the order. While we waited, I dove into the albums, eager to learn more about Mary Catherine—Kate—and hoping I'd learn her maiden name in the process.

"Tell me about your grandmother," I said after finishing the first album. The pictures were much too new to be of help, but I wasn't going to pass up a chance to look at photos from Ken's childhood.

"Wow, where do I even begin?" He rubbed the back of his head. "She was a funny woman, always smiling when I was a kid. She told lots of jokes. It played off my grandfather's seriousness. It's not that he never laughed—sometimes he did at my grandmother's antics—but he was quiet where she was loud, stern where she wasn't, and reserved in dress where she was bright with color and pattern."

I flipped through the pages of the second album. Photos of Danny in high school, his graduation. Kate was wearing a bright-red outfit that matched the school's colors, a large flower in her hair. Her husband had a muted suit with a black tie.

"They worked well together, my grandparents. Dad said they were a team. My granddad was an insurance adjuster. He'd go out after accidents to take photos of the scene or of damage done to houses because of storms. He was handy around the house. Fixed anything that broke. Taught my dad how to throw a football."

He sounded like a good man. I continued flipping through the album as Ken talked.

"Grandma Kate was a quintessential housewife. She baked cookies, or whatever else, so my dad and his friends would have something to snack on when school was over. She made dinner each night. But there was this other side of her. She read all the time. She followed the news and wrote letters to politicians."

This was the Kate I had expected after meeting her in her hippy outfit the night she came to me.

"I think she would have gone out and been civically engaged—protested things that others protested—had my grandfather let her. He didn't see it as a woman's place, if you know what I mean."

With an *mm-hmm*, I handed him the second album before reaching for the third. This one was older.

Ken paged through the album, smiling at the photos of his dad. "They loved my dad, no doubt, but I don't know if they really loved each other. They slept in separate twin beds in the same room like you see on TV shows from that time. Did it when I was a kid too, and by then, that wasn't the norm anymore."

The doorbell rang, and Ivy came running out of the kitchen, a fork still in hand. "Ivy! No running with your hands full!" Ken half shouted at her. She skidded to a walk and opened the door to the delivery driver.

"Daddy, it's for you," Ivy said before spinning on her heels and skipping back into the kitchen. She had found her loophole, and Ken knew it. He rolled his eyes as he stood up, shaking his head slightly. She had bested him.

He met the delivery guy, Larry, at the door. He didn't talk much, though I always tried to be conversational when he brought me my food. Ken removed his wallet from his back pocket and grabbed a five out of it. He swapped the five-dollar-bill for the receipt and a pen, then signed the receipt and handed it back to Larry, taking the brown paper bag from him.

Ken closed the door. "If you don't mind, can we eat this in the kitchen?"

"Absolutely. I wouldn't want to spill anything on the

photographs, anyway." I got up and followed him into the other room, where Ivy was finishing up her dinner.

Her nose wrinkled as she saw the Chinese food bag. "Can I go play outside?"

"Sure thing, kiddo."

Ivy slid off her seat and then put her dish in the sink. She jumped up and grabbed a pink jacket off the hook next to their back door and slipped it on as she pulled the door open. The door shut with a bang.

"It's off-balance. Shuts on its own," Ken explained as I glanced at the closed door. "I have to fix it one of these days. When it warms up a little more. Then I can have the door wide open for as long as I need to work on it."

I nodded in understanding, my mouth already full of a cheese wanton that I'd popped into my mouth as soon as I'd grabbed the container of them from the bag. As we settled into dinner, we drifted into conversation about various subjects, the photos semi-forgotten as we got to know one another better. But as soon as we'd finished cleaning up after eating, we returned to the photographs.

In the fourth album, the first from the second box, I pointed to a photo of Kate with a young boy. "Is this your dad?"

Ken leaned over to have a look, and my body went on high alert as he drew near. He smelled of bar soap and some sort of aftershave. I couldn't quite put my finger on what it was exactly. I hadn't been within this close of smelling distance with a guy in years outside of Ken's friendly good-byes recently. But those were quick. This was longer, giving the smell plenty of time to invade my senses.

"No. It must be my uncle. He was several years older than my dad, and he didn't live in town by the time I came along. They didn't talk, he and my dad. Nor really he and Grandma

Kate. I guess he visited once when I was two, not that I remember it at all, but I guess he got into some big bar fight and was thrown out by my granddad after that. He left, and they never talked about him." He shrugged. "I only know he exists because my dad slipped and mentioned it one day. I was a teenager at the time."

"I have family members out there I don't know much about either. My dad, for one." It was something I didn't like to admit, but it was easy to tell Ken. It had been comfortable talking to him from the start, something I'd achieved with only a few people as quickly in my four years here. Though they still didn't know everything about me. Ken though? If we did get into a relationship, I'd have to tell him. It wouldn't be right to keep that from him. Was I already contemplating telling him everything? Was I ready for that?

The back door opened and banged shut, and then Ivy trampled into the living room. She hopped onto the couch next to Ken and grabbed one of the photo albums. As she flipped through the pages, she wanted to know who this person was, and that person too, but she was soon rubbing her eyes.

That was my cue to leave. It was already dark. I helped Ken put away the albums, packing them back into a single box this time to keep them all together.

"Night, Joanie," Ivy said sleepily as her father led me to the door, his hand at the small of my back. She had pulled her feet up onto the couch and way lying against the armrest.

"Night, Ivy. It was fun to see you tonight."

"Why don't you go get ready for bed, kiddo. I'll be right up."

"Okay, Daddy." Ivy slowly slid off the couch and walked toward the stairs, passing us as she turned to climb up the staircase set into an alcove in the center of the house, sandwiched between an open doorway leading to the dining room and a closet. It was the slowest I'd ever seen her move, though it was probably a normal pace for others.

"Thanks for letting me come over tonight to look at photos," I said, turning around to face him after stepping outside. "It was nice getting to learn a bit more about you."

"It was fun. And thanks for being so agreeable to getting Chinese. Can we do it again sometime?" He ran his hand through his hair. "Maybe you have some photo albums you need to go through?"

I laughed but then realized it *was* time to invite him into my world a little. Best to show him what he was getting into now before either one of us got too invested. But there was another reason too. "You know? Why don't you come over tomorrow? Ashley and Rich are stopping by to wrap up what we were working on the other night, and since you are connected to it now, you might be able to help. In fact, you might be exactly what we need."

His smile fell slightly, but he recovered. "I'll admit it's not quite what I had in mind, but I'm intrigued."

"Great. I'll call you when I get home from the bakery."

He leaned down and kissed my cheek. "I'm looking forward to it."

As I walked home, the little boy in the photo with Kate was still in the back of my mind. If Ken was twenty-seven, his uncle would have last visited about twenty-five years ago. Ashley was twenty-four. The timing was right. Was Ken's estranged uncle, Nick, her biological father?

CHAPTER 39

I had one delivery to make to the inn before I could go to lunch and get the last answer I needed to hopefully set Rosa—no, Kate—free. Fortunately, Billy met me in their kitchen, which meant little conversation for me. Talking with Libby was great on most days, but today I needed all the time I could get.

At Town Hall, I knocked on Courtney's window, holding up a bag of goodies for her and Jill. I didn't need help with the massive doors today and could have walked in on my own, but I liked seeing if I could make her jump. Today it worked, and as she settled back down, I strolled into the office to her shaking her head at me. Jill sat laughing at her desk, which was kitty-corner to Courtney's across the room.

"One of these days, I'll figure out a way to surprise you."

I laughed. "Not going to happen." She had this energy about her that I swore I could feel as she approached. Even with my back turned, I could always tell when she entered the bakery.

"So what brings you in today? You want to head to lunch?" She looked hopeful.

"Sure, in a few, but I have a work favor to ask first."

She raised an eyebrow. "What could you need from me here?"

"Could you look up a record for me on a Mary Catherine Dawson? Her first married name was Coogan, married to a Nick Coogan, but I need to find out what her maiden name was."

"Who is that?" She folded her hands on the desk in front of her.

"Ken's grandmother."

"He's from here?" Her mouth dropped open. "How come I don't recognize him?"

"He lived the next town over, but his dad and grandma were from here."

"Oh, that would explain it." She looked at me straight-faced. "You know I can't give that sort of information to you, though. The records I have can only be requested by family members or a representative like a lawyer, social worker, etcetera."

I sighed. "I figured as much, but I had to try."

"Why don't you try one of those genealogy websites?" Jill asked from her desk, typing away on her keyboard.

"You think they'd have that?"

She shrugged. "Worth a shot. They have census images and vital records. Some even have high school yearbooks if someone had uploaded those." She motioned me over.

Her screen already displayed one of the websites she'd mentioned. "Okay, what do I need to do?"

"Type in what you already know. I recommend going with her first married name to hopefully pull up that marriage record."

I leaned around her to type in the information. "I don't

know when it was, just a guess of the mid-to-late nineteen-sixties."

"You can give a range. It's going to pull up any close matches anyway, even without it."

I added a five-year span to the boxes asking for a date, then clicked enter.

There were several results. I had no idea how common of a name Coogan was, and Mary and Nick weren't uncommon names either. Two of the top ten results were from the state capital. I'd fall back to those if needed, but two looked more promising as they were from this county.

The first wasn't what I needed. Turned out Mary was that woman's middle name. I clicked on the second and crossed my fingers as the page loaded. Nicholas J. Coogan married to Mary C. Turner, June 25, 1966. "This has to be her." I tapped on the screen.

Jill clicked on the name to see if we could find more information on her. It brought up another marriage certificate for a few years later as well as her social security death record. The marriage certificate loaded on to a man named Edward Dawson.

I jumped up and down. "It's her, all right. That's Ken's last name." I clapped Jill on the shoulder. "Thank you so much for your help. I owe you a pastry or something the next time you stop in to see Sarah. Beyond the one I brought you." I'd forgotten I was still holding the bag of treats so handed it to her now.

She peeked inside. "Oh, yum, thanks. I'll have it with my lunch. Do you need this printed out?"

"Nope, only needed the name."

Courtney walked toward me, her purse already slung over her shoulder. "Speaking of lunch, now that you have your information—and faster than I would have been able to get it to you even if I could have—you want to go grab something to eat?"

"Sure." I hiked my bag back up and straightened my jacket. "Thanks again, Jill."

"Don't mention it," she said, smiling. "Tell Sarah I'll be in later. I can grab a ride back to the apartment with her."

I nodded before ducking out of the office, following Courtney's footsteps.

Since we had the time and the day was nice for this time of year, we walked to lunch. I spent the whole time filling her in on what had been happening with Rich and Ashley and the latest discovery of Ken being involved.

"Sounds like you are solving family mysteries left and right."

I had to agree. What seemed like one mystery originally had quickly spread off into finding out who Ashley's dad was, learning Rosa's real name—there I was calling her Rosa again —and solving how she and Daniel were connected. I looked forward to seeing how everything would come together. With any luck, tonight would lead us all to some answers.

CHAPTER 40

After lunch and a busy afternoon at the shop, thanks to everyone buying treats for the weekend, I sped through the closing tasks and hightailed it back home. As soon as I walked into the house, I called Ashley, Rich, and Ken. Then I set up the kitchen table in what was becoming a familiar setup with the brush at the center flanked by black and white candles. Saffy inspected my setup, I assume deciding it adequate since she jumped from the table and down to her early dinner.

Ashley and Rich arrived first, quietly settling into their seats at the table as I smudged the room, still using dried sage leaf from a spice jar. Based on Gram's suggestion, I'd put in an order for a real smudge stick, one that had several kinds of plants, but it hadn't come in yet. The spice jar had worked well enough so far, so I wasn't too worried.

Daniel, who'd been able to follow Rich inside without needing an invitation. stood behind his grandson.

"I invited Ken to come," I told them all. Daniel rolled his eyes. "I understand your feelings toward him now, Daniel"— Rich whipped around to see the empty space I was talking to

—"but you need to be on your best behavior. What happened is not his fault any more than it is Ashley's."

Ashley cocked her head to the side as she heard her name, and Daniel nodded and looked to the ground, properly chastised for his prior behavior.

"But you and Mary Catherine"—ha! I'd said it correctly—"or Kate, as you probably called her, will be together soon enough." Daniel looked back up at me, a smile on his face.

"I guess you've been busy sorting things out, Joanie," Ashley said.

"It's been an enlightening last couple of days, you could say."

"So how do I fit into all of this?" Ashley pointed to herself. "What's not my fault?"

"All will be revealed shortly, I promise. Let's wait for Ken to get here."

At that moment, the front door opened and closed, then footsteps approached the kitchen. Ken popped his head through the doorway, a big smile on his face until it was quickly replaced by a quizzical expression as I blew smoke into the corner of the room.

"Um, Joanie?"

I glanced at him, smirking. "Welcome to my world, Ken. Take a seat."

He hesitated slightly as he sat in the open chair closest to him.

I placed the remains of the smoldering sage on the table next to the white candle, then sat down in the chair next to Ken. "I thought it fair for you to find out early on." Saffy nudged my leg, prompting me to take a deep breath. "Sometimes, weird things happen when I'm around."

"And this is one of them? Joanie, it looks like you're

having a séance. Is that what you're doing? Don't you need a Ouija board for that?"

I shook my head. "Don't need one, but that's because I see ghosts. And right now, one needs our help. And she's your grandmother."

"You're kidding me, right? This is just some elaborate setup to test me or something, isn't it?" His gaze bounced between Rich and Ashley. "And you two, for some reason, agreed to help her." He stood back up, and my heart sank.

"She's telling you the truth," Ashley said, a hint of attitude behind her words. I didn't think she appreciated being accused of being a part of some ruse. "She's been helping me and Rich, and what she says is true. So stay and help or you can leave, but you'd be missing out on a great person if you did that."

Ken seemed somewhat scolded as he settled back into the chair.

"A lot of this is all new to me." I waved my hands in front of the table. "This whole setup, anyway. Usually I can see ghosts without a problem. Have been able to for years."

"And I'm just supposed to accept that?"

"No, you don't have to, which is why I wanted you to know now. You have Ivy to consider, and I get that. But I like you, and I hope you stick around. Perhaps once you see it, you won't be afraid."

"I'm not afraid," Ken quickly retorted.

"Certainly looks like you are," Rich stated, an eyebrow raised in challenge.

"Well, do what you are going to do. Let's see it." His tone wasn't angry. If anything, he was resigned.

I lit the candles and instructed everyone to join hands. Rich flapped his at Ken as he hesitated to take both mine and his. Finally, Ken slipped his hand into my waiting palm. I gave it a soft, reassuring squeeze and smiled at him. His mouth ticked up slightly.

I spoke the words Gram had taught me, ending the recipe —I still wouldn't call it anything else—with the command of "Mary Catherine Turner, I summon thee to appear before us."

CHAPTER 41

Mary Catherine's spirit rose out of the brush almost immediately as if she'd been waiting for us. Nothing more than a wisp, the apparition expanded and took form. After a few moments, she stood completely on the table. My friends' jaws dropped as she turned around to take in everyone there.

"Oh, Kenny, look how much you've grown! I wasn't expecting to see you here at all."

Kenny? How cute! He definitely seemed like a Ken to me now, though.

Ken blinked rapidly, likely not believing what he was seeing. "Grandma Kate? You look—"

She raised her arms up slightly, palms out, and studied them. "Dead?"

"I was going to say younger, actually. You don't look like a ghost."

She laughed, throwing back her head. "Well, have you ever seen one before?"

He shook his head, then looked at me. "How is this possible?"

"I don't really understand it myself," I admitted.

"I've been trapped in that brush since I died. Cursed," Kate stated matter-of-factly.

Now my mouth dropped open. *Cursed?* Did we have something much bigger on our hands?

"Before you go thinking someone did something, know that I did it myself." Kate glanced over at me before pivoting to face Daniel, who had tears in his eyes. Her posture relaxed. "Oh, my love, don't cry." Daniel wiped the tears from his eyes. "I couldn't see myself moving on knowing you were still here. Thought that by attaching myself to the brush, I'd be able to be nearby and wait for you until it was your time. It was a risky move, and I certainly wasn't expecting Nicky to take the hairbrush with him after I passed."

She spun to face Ashley. "Who knows how long I could have stayed in the back of that closet if that woman hadn't dug that brush out and mailed it to you."

Ashley closed her mouth and pointed at herself. "Me? But why me?"

"You're my granddaughter. Oh, how I wish I had known that when I was alive. I remember seeing you playing, riding your bike through the neighborhood. Always such a cute thing. We would have had fun together. I had wondered for a time if it were possible. Your mom hung out with my Nicky when they were in school together, and they reconnected that summer he came back. Your dad, the one who raised you, never let on that he was anything but your real dad, so I let the idea go. And really, who was I to question it or upset your family?" She sighed. "Nicky and I had a falling out that summer, and I never saw him again. So I never knew, but he must have found out at some point, or how else would the brush have gotten to you?"

Ashley had grown teary-eyed. "So how did you realize who I was?"

"The moment you touched the brush, I knew. I knew you were my granddaughter." She glanced at me then. "Sorry for the mess in your bakery that day. I couldn't quite control myself, and my energy went haywire. After that, my energy continued to build, but it wasn't until the other night that I could finally speak." She smiled warmly. "Thank you for doing all you could to set me free and for all the help with my granddaughter."

"So wait," Ken interrupted. "Does that make Ashley and me cousins?"

Kate took a step back so she could see the two of them together. "It does. I'm glad you've found one another. You could both use some more family by your side." Kate pivoted to face Rich. "Although, it seems you have someone else who wants to be next to you, dear. My beloved Daniel's grandson. Funny how you two would end up together."

Daniel stepped forward and placed a supportive hand on Rich's shoulder. "He's a good boy, Katie. I'm real proud of you, my boy. Continue to make your mama proud." It was the first time he had spoken. Rich's mouth dropped open, and he gazed up at his grandfather, tilting his head all the way back.

"I'm sure he is," Kate answered. "I saw how well you raised your children. It doesn't surprise me that would extend to him. But we need to let them be now." She motioned between Ashley and Rich. "We can't keep using them to rehash our old fears that kept us apart. It's not the nineteen-sixties anymore. They can be together if they want to be. It's not like the way it was then. Other people don't matter. They don't get a say. Sure, others might judge, but they'll judge anyone. It's time for them to be happy."

Daniel nodded. "Say the word, my love, and we can finally be together too."

"Is that what happened?" I asked. "Other people got to have a say?"

Kate sighed. "It is. My parents forbade it. Putting it politely, they didn't want their little girl with a Black boy. Many frowned upon the idea. That's the time we lived in. We had to sneak out to be together. Kept it a secret from our friends and family until the truth got out. Secrets always come out in the end. Then we argued about the risks of being public, of losing my family because other people had problems with our relationships, saying we were too different."

"Then your grandad came along, dear." She looked back at Ken. "Wow, I can't get over how much you look like your dad when he was younger."

"How did he come first, though, Grandma Kate? You were married before him."

"It's true, I was. But I met your grandfather before Nicky. I'd known your grandad through school. Much like I knew Danny." Her gaze settled back on Daniel. "They even played football together. Somehow, Eddie knew, but he didn't care that he'd play second fiddle in my heart. He picked up the pieces when my family prevented me from seeing Danny and made me break up with him in front of them. It nearly killed me to hurt you like that."

She reached a hand out for Daniel, but the circle we'd established prevented her from escaping. Daniel couldn't get in either.

"When Eddie went to war, Nicholas and I got together. He did right by me when I ended up pregnant with Nicky. But that was it. Then Nicholas went to war, and he never came home. Eddie did, though. Such a good man. He came back to me and had no qualms about raising Nicky. When we finally had your dad, Kenny, our family was complete. Nicky rebelled as he got older, and he left as soon as he could. Like I said, he came back home only that one time. But it was enough." She smiled lovingly at Ashley.

"I apologize for not liking you at first. I knew who you were all along, and you were a reminder of what I didn't get to have," Daniel said to Ken before focusing on Rich. "I'm talking about Kate, not a family. I'd never wish you and your ma away."

"Oh, um, it's all right," Ken replied as Rich nodded.

Kate pointed at Rich. "You take good care of her, you hear me?"

"I definitely will," Rich answered. Daniel clapped him on the back.

"Are you ready, Katie?"

"I think it's finally time." Kate turned toward Daniel and held her hand out. She grinned from ear to ear. Daniel's smile matched hers.

It was time to reunite them.

"Oh, one more thing." She looked back at Ken. She quickly tilted her head toward me before straightening. "This one is special. Don't let all this stop you."

He nodded and glanced my way, his gaze softening.

"Drop your hands," I whispered to him and Rich.

They did as asked, breaking the circle, allowing Kate to go free as soon as she was ready.

Daniel took his hand off Rich's shoulder and stepped in front of the opening. He held his arms out for Kate. She hopped off the table and into his waiting embrace. Before our eyes, Daniel became a young man again, matching Kate's age. He spun her in a circle as she wrapped her arms around him.

"Oh, it feels so good to be able to be in your arms again, Danny."

"I completely agree, Katie. I don't plan to let you leave them anytime soon."

Kate turned to face us all, still in Daniel's arms. He buried his face in her hair and took a deep breath through his nose. I had never noticed if ghosts had a smell, but if they looked like living people, maybe they smelled like them too. I wondered if it was something he used to do when they were together. But the action was cute and one of pure bliss on his part.

Daniel picked up his head and leaned it against the side of hers. Although Daniel's mustache partially covered his mouth, I could easily tell where Rich had gotten his megawatt smile from. "Thank you for not giving up on this, Miss Joanie."

"I couldn't leave her," I replied. "No one deserves to be trapped like that, even if it was done on purpose. I'm glad you two can finally be together."

Kate patted Daniel's top hand that was wrapped around her middle. "Why don't we let these kids get back to what they were doing. I'd like to go for a walk and see how things have changed around town if you don't mind. After being cooped up for so long, it will be nice to stretch my legs a bit. Then we can be on our way."

Daniel turned toward her hair once more and kissed the side of her head. "Anything you want."

Kate looked at me straight on. "Thank you. I can't even begin to tell you what this means to me."

"You're absolutely welcome. I wish you the best where you're going."

She winked. "The best is just beginning."

She stepped out of Daniel's embrace but held on to one of his hands as she moved around the table. She patted Ken's cheek. "Remember what I said, now, you hear?"

Ken nodded. "Yes, Grandma Kate."

"Good boy." Her pat turned into a caress. "It was so good to see you again. I love you."

"Love you too. Say hi to my parents, will you?"

She nodded, then stepped toward Ashley, who had tears in her eyes.

"Oh, sweet girl. I wish we had more time together. Someday, yes? But not for many more years." Kate pulled Ashley into a hug. "Have a wonderful life."

Ashley threw her arms around Kate, her tears now falling down her cheeks. "Goodbye, Grandma Kate."

Kate pulled out of Ashley's embrace, then stepped over to me and wrapped me in a hug. "Anyone who goes through that much trouble for me is a part of my family. I'll see you again, I'm sure."

"Not if I see you first," I joked to keep myself from adding to the tears in the room. "I can see ghosts, after all."

Kate barked out a laugh. "Use it for good."

"I will." Perhaps it was time to start helping those ghosts who needed it again. Within limits, of course. I didn't want to open up to everything again. We had locked away part of my abilities for a reason.

Kate moved on from me to Saffy. "Can't forget you, money cat," Kate said, petting my calico who had remained at my side the entire evening. Saffy leaned into the affection. After another moment, Kate ran her hand all the way down Saffy's back to the tip of the tail, the same way the hairbrush had done the other night. "I had a lot of fun with you."

She stood, then approached Rich. She patted his cheek, much like she had Ken's. "Oh, Danny, he really does look so much like you."

Daniel stepped forward and hugged his grandson. "I'm so

proud of who you've become. You take care of that young lady over there? Your mom too."

"I will, Grandpa. You can count on me."

"I know I can, son."

Daniel let Rich go. Then it was Kate's turn as Daniel stuck his hand out to Ken. Ken took it, and they shook. Peace seemed to settle over Daniel as he let his old grudges go against Ken's family.

When Kate let go of Rich, she stepped back into Daniel's waiting embrace. "Thank you all. For everything. Let's go, Danny." She lifted onto her toes and kissed him softly on the lips.

They faded into nothingness.

CHAPTER 42

The four of us stood there for a few moments in silence, basking in the warm, peaceful feeling they had left behind.

Ken was the first to break the silence. "That was amazing! Do you do that all the time?"

I hadn't been sure what was going to unfold when he'd first stepped foot into my kitchen. Now relief flooded my system that I'd told him the truth and he'd stayed to witness it and take part. He'd made a complete one-eighty after the experience. I chuckled. "No. That was a first for me." I leaned forward and blew out the black candle.

"But you can see ghosts? All the time?"

I turned slightly and blew out the white candle. "If they're around."

"That's incredible. It really is."

"I agree, Joanie," Ashley said. She'd already found her way into Rich's arms. They were mirroring Kate and Daniel's earlier embrace as they both faced Ken and me. "Thank you. I had no idea when I left that brush with you that all of this would happen."

Rich nodded. "You really went above and beyond. Thank you for helping my grandfather."

The telltale heat of a blush crept onto my cheeks. "Well, I'm glad I could. And you two should be okay now. No more puppets."

"No more puppets," she repeated with a light laugh.

Rich turned to Ken. "So you're from here?"

"Yeah, Knoll's Grove," Ken answered.

"Did you play football in high school?" Rich asked.

Ken nodded. "Yeah. Defensive back."

"You know?" Rich started, wagging his finger at Ken, "I thought you looked familiar that day in front of the general store when we officially met, more than just from the day you picked Joanie off the floor." He chuckled at the memory. "I played offense."

"I don't know if I like you anymore," Ken stated with a wide smile before breaking out into a laugh.

I'd only lived here for a little over four years, but there was no missing that Heartwood Hollow and Knoll's Grove were each other's biggest high school sports rivals. The whole town turned out for home games between the two teams.

Rich's chuckle turned into a hearty laugh. "Feeling's mutual." Ashley ducked out of his embrace as Rich stuck out his hand.

Ken took it, and the two exchanged a bro hug.

"To think I could have grown up with a cousin," Ashley said somewhat somberly.

Ken stepped toward her and pulled her into a hug. "I'm glad we can get to know each other now. Feel free to come over anytime. I can tell you stories about Grandma Kate."

She nodded, returning his hug. "I'd like that."

Rich placed his hand on the small of Ashley's back. "What do you say we get going, Ashley? I'll walk you home."

She turned to face him. "How about we grab something to eat first. I'm starving."

"I think that can be arranged." He nodded at both of us as he took her hand. "Goodnight."

"Goodnight," Ashley echoed, looking over her shoulder at us. They walked out of the kitchen hand in hand.

Ken and I followed. As they reached the front door, Rich pulled Ashley toward him and bent his head forward to kiss her. She wrapped her arms behind his neck as she kissed him back.

After a few moments, Ken coughed. "You guys have an audience, you know."

Ashley and Rich stepped away from one another, ending their kiss. Ashley looked down, her face beet red. Rich ran a hand through his hair.

"Sorry. Got a bit carried away. You two have a good night."

"Do you want the hairbrush back?" I asked Ashley as she put her hand on the doorknob.

"You know? Why don't you keep it? It seems to have found a home with you. Had I kept it, I would have ended up burning it, and then where would we be? Thanks again, Joanie."

Ashley opened the door, and she and Rich stepped outside, leaving Ken and me alone.

I couldn't quite meet Ken's gaze. "Well, that was certainly something."

Ken tucked a lock of my hair behind my ear. "I meant what I said. That was amazing."

I glanced up at him. Part of me still expected him to be hesitant, disbelieving. It was why I didn't tell people I could see ghosts. I'd lost my best friend from elementary school that way. She thought I was crazy. I'd felt it at the time.

My gaze was met with a wide smile and bright eyes. "*You*

are amazing." Ken lifted my chin so I was facing him head-on. He leaned down slightly and brushed his lips against mine. Tingles shot down to my toes and back up, but they were different than those I felt when I was near two people meant to be together. Was this what people experienced when they said they felt butterflies?

He broke the kiss all too soon. "I like Ashley's suggestion. Dinner? I wasn't sure how long I'd be here, so I have the babysitter until ten. We have plenty of time as long as her grandma's dog doesn't get out again."

I laughed. "Dinner sounds wonderful."

CHAPTER 43

The weekend flew by, and I breezed through the few days with a lightness I hadn't felt in some time. Even Sarah picked up on it. Of course, I didn't confess to her what had happened as far as setting the soul of one ghost free into the waiting arms of another, but I did confirm that the witchy business with the hairbrush was over.

And I may have told her Ken and I kissed. She was more excited by that than anything else I had said.

On Monday afternoon, Ashley and Rich came in together after school was over, arm in arm.

"Well, hello, you two. How is everything going? Looks like it's all good to me."

Ashley dropped Rich's arm as she walked over to the case to see what I had. "It was such a great weekend, Joanie. We hung out together the whole time. He even came with me to pet the cats."

Rich stepped up to the counter. "It's like night and day. No arguments. No feeling like I'm not myself. Just fun and"—he glanced over at Ashley, his gaze one that I had seen with all of my matches, full of happiness and the blossoming of love —"getting to enjoy one another's company."

My toes tingled. Everything would be okay between them from here on out. "That's so wonderful. So what can I get for you?"

"I need to place another order of test-taking muffins for Wednesday. My AP class last week all got ninety-five or higher, and I'm hoping to say the same for my Western Civ class this week."

"Sure thing. How many do you need?"

"Fifteen." He paused. "No, make it sixteen. I want one for myself."

I raised an eyebrow at him, and he shrugged.

"What can I say? After what I saw this last week, I may believe in the power of your muffins now."

Chuckling over his change of heart, I wrote his order down on my slip. Even I wasn't sure if my belief went that far. My muffins had nothing to do with ghosts.

"And a cookie, too, please," Ashley added, pointing to a black and white in the case.

I grabbed the biggest cookie on the tray, then handed it to her. She broke the cookie in half and gave Rich one of the pieces. Each had half of the chocolate frosting and half of the vanilla frosting.

"Sure you don't both want one?" I asked. "I have a few more."

"Oh, I love them so much, but I don't want to ruin my appetite. We're going to grab dinner together at the Maplelick Taphouse."

"Oh, is that the new one at the edge of town?"

She nodded excitedly.

"Let me know how it is." I needed to come up with an idea for my next date night with Ken.

Rich paid for the cookie and his order as Ashley said she'd give me a full report on what was good at the restaurant.

They left in the same way as they entered, arm in arm.

"You really do have a knack at this whole matchmaking thing," Sarah said from behind me. She'd been quiet the whole time Rich and Ashley were here, and I was glad our conversation hadn't strayed to Kate and Daniel. No way could I have explained that to her. She leaned a broom against the counter as she opened the case next to me. "I have to admit, I kind of doubted you on this one after hearing about that disastrous date. But you've proven me wrong. I should have believed in your witchy ways."

I ignored her witchy reference and began compiling cookie trays together so the empty ones could get washed and ready for tomorrow's baked goods. "You said it, I have a knack for that stuff. But we'll see how it goes. They have a few months before I can call it a success." This pair didn't need a few months, however. They were well on their way to a happy life together. It didn't hurt that Rich had made a promise to the ghost of his dead grandfather that he'd be sure to take care of Ashley.

I walked home thinking of what to make for dinner that a seven-year-old would approve of. I should have thought to ask Ken when I invited him and Ivy over to meet the other man in my life. Ken had quirked his eyebrow when I said this, but I told him to trust me, and he nodded in agreement. He probably thought I meant another ghost. I just meant Matt. At least if Ivy disliked what I cooked, I'd be able to make it up to her with the cookies I'd taken from the shop for dessert. They'd go great as the sandwich portion of the ice-cream sandwiches I planned on making. I had to go to the grocery store first, but I was taking my car. Saffy was already running low on cat food.

Matt showed up right when expected, halfway through my cooking. "You burn your TV dinner again?" I asked as I stepped aside so he could enter the living room.

"I swear that microwave goes on the fritz at least once a week. It's like it knows you're cooking up something much better than I could make on my own."

"You're always welcome at my table. Set two extra places, will you? I've invited a friend and his daughter over."

Whereas Saffy glared at me as she slowly ate her early dinner over the mention of Ivy, Matt raised an eyebrow. "Is it the little girl who screamed in your backyard for what seemed like an eternity last week?"

I nodded.

"She woke me up from my morning nap."

Heat flared up my neck and across cheeks. "Yeah, it wasn't pretty, but we got that all sorted out. I don't know if her dad knows that happened, though, so—"

He made a motion of zipping up his lips. "You know I don't like to gossip. Your secret is safe with me."

I transferred the meatballs from the oven to a pot of sauce I had simmering on the stove. "Thanks, Matt."

After he'd set the table, he took up his usual seat, and we chatted as I salted the water and set it to boil for the ziti. I was seasoning the garlic bread as I broke the news to Matt.

"So remember how I was asking you about Daniel the other day?" He grew quiet.

"I do. I'm sorry I don't have more to say about that."

"Oh no, that's totally okay. I wanted to tell you that his grandson, Rich, Ashley, and I learned who the girl was."

His eyes grew wide. "You did?"

I poured the box of ziti into the boiling water, then sat down at the table in the seat across from him. "We did. Mary Catherine Turner."

"You don't say." He ran both hands through what little hair he had at the sides of his head. "Wow. She lived across the street from me growing up, the next street over from this one where my sister still lives. I had no idea."

"You never told me you had a sister," I chided him as a way to not dwell on how much easier this case could have been if I'd knocked on Matt's door first thing when I got the photo. I'd been so focused on showing as many people as possible, I'd never considered a more targeted approach. At least it had all worked out. "Do you burn your TV dinners to go over her house for dinner too?"

He dismissed my comment with a wave and stuck out his tongue partway in disgust. "Only if I wanted her to kill me. She's a terrible cook." He paused. "I wonder if Betsy knew. She was great friends with Katie. I always thought it was odd that she up and got married right after high school when she and Nick hadn't even dated. It wasn't some shotgun wedding either."

"Turns out their son, Nicky, is Ashley's biological father."

"Well now, isn't that something. You've been solving family mysteries left and right, haven't you?"

I laughed as I stood to stir the pasta and toss the garlic bread in the oven. Ken and Ivy would be here any minute, and I hoped I'd timed everything properly. "And that's not everything."

"There's more?"

"Ken helped solve it all too, and he's Kate's grandson through her son Daniel. That part was never a mystery, but now he has a cousin."

"She named her son after the man she loved, didn't she?"

"I didn't ask," I replied sitting back down.

He cocked his head to the side and squinted at me. "Ask who?"

At that moment, the doorbell rang, saving me from my blunder. Matt didn't need to know about my abilities.

Saffy scampered past me as I went to answer the door for Ken and Ivy, and she bolted up the stairs. Someday maybe she'd be friends with Ivy. I expected them to come over a lot more now. Maybe if Ivy helped me bake some cat treats. Bribes went a long way with my sassy cat.

Ken held up a bag with two half-gallons of ice-cream. He'd called to ask what he could bring, and I did not want to end the evening on a bad note by not having Ivy's favorite.

We stepped into the kitchen and Ivy plopped herself in the chair next to Matt. "Hello," she said in a sing-song voice. "I'm Ivy."

"Well, hello there, Ivy. I'm Matthew, but you can call me Matt."

"Matt, this is Ken. Ken, Matt." I walked over to the stovetop and turned off the burner.

Ken stuck his hand out toward Matt. "Pleasure to meet you."

Matt shook his hand with three strong, short strokes. "Likewise. You look like your father."

"Thanks. I've heard that a lot lately."

I poured the pot of ziti into a colander in the sink, then let it drain as I pulled the garlic bread out of the oven. "I was just telling Matt that you're Kate's grandson."

"Oh really," he said. "Did you know her?"

"Grew up with her. We were neighbors."

"Huh. How about that?" Ken plopped into the seat next to his daughter.

"Ivy, do you like your sauce mixed in or on the side?" I

didn't want to ruin her dinner for her by messing it up at the last minute.

"Side, please!" she chirped.

"You got it." I grabbed a bowl from my stack on the counter and added a few scoops of plain pasta to it. Then I took my ladle and placed a spoonful of sauce on the side of the bowl and added two meatballs on top of the sauce. I poured the remaining pasta into the pot of meatballs and sauce, then gave it all a big stir. "Okay. That should do it. Just have to cut the bread. Come serve yourself."

I sliced the garlic bread as Ken and Matt stood to get their dinners, loading their bowls to the brim. Ken set Ivy's bowl in front of her, and she immediately dug in. Once the bread was done, I placed the tray of it in the center of the table, then filled my bowl with pasta and sat down to join everyone.

We sat and talked the evening away, Matt regaling us with stories of Ken's grandma in her youth. She sounded like she'd been a spitfire. No doubt I would have liked her.

Nearly two hours later, Ivy began to rub her eyes, not surprising given how late it was getting. I had to give her credit. Ivy had been a delight throughout dinner, even taking part in the conversation. I doubted I would have been able to stay engaged for that long once it became about people I didn't know. I wondered if she was finally settling in after her move. Or maybe Matt had something to do with it. Since first saying hello to him, Ivy seemed enamored with him. It was cute.

Ken glanced at his daughter. "Guess that's our cue to leave. Ready to go, kiddo?"

Ivy nodded. "Okay." She rubbed her eyes once more. She slid from her chair and shuffled over to Matt, then wrapped her arms around him. "Goodnight, Mattie." She'd been calling him that throughout dinner.

"Goodnight, Miss Ivy." Matt patted the back of Ivy's head. "I'm sure I'll see you again."

"I'm sure too," Ken said, glanced at me, the smile on his face sending heat into mine. He turned toward Matt, his hand extended. "It was nice to meet you. Thank you for the stories about my grandma."

Matt took Ken's hand, and the two shook. "Anytime."

Ivy gave Matt one last squeeze before stepping away and walking toward the living room.

"Thank you for coming," I said as I walked Ken and Ivy to the door.

"Of course." He looked down at Ivy. "Say goodnight to Joanie."

Ivy stepped forward and, like with Matt, wrapped her arms around me. "Night, Joanie," she said sleepily. "Thanks for dinner."

"You're welcome." I stooped slightly and gave her a quick hug.

She pulled away and then leaned into her dad. Ken placed his hands on her shoulders, but his gaze was fixed on me. "Lunch tomorrow in the cafeteria?"

I nodded, grateful I had off tomorrow. "It's a date."

Ken smiled, then kissed me goodnight, a quick peck on the cheek. I wondered if he felt weird with Ivy watching. I did slightly, but it would be something we'd have to get used to if we continued seeing one another. He pulled away with a smile on his face. "It's a date."

He turned toward the door, then pushed it open and guided Ivy outside. I headed back into the kitchen once they'd reached the sidewalk.

"You know," Matt started as I dished some leftovers into a container for him, "I didn't want to bring it up at dinner since no one likes to talk about such things, but did you know Daniel and Kate died three days apart from one another?"

"I didn't."

"Guess they couldn't bear being apart any more than they already had been and could finally be together that way."

He had no idea what lengths they went to even after that.

"It's sad when you think about it," he continued. "They couldn't be together while alive. I wish I'd known. I would have been okay with it. He was my best friend, and she was my sister's."

I placed the remaining leftovers in the refrigerator. They'd make a great dinner tomorrow night. "Well, you can imagine them happy together now, if that eases your mind. I'm sure they wouldn't want you upset about it after all these years."

"You're right." He smiled at me, and as I handed him the container of leftovers and some garlic bread wrapped in foil, the grin grew wider. "Now *this* makes me happy."

"You and your stomach, right?"

He barked out a laugh. "Indeed. And now that I have this, I'll be on my way. Goodnight, Joanie."

As soon as Matt left, I collapsed onto the couch. Cleaning the kitchen could wait until morning. Saffy jumped up, having come out of hiding now that Ivy was gone, and curled up next to me. I grabbed my book and read until my eyes grew heavy.

CHAPTER 44

The next morning, I slept in. Unlike last week, there were no ghosts to wake me up, no upset couples knocking on both doors to my house. Even Saffy let me sleep as long as I wanted, a real feat for her and her appetite. When I finally made it downstairs, she was sitting in front of her bowl, waiting for me to feed her breakfast.

"You get extra treats today for not demanding breakfast before dawn." I turned the burner on and fed Saffy as my tea water heated up. She chirped happily as I set her food down. Right before it started to boil, I poured the water into my teacup, then took it out into the living room to steep. There was no better way to spend the rest of the morning than to curl up under my blanket and dive back into my book.

Saffy had just joined me when there was a knock at the door. She didn't react in the slightest to the noise, which wasn't like her at all. Unlike with the doorbell, she'd usually jump into the window to see who it was, especially since today there was no engine noise to clue her into whoever it was. They must have walked. Was it Matt? He was the only person who reliably avoided the bell. Even as I pulled my legs out from under her, Saffy only grumbled at my disturbance.

Questioning my cat's sudden attitude shift, I shuffled to the door and then looked through the peephole. No one was there. I opened the door and stepped out onto the porch, nearly tripping over a brown paper package. Curious, I studied the delivery. It looked harmless, but I wasn't going to take it inside until I'd found out what it was. I lifted it onto the porch swing, then opened one side of the parcel to peek inside.

Recognizing the contents immediately, I pulled the bundle of paisley fabric out of the wrapping. A note fell to the ground. I bent to retrieve it, then unfolded the piece of paper.

For your pillows.
XO, K&D

I dashed down my steps and to the sidewalk, looking both ways. Nothing. I ran to the corner of the street at the end of my yard and looked again. In the distance, Kate and Daniel walked hand in hand. If not for Kate's pants, they could have been anyone.

After a few moments, they disappeared from sight.

They were gone. I wouldn't be seeing them again.

I headed back inside, clutching the fabric to my chest, note still in my hand.

Saffy glanced up at me briefly as I walked over to the coffee table and set the bundle down. She grumbled again as I sat back on the couch and slid my legs under her, but she settled quickly.

I'd have to dig out my sewing machine later. After I met Ken for lunch.

But first I had a cup of tea and a book to finish.

There's more to Heartwood Hollow than meets the eye. Find out what as Joanie's story continues in *Scones and Spells*.

WHAT'S NEXT?

Some secrets don't go to the grave... they come to my bakery.

I thought ghosts meddling with the last couple I got together was a one-time situation. But the spirits are interfering again, and my current mystery is more complicated and even a little dangerous.

Nothing is quite what it seems in my small town, and everyone has something to hide. Even me. When the case leads me to a forest where six townspeople disappeared, or worse, I learn I must uncover the truth of what happened there to heal Heartwood Hollow and help my latest match find love. It won't be easy.

To do it, I need to accept there's truth to the rumors about me. I'm a witch. But can I turn to magic I didn't know I had to get my answers?

There's more to Heartwood Hollow and its residents than meets the eye.

Scones and Spells is now available.
Grab it today to start uncovering Heartwood Hollow's secrets.

ACKNOWLEDGMENTS

So many people deserve to be thanked for their help in the creation of this book, for without them, this book would not have been possible. Thank you to my family for their support of this dream of mine and listening to me talk about these characters as if they were real people. Then again, to me, they are.

Thank you to Frankie Blooding for bringing the spark of Joanie and her friends to life. You are awesome. Thank you to Tamara Beard for her beta reading and Kay Springsteen, my editor, for making my words shine.

Cookies and Curses started out as a NaNoWriMo project. It was the first time I've ever won, hitting 58k words that November. It took an additional two weeks to finish the story.

It was, by far, my most ambitious pace for any project. It would not have happened without the amazing groups of word sprinters I had a chance to virtually hang out with as we challenged ourselves to write faster and more productively. My word counts easily tripled during sprints as opposed to me writing solo. So thank you to the awesome authors in the *Writing Sprints for Authors* and the *Let's Sprint* groups on Facebook.

Sprinting also wouldn't have been possible without the wonderful napping schedule my six-month-old daughter had at the time or the bouncer she was so obsessed with playing in next to me while I finished whatever scene I was working on.

And finally, thank you to *you* for reading this book.

About the Author

Rosie Pease is a native Rhode Islander but has lived in Vermont, New York, and Ohio. She uses the places she's traveled to as inspiration for the settings of her cozy mysteries, pulling the theater from one, the cider mill from another, the river from another to create a fictitious town that feels familiar.

She collects Funko Pops of the Harry Potter, Hunger Games, Doctor Who, DC TV, and Marvel variety, with a few others thrown in for fun. Her desk is a mess, but she can find everything on it, so it works for her as long as things aren't falling onto the keyboard as she writes.

When she's not crafting cozy mysteries, she's playing with her daughter, hanging out with her husband, or being amused by her two crazy cats.

Come find Rosie online:
Website: https://rosiepease.com
Facebook, Instagram, Twitter, and Pinterest:
@WriteRosiePease

Also by Rosie Pease

The Matchmaking Baker

Coffee and Calicos

Sweets and Santa

Mixing Up Magic

Cookies and Curses

Scones and Spells

Weddings and Witchcraft

Potluck and Powers

Purrfect Travel Companion

Catastrophe on the Road

Catastrophe in the Kitchen